"Action, romance, suspense, love, betrayal, sacrifice, magic, and sex appeal to the nth degree! Her heroines kick butt and run the gamut from feminine to tomboy, and her heroes . . . well, they're all 200% grade-A male. YUM! Her love scenes left me breathless (and wanting a cigarette) and I'm surprised I have any nails left after the suspense in this last book."

—*Queue My Review*

"Vivid battles, deceit that digs deep into the coven, and a love that can't be denied."

—*Night Owl Romance*

"Besides a fabulous finish to a great urban fantasy that subgenre fans will relish as one of the best series over the past few years, the romance is the one readers have been waiting to see how it plays out since almost the beginning. Master magician Cheyenne McCray brings it all together in a superb ending to her stupendous saga." —Harriet Klausner

SHADOW MAGIC

"A sensual tale full of danger and magic, *Shadow Magic* should not be missed."

—*Romance Reviews Today*

Other St. Martin's Paperbacks Titles By
CHEYENNE MCCRAY

Lexi Steele Novels
The First Sin

Night Tracker Novels
Demons Not Included

The Magic Novels
Dark Magic
Shadow Magic
Wicked Magic
Seduced By Magic
Forbidden Magic

Romantic Suspense
Moving Target
Chosen Prey

Anthologies
No Rest for the Witches

THE SECOND BETRAYAL

Cheyenne McCray

St. Martin's Paperbacks

This is a work of fiction. All of the characters, organizations and events portrayed in this novel are either products of the author's imagination or are used fictitiously.

THE SECOND BETRAYAL

Copyright © 2009 by Cheyenne McCray.
Excerpt from *Luke* copyright © 2009 by Cheyenne McCray.

Cover photograph © Royalty Free Image / Veer.

All rights reserved.

For information address St. Martin's Press, 175 Fifth Avenue, New York, NY 10010.

ISBN: 0-312-94645-7
EAN: 978-0-312-94645-6

Printed in the United States of America

St. Martin's Paperbacks edition / August 2009

St. Martin's Paperbacks are published by St. Martin's Press, 175 Fifth Avenue, New York, NY 10010.

10 9 8 7 6 5 4 3 2 1

To Jo Carol Jones for being a good friend and kicking my ass into gear.

ACKNOWLEDGMENTS

They say it takes a village . . . and I have a wonderful support system of individuals who help me with the smallest of details. In every book I write I thank those who are a part of the genesis, the foundation of my writing career—because without them this journey wouldn't be the same.

Writing for the most part is a solitary career. Many authors sit in a recliner at home, or at a PC on their desk, or with a headset on while at a table in a coffee shop. Perhaps they write in a library where it's ultra-quiet. Some are even able to write with a roomful of noise and the TV on. (I don't fit the latter group!)

For many of us, our closest friends are the authors, readers, and booksellers whom we have come to know so well online. Sometimes we get to meet them in person at conferences or conventions—and if we're lucky enough to live near each other, we can meet over coffee.

We have the World Wide Web to thank for bringing us all closer and making this a smaller world where together we can be a part of the fruition of a novel.

When I thank those who are a part of my career as an author, I do so with love, respect, and gratefulness to have each and every person as a part of my life.

Jo Carol Jones, this book is for you, and I want to thank your family, too, for your wonderful hospitality in offering "the cave" and your entire upstairs as my writing retreat and making me come down every now and then for air. Especially Johnny for your home-made ice cream and chocolate chunk bread pudding! Oh, and I cannot possibly forget Jo Carol's fabulous chocolate martinis. I want the recipe!

My critters Anna Windsor and Tee O'Fallon, and of course my editor, Monique Patterson, and my agent, Nancy Yost. Always. Each and every book.

Mop and Pops with love from Dop. You are the most amazing parents in the world, Karen and Robert Tanner. Mop, you are a lifesaver in too many ways to count.

Tracey West, what would I do without you? You can never leave me! Phyllis, you are awesome and you have to stay, too!

My sons, Tony, Kyle, and Matthew, for putting up with Mom's hiding away to write and escaping on writing retreats, and for being proud of their mommy. Er, Mom. Even though my twenty-one year old likes to call me Mommy. ☺

To Frank. You will *always* hold a special place in my heart.

Every person at St. Martin's Press: I can't possibly

begin to list all of you who touch my novels, but I want you to know how much I appreciate you for the magnitude of what you do. Every single one of you.

To my readers and booksellers. I think of *you* when I write and craft my novels and hope they bring you enjoyment.

Thanks beyond thanks to the following gentlemen for answering my often inane law enforcement questions:

Officer T. J. Leonard, patrolman with the Boston Transit Police Department—my Bostonian education is all the better for you!

Texas police officer Jerry Patterson Jr., you totally rock.

Phoenix police officer Kenneth J. Meadows—what a match. ;)

RED wouldn't be the same without any of you.

Of course, all the stuff I make up that strays from reality is my responsibility and mine alone!

Ha!

AUTHOR'S NOTE

One of the little-known facts about New York City is that no helicopter can land on any building in Manhattan as a result of 9/11. Manhattan has three public heliports that are used for any helicopter-related transportation.

The hotel used in this novel has a helicopter pad thanks to my imagination. I also made up a few other things, like how to get to the imaginary helicopter pad via the fifty-second-floor penthouse.

Unfortunately, I've never had the opportunity to visit said penthouse. Or any penthouses that live up to the luxury of the Trump Tower. I really would like to, though. I'm willing to accept any legitimate offers . . .

When churchyards yawn and hell itself breathes out
Contagion to this world.

—Hamlet
by William Shakespeare (1564–1616)

THE SECOND BETRAYAL

PROLOGUE

Dasha

A new life. She would no longer live in poverty as she had in Moscow from the time she was born. Now she was in New York City, a place that would give her a new beginning.

Cold late-September rain slashed against Dasha Orlov as she stepped out of the bus and moved past the other girls to get a look at the magnificent sight.

The cold stung her cheeks and her bare legs, yet the chill was nothing but enticing wet kisses compared with the freezing temperatures she had known in Russia.

Only twenty girls had been chosen by the American modeling agency that came to Moscow. It seemed almost unreal that the Americans had paid her way to New York City and would give her money to model beautiful clothes. It could be nothing more than a perfect dream.

"Can you believe it?" Yulia squeezed Dasha's fingers as she laughed and looked up and around at what the bus driver had told them was Times Square. "That we are finally here?"

"It is so . . . ," Dasha answered in Russian as she searched for something to say that could put into words every feeling of hope, joy, excitement that she felt at that moment. It didn't matter that she was nervous, too. All that mattered was that she was finally in America. "It is all so magical," she said, then grinned at her brown-eyed new friend.

Yulia laughed, her long brown hair swinging into her eyes when she rose up on her toes and swept her gaze around them. The petite girl's face, hair, and plaid coat were as wet as Dasha's own, but it was too precious of a moment for either of them to care.

"When do you think they will take us to the modeling agency?" Yulia asked.

"I hope now." Dasha grinned. "It seems so much time has passed since we were chosen." Her words were almost drowned beneath the sound of the deep-throated throb of the bus's engine, the other girls' giggling, and the voices of the men who had taken them all on the bus from John F. Kennedy Airport.

Yes, Dasha thought again, *into what must be a dream. A perfect, beautiful dream.*

Thump after *thump* from luggage being unloaded from storage bins beneath the bus and thrown onto the concrete sidewalk made her turn slightly. She hugged her handbag to her chest. Three men were tossing their luggage out of the bus so hard she was afraid the suitcases would fly open and all of the girls' belongings would be strewn across the dirty asphalt street. The men flung the cases as if they were garbage.

She shook her head. Silly. They were just in a hurry.

Gray exhaust puffed from the back of the bus. Hard slamming sounds could be heard over the girls' laughter as the men shut the doors of the luggage compartments.

Dasha looked back at the amazing flashing signs around them. ABC News, Target, Coca-Cola, Virgin (an odd name to be flashed in the street), Cingular, Swatch, Planet Hollywood, CNN, NASDAQ . . . And there were the familiar golden arches of a McDonald's! Along with a hundred more advertisements.

"Into the vans." A man's rough voice came from behind Dasha as she was shoved toward one of the two long, white, and windowless vans.

Dasha stumbled when the man pushed her, but Yulia had a hold on her fingers and Dasha didn't bump into Jenika who was in front of her. Who was this man with the rough voice and even rougher hands?

Dasha glanced over her shoulder and saw that the man's expression was as hard as his voice. Her belly clenched as he met her gaze with a strange look in his eyes. She didn't want to know what it meant—it was almost as if she were staring into the eyes of the devil. She shuddered and hurried to sit in the van with Yulia, Jenika, and at least seven other girls. The harsh man climbed into the front next to the driver.

Disappointment stirred inside her as she sat in the confines of the van. No windows. She wouldn't be able to see much of her new city on the journey to the modeling agency, because it was difficult to get a good look through the front windshield from where she was sitting. Well, there would be time enough for sightseeing later.

The driver pulled out behind the other white van, ~~and they started~~ moving through traffic. Excited chatter filled the enclosed space as most of the girls spoke in Russian about their new lives in New York City.

Bubbles of excitement tumbled in Dasha's belly as Yulia chatted next to her. Dasha barely heard her friend as thoughts of earning lots of money made her excitement grow. She would be able to send Matushka and Otets, Mother and Father, money to make their lives better. Her father had lost his job months ago, and they barely got by with her mother working as a maid in a Moscow hotel.

The van came to a stop that caused Dasha to jerk forward and back in her seat. She grabbed the seatback in front of her to steady herself. The harsh man jumped out of the passenger seat, and the driver turned the engine off and got out, too. The van door slid open, and she met the gaze of the harsh man.

"Get out," he said to all of the girls in a way that made Dasha flinch.

She hurried to climb out with the others, who suddenly went quiet when they all stood on the sidewalk. One of the men walked from the vans and through a polished wood door after passing beneath a red awning with ELITE GENTLEMAN'S CLUB scrawled across the street-side flap of the canvas.

A sick feeling that something wasn't right churned Dasha's stomach. She glanced at buildings to either side of the club. The buildings were made of brick coated in grime from pollution; shuttered windows were like staring, blank eyes.

To the left of the building they faced was Rocco's Pizza. On the right was another business—One-Day Dry Cleaning. Garbage bags were piled on the sidewalks up and down the street in front of the buildings, probably to be taken away.

Where was the modeling agency? Dasha's English wasn't perfect, but it was good enough to read each sign and not one business had a name that would tell them they were at a modeling agency. Dasha tipped her head up to look at the blank windows again. Five stories. Maybe there were apartments above where they would live when they weren't working.

She looked at the sign that said ELITE GENTLE-MAN'S CLUB again. A sudden cramp in her belly shouted at her that something was wrong.

Dasha clutched her handbag tighter and took a step back. She bumped into someone hard and tall, and she looked over her shoulder to see the harsh man.

He grabbed her upper arms, leaned down, and pressed his lips against her ear, his breath hot and foul. He said in accented English, "Don't make a sound or I will kill you."

Panic rose in Dasha so fast her heart throbbed hard enough to hurt. Kill her? Why would he kill her?

The harsh man gripped her upper arms tighter and shoved her forward through the now silent group. Men surrounded the twenty girls. At least ten or eleven men, all hard-featured, and all had eyes filled with threats . . . and something she couldn't read. Maybe she didn't want to read.

Shudders started racking Dasha's body as the harsh man pressed his fingertips hard enough into her arms that she gasped. He propelled her forward. He didn't take her into the gentleman's club, but opened a recessed door to the left of the building and shoved her through the open doorway.

Dasha stumbled in a darkened hallway but didn't fall. What was going on? What was happening? Her heart raced and her throat tightened. She blinked to get used to the dim lightbulbs strung down the length of the hallway. It smelled of filth and as if someone had urinated on the cracked, chipped, and stained linoleum tile.

Her heart beat impossibly faster and faster and her chest hurt. This wasn't right. This couldn't be right. The man pushed her past closed doors on their right and took her all the way to a staircase. He pushed her up the staircase, and the sound of all the girls' shoes clinked against the stairs as they went up past floor two, then three, and stopped at the fifth and final floor.

The harsh man opened the first door on the right before he flung her to the floor.

Dasha cried out as she landed hard on her hip and elbow. Her handbag flew from her fingers, and the contents scattered across the floor of a large room that was just as ugly and smelled as bad as the hallway.

Vaguely she was aware of two brown tattered couches with stuffing squeezing through tears. An old television was on a stand against one wall, a long table behind one of the couches.

She couldn't take her eyes off the harsh man as all

the girls were shoved into the room and the door slammed shut behind them. The way the harsh man looked at her made her want to scrabble back on the floor away from him, but something in his eyes told her that wouldn't be a good idea. He would hurt her if she did. She knew it with everything in her heart.

Instead of giggles and laughter, mostly silence crowded the room. A few whimpers and sobs made her blood chill.

"Take their passports and other belongings," the harsh man said without breaking eye contact with Dasha. From the corner of her eye she saw men ripping away handbags and coats from the girls, and she heard their cries and screams.

"Forget anything to do with modeling right now," the harsh man said next. "Instead you'll be working off the cost of the plane tickets and other expenses we paid to get you to the U.S."

Confusion and fear tore through Dasha. Working off the costs, how?

The harsh man reached into his pocket and pulled out a handful of syringes. He started tossing them to some of the other men then grabbed more out of his pocket and gave the rest of the men syringes, too.

Tears rolled down Dasha's eyes as the harsh man approached her then knelt at her side. She tried to scramble backward, but he grabbed her arm and jabbed a needle into a vein on the inside of her elbow.

Dasha cried out as she felt a burn in her vein that slowly died. Almost immediately after that, she relaxed as her mind turned fuzzy. The harsh man's words seemed distant, far away, and too unreal to believe.

No. Soon she would wake from this nightmare. She would be back in her small home in Moscow, asleep in her own bed.

CHAPTER ONE

Little Red Riding Hood

It had been a mistake having totally wild, raunchy sex with Nick Donovan during our first assignment together.

Including the hundred or so times we ended up in bed—or up against a wall, on the kitchen table, on the floor, in my office—when we weren't working on *Operation Cinderella*.

The breath I sucked in burned my throat as I tried to control my lust while I watched Donovan. His jeans tightened against his muscular ass as he bent over the shoulder of Agent Chandra Kerrison to look closer at the wide-screen monitor in front of her.

Donovan had become like a drug to me. An addiction. I couldn't get enough of him.

I pushed my hair out of my face in frustration. Lexi Steele had never allowed distractions like Nick Donovan. I had to get a grip.

I'd been telling myself that for a good six months

now, since June, a couple of weeks after we finished our first op together. Here it was, the end of November, and I still couldn't get enough of Donovan.

"Damnit," I said under my breath. This infatuation had to stop. It was like being a freaking teenager.

Another thought crossed my mind as I watched Donovan, a thought that was always there and wouldn't let go of me. The big man held so many secrets tight to his chest and had never let me in far enough to know what any of them were. I had spilled my guts about what had happened when I was in Army Special Forces, and how I'd been forced into being an assassin. Why was Donovan keeping a big part of his past from me?

I shook off the thoughts. This wasn't the time for lust or secrets. It was time to get back to work. I turned my attention to the current op and headed toward David Takamoto.

Takamoto stood at the opposite side of the banks of monitors and screens of our Team Center, TC. A blue glow encompassed the whole of the Command Center, the glow given off from walls of screens in the CC where various teams tracked activity on their assignments.

Agents had put up holiday decorations here and there, some for sheer amusement, like a small Santa who dropped his pants every time someone walked by.

There were also decorations on agents' desks reflecting their own holiday beliefs. A silver-and-blue depiction of a Jewish menorah with its white candles. A picture of a Kwanzaa kinara with its colorful candles—three red, one black, and three green.

Some wiseass had put up a Mexican donkey piñata in a corner of the CC—a picture of Special Agent in Charge Morris Carter on its ass. Our SAC would be entirely oblivious considering he spent his time in his first-floor office playing computer card games as he waited out the last year until his retirement.

Of course our Assistant Special Agent in Charge might not find it amusing. Our ASAC, Karen Oxford, was tough, fair, and had no obvious sense of humor. Then again, the picture was still up, and the donkey had been there since two weeks before Thanksgiving. Maybe she had a sense of humor after all.

A soft buzz and hum filled the CC as agents spoke into headphones and kept track of their assignments on the enormous high-tech screens. I smelled pine from a small Christmas tree that overpowered the familiar scent of climate-controlled air as I passed the tree.

"Steele." Takamoto caught sight of me, and I tilted my head to meet his brown eyes when I reached him. "I was just about to find you and give you the news. It's about *Wolf*."

A petite five-four, I had to look up at most of the guys at the Recovery Enforcement Division. Seemed that Oxford liked to hire male agents six feet and over. Or maybe it was a coincidence.

Ha.

Most of the guys on RED task forces made me feel like I was in the land of the giants—just like my four older brothers did. Even my twelve-year-old brother towered over me. Little shit. Make that big shit.

"I'd give anything for news on Hagstedt." I put my

palms on my hips as I met his Takamoto's gaze. "Tell me you have something on that bastard."

Takamoto was excellent at schooling his expressions, and right now I wanted to shake him for looking so calm. He slipped his hands into the pockets of his slacks, causing his shirt to pull against his athletic runner's physique. He pressed his shirts and slacks so stiffly I don't think a wrinkle would dare sneak in. I managed not to look down at my T-shirt and Levi's that I'd snatched out of the laundry basket this morning and felt the material almost crawl with wrinkles.

"*Operation Big Bad Wolf* looks like it could be hot in Manhattan just like we expected." Takamoto glanced in the direction the group of agents on his intel team. "Rublev just reported in after she sent us the coded message. She said the Elite Gentleman's Club is definitely Hagstedt's. She overheard a conversation that verifies what info Johnny gave us. And if we can crack that coded message she intercepted earlier, that may give us all we need to get in there and get to Hagstedt."

I wanted to grip my fist and jerk my elbow back in a *yes!* motion. We'd known the key men were involved in kidnapping and prostituting young women in their club, but we hadn't known for sure if that operation was part of Hagstedt's enormous human trafficking ring. "Thank God. We've been working that club for how long once Rublev was in?"

Takamoto shook his head. "At least two months."

"About friggin' time." I breathed a sigh of relief. "I can't believe it's been over six months since we brought down his man Cabot in *Cinderella*."

Operation Cinderella had been a huge coup for the Human Trafficking and Sex Crimes Unit, which was part of the Recovery Enforcement Division. RED was a clandestine offshoot of the NSA, and we had clearance to do any damned thing we wanted to.

Yeah, *Cinderella* had been a success, but *Wolf* had *not* been going so well. Beyond six months of fruitless searching over the summer for Anders Hagstedt grated at me more and more every single day. The so-called mastermind of countless human trafficking rings in China, Russia, Switzerland, and the United States needed to be brought down. *Now.* We doubted *Hagstedt* was his real last name, but we'd still run all the leads we could on anyone with that surname with no luck.

Takamoto inclined his head in the direction of the "dungeon," as we liked to call our geek squad's domain. "Now if the geeks can decipher the coded message, we might get some more detailed info. It's been six hours and the geeks are still working on it."

"The new agent, Kerrison, thinks she can crack it," I said. "She's only had it fifteen or twenty minutes, though." My chin-length hair brushed my cheeks as I looked over my shoulder and saw her talking with Donovan just a few feet away.

I swiveled my gaze back to Takamoto. "I think we're real close to putting *Little Red* into play."

Before Takamoto could respond, I sensed Donovan behind me and caught his musky, spicy scent. My body immediately responded to his presence with an aching desire that made me want to moan in frustration.

Oxford had paired Donovan and me up as Team

Supervisors during *Cinderella,* and she'd decided to keep us working together instead of giving Donovan his own team. Karen Oxford was one incredibly savvy, observant woman, but I don't think she knew about ~~my sexual relationship with Donovan, or she would~~ have separated us. Or canned one of our asses. Hell, probably both of us.

Donovan's blue eyes didn't show any emotion that might tell me how he felt about the two of us. No, his gaze was entirely professional. Good. That's how it should be—I hoped I looked just as professional.

Donovan glanced from me to Takamoto and back. "Kerrison deciphered the communication."

It took some effort, but I managed to keep my jaw from dropping. "She decoded the message in twenty minutes?"

"Fifteen." Donovan's expression bordered on grim as he continued. "Hagstedt's operation isn't relegated to one or even a few clubs. It looks like he's doing exactly what we've been able to gather from intel," Donovan continued. "He imports girls from Switzerland, China, and Russia, and forces them into prostitution in clubs in all of New York City's boroughs. The club we've been watching on East Sixtieth Street is more or less the headquarters for his New York op."

Rick Smithe gave a low whistle behind me, and I cut my gaze to my left to see that he and George Perry had joined Takamoto. "What do you know? We finally got something," Smithe said.

Women being lured into the wrong hands with promises of jobs in America, then being prostituted once they arrived was nothing new—other teams on our task force were working on various ops related to all types of human trafficking, including that.

But to finally find a ring firmly tied to Hagstedt was like raking in the dough from a billion-dollar lottery. No—giving the slimeball a bullet in the brain would be the winning ticket. This was more like watching each Powerball number start to fall into place.

A shiver of excitement tickled my skin from anticipation of getting my teeth into the *Wolf* op that was finally going somewhere. Hagstedt was a big fish. Probably the biggest mastermind of human trafficking in the world from the intel we'd gathered.

I gave Donovan word on the latest Takamoto had just relayed. Adrenaline started rushing through me from the excitement of an oncoming hunt. "What do you have that Kerrison came up with?"

Donovan was holding two pieces of paper, and he raised his hand. For a moment I couldn't take my eyes off his thick wrist and the black hair on his forearm, and I could almost feel myself tracing my fingertips over the back of his hand. I swallowed and met his gaze. Damn.

He handed me the pages. I skimmed the gibberish on the first piece. "The code's so complicated that Taylor and his geek squad couldn't make sense of it in six hours. And Kerrison did it in fifteen minutes?" I repeated more to myself than any of the men standing around me.

Oxford had told me that Kerrison had one of the highest IQs in the world and had also sailed through Quantico's intense physical tests—supposedly she could kick major ass. A Harvard graduate at twenty with an IQ as high as Stephen Hawking or Marilyn vos Savant, Kerrison made an incredible addition to my and Donovan's team. On top of that she was model-beautiful, which could work to her advantage in some undercover ops.

My skin prickled as I read the decoded message on the second page. "Hagstedt is supposed to arrive in Manhattan within the next couple of weeks weeks," I said.

I glanced from the paper to Takamoto, Perry, and Smithe as I continued. "It actually names the Elite Gentleman's Club and names the asshole who oversees Hagstedt's entire New York City human trafficking ring. His name is something we've never been able to get. He doesn't talk with anyone but a couple of his men and the madame, from what Rublev has managed to see. And they call him Mr. G."

"Holy shit." Smithe's grin was almost dangerous. "We're going to put that bastard's ass in a grinder."

Perry tilted his head to look at the paper as he rubbed the back of his neck. "What kind of name is Beeff Giger?" Perry touched the sides of his dark GQ haircut. "Sounds almost cliché, like Rocko or Shorty."

A metrosexual, Perry was always primping. He was supposed to have been my submissive in the last op—I'd ended up being the submissive, but to Nick Donovan, who'd been my "Master" in a private BDSM circle. Not something I wanted to repeat. I'd been whipped enough in my former life as an assassin, and even though things had gotten pretty erotic with Donovan, I'd skip floggings any day. Especially bamboo. That hurts like a sonofabitch.

Takamoto shrugged in response to Perry's question. "*Beeff,* is actually a Swiss variant, like *Giger,* his last name." Takamoto pronounced the names perfectly as he looked over my shoulder at the page, too.

"We think our inside cooperative, Jenika Rublev, has been doing her job in finding ways to make the handlers suspect that the club's madame is catching on to their real operation—that it's not a strip club with willing prostitutes." Donovan glanced at the three men beside me. "These boys are probably starting to feel a little uncomfortable with the madame."

"We need to pull her out or she'll end up permanently visiting the fishes in the Hudson," Takamoto said.

I nodded. "We'll be able to roll *Little Red* into gear in no time. But we've got to hurry." I glanced at the huge atomic clock on one wall with its glowing blue numbers. Almost two in the afternoon. I looked back at the guys. "Smithe, grab Weiss, Fairbanks, and Jensen and meet me and Donovan in Conference Room Four. Three sharp. Takamoto and Perry, I want you there, too."

"Can't wait to see what you're cooking up in that ruthless head of yours, Steele," Perry said with a grin.

Same here. "Three," I repeated before I turned to head up the steps to the catwalk that led to the Team Supervisor offices.

Damn, a hot lead. But we had to hurry and get "in"

before Hagstedt arrived. We needed to make our case solid to tear down his entire house of cards.

Donovan fell into step beside me, and as always he made a point of shortening his normally long strides so that I wouldn't have to jog to keep up with him. As my partner he'd be going in on any op we put together, and the thought sent something indefinable curling in my belly. Or at least something I didn't want to define.

My new running shoes squeaked on the metal stairs that led out of the Command Center. I glanced up at Donovan as we stepped on the black-and-white-tiled catwalk at the same time. He was looking at me with such intense scrutiny that hair pricked at my nape.

"Hold a second," Donovan said. We came to a stop in front of the glass-walled offices of four other Team Supervisors. Donovan was already walking back to Kerrison, who now stood at the top of the stairs we'd just taken from the CC to the catwalk.

I didn't follow him. I figured he'd relay whatever message the junior agent had.

I couldn't resist admiring Donovan's biceps, which bulged as he braced his hand on one of the rails that ran along the catwalk as he spoke with Kerrison. The powerful muscles of his shoulders flexed beneath his black T-shirt when he moved, and his short, dark hair needed to be ruffled.

My mouth watered as I trailed my gaze down his athletic physique—all six feet, four inches of him—to the Levi's that were snug against his tight ass and muscular legs. When I moved my gaze up again, I studied his almost harsh but incredibly sexy profile. I couldn't see his vivid blue eyes, but the stubble on his strong jaw made me itch to caress his cheeks, to see my fair Irish skin against his darker flesh.

Donovan headed back toward me while Kerrison returned downstairs to the hub of our RED unit. I went into my office, Donovan right behind. He closed the door.

My gaze fell on the red heavy-duty Everlast punching bag that I kept in my office. I could sure use it now to work off the sexual tension.

I plopped onto the padded leather seat behind my desk. Besides the punching bag, my large-screen monitor, and my desk, my office was almost bare. The exception being a framed photograph of my entire family taken two years ago. All five brothers, my sister, Mama, Daddy, and me.

"If we hurry and make our move," I said as I swiveled slightly in my chair, "I think we can put *Operation Little Red Riding Hood* into action."

Donovan folded his arms across his broad chest and hitched one shoulder against the frame of the door he'd just closed behind him. The floor-to-ceiling windows were currently covered by my office's sleek black vertical blinds. "Agreed."

Enthusiasm for our plan took over. I rested my forearms on my modern, sleek black desktop and leaned forward. "Smithe's team just needs to put the finishing touches on the fictitious history for me." I almost rolled my eyes at the thought of Smithe, who was always up to something.

With a very unladylike snort, I continued. "Of course Smithe embellished the rap sheet, but it is good. Still comes down to me having run a successful cathouse for nine years here in Boston. Smithe even managed to create fake articles in the *Boston Globe* and several other rags about me being busted for my girls having sex with clientele willing to cough up the money."

"How long since the bust?" Donovan looked so sexy the way he leaned up against the door . . .

"A year. Long enough to be sure no one would pay any attention to me now. I've had plenty of money to last me, blah, blah, but now I need the income to continue my comfortable lifestyle."

Donovan nodded. "Exactly what we wanted."

I rocked back in my chair. Nothing on the rap sheet that would put me on the radar with any government agencies. This Beeff Giger bastard will see my solid history of handling girls. I'll have moved to Brooklyn to get away from the heat in Boston and stay low for a while."

"I don't think we'll have a problem getting you in once the current madame is out." Donovan looked thoughtful. "I assume Smithe has my background set up so that it shouldn't be too big of an issue getting on as one of the handlers."

"You'll have to rough yourself up a bit, Donovan." I appraised him and tried not to smile. "You don't look like a hard-core prostitute handler."

"And you don't look like a hard-core madame," he said, his tone dry but almost amused.

"All it will take is a little wardrobe change and just

the right made-up look." Georgina, my best friend and fellow RED agent, was brilliant at helping me with that kind of thing. Plus she currently wasn't on an undercover op. "Yeah, makeup and adding about four inches to my height." Thank God for stilettos.

The corner of his mouth quirked in one of his rare smiles. He look so incredibly hot and sexy that I instantly wanted to jump his bones.

If he took me hard and fast, we could do it in a few extra minutes . . .

I caught my breath as Donovan read the desire in my eyes. His gaze darkened and I heard the lock click as he reached behind him. The floor-to-ceiling blinds were drawn and it was just me and Donovan.

He moved toward me with clear determination. He wanted me as much as I wanted him.

I shoved my chair back and it rolled across the tiled floor with a clatter as I stood. When he reached me, I was in his arms before I could catch my breath.

Our mouths met, his taking mine hard and fierce. I returned the kiss equally as fierce. He always tasted so good. Felt so good. Smelled so good.

He raised his head, his expression primal, his eyes changing to a deep cobalt blue. "Right here, Steele. Right now."

"You talk too much." I reached for his belt and started to unfasten it.

Donovan pulled up my top and jerked down my bra so that it was beneath my breasts

Cool air met my nipples and I gasped from the delicious sensation. Donovan grasped my hips, lowered his head, and covered one of my nipples with his warm mouth. I gave a low moan when he sucked hard on one nipple.

As much as I wished they were, the walls weren't soundproof and I had to bite the inside of my cheek to hold back whimpers and moans of pleasure.

I finished unbuckling his jeans and had the top button undone with a twist. His long, thick cock felt like satin-covered steel when it escaped the tough cotton. If we had enough time I'd have gone down on him because I wanted to taste him so badly.

Instead, I continued to gasp and moan as I kicked off my running shoes then unfastened my own belt and jeans. I shimmied out of them, but slow enough so that my holstered weapon didn't hit the floor too hard. Still, it and my two cell phones thumped as I kicked the jeans aside.

Donovan raised his gaze to meet mine as he picked me up by my hips and set me on the edge of the desk that was cool beneath my ass. Thank God for keeping my desk bare.

He pushed my thighs wide and gripped me with one hand while he grasped his erection in his other.

"Hurry, hurry, hurry." I wiggled on the edge of the desk, closer to him. "You can't be inside me fast enough."

Donovan smiled his most dangerous smile and entered me in one hard thrust.

Jesus. I wanted to cry out at the exquisite pleasure of him inside me and it was almost impossible to keep from letting myself let it rip. The feel of his jeans and holstered gun and phone on his belt added to the eroticism of the moment.

I clung to his biceps as he began pounding in and out of me so deep and incredible that I felt like saying to hell with it. But I did like my job a whole lot.

"Come, Lexi." Donovan's words came out in a growl. He called me Lexi when we were intimate even though I always called him Donovan, and it turned me on. "I want to feel you around my cock when you climax."

He didn't have to tell me another time because I was already there.

A rush of pleasure rocketed through me, expanding from my core to my fingertips, my toes, my scalp. It was hot and molten and felt beyond fantastic.

My head almost ached from clenching my teeth so tightly to keep from really crying out. His continuous thrusting movements drew my climax out and I enjoyed the ride.

He came with a harsh but low sound and his cock throbbed and pulsed inside of me while my core continued to clench him.

His breathing was rough and hot against my hair as he rested his chin on my scalp. While he stayed inside me, I pressed my cheek to his T-shirt and heard the fast beat of his heart.

I tried to catch my breath well enough to talk. "We did order our agents to be in the conference room at three."

"Unfortunately," Donovan murmured against my head.

We adjusted positions and I tilted my head back to meet his gaze. "The team needs to move now. We've got to get on it."

Donovan rubbed his thumb across my cheek. "Trust you to follow great sex with work."

I grinned. "Hey, but we had sex first. Priorities, you know."

He gave me one of his adorable and rare smiles as he drew out of me and adjusted himself before zipping up. After he moved far enough away, I slid off the desk and climbed back into my jeans before slipping my running shoes back on.

When we made sure each other looked decent enough to not appear like we'd just had sex in my office, we sat down to get to work.

My core still felt sensitive, but I forced myself to be the senior agent I was. A senior agent who had just fucked her fellow senior agent.

I took a deep breath as I queued up the op on my large computer screen. I turned it slightly so that Donovan could see it from where he now sat in a chair in front of my desk.

"Twenty-four hours after the meeting," I said, still trying to catch my breath, "our team better be fully prepared and standing at the gates to board the plane to JFK to put *Operation Little Red Riding Hood* in motion." I cocked my head. "Once we get our claws into enough meat to get Hagstedt, we shift to *Operation Big Bad Wolf*."

Donovan studied me with his damned incredible blue eyes but no discernible expression on his harsh but handsome features. I knew he hated it when I took control and didn't ask his opinion. But even after working so many months together, I couldn't help my natural inclination to make decisions on my own.

"We'll change things up a bit and bring Kerrison in on *Little Red* to replace Jensen," Donovan said in a way that sounded like he considered his statement a done deal. "She's new, but from everything I've seen she's got what it takes, and the fieldwork will be good experience for her."

I didn't let my surprise show that he'd recommended the new agent, *and* that he wanted her on the inside with me. "That's not a good idea, Donovan. Kerrison's untrained and not ready for this kind of undercover op."

Donovan gestured to my glass wall that would give a perfect view of the CC if the blinds were open. I pictured Kerrison sitting in front of her monitor, her long sunset-red hair pushed over her shoulders. "She'll be perfect for decoding any messages that might come your way when we get you two on the inside," Donovan was saying. "Plus, we can really use Jensen in surveillance."

Of course he was right. If Kerrison could decode anything as fast as she'd taken care of today's intercepted communication, she'd be an incredible asset on the inside. Marti Jensen was top-notch, but she could be used on the surveillance and raid team just as easily.

Still, I found myself pushing it. "I know I wouldn't have a problem with Jensen avoiding the kind of attention the bastards might try on her. If anyone got rough with her, she knows how to take care of them."

"Kerrison can do the job." Donovan met my stare with a solid look. "Martinez can prep her on using the same bracelet Jensen would have worn, and he can size a ring for Kerrison. It won't take him long to brief her on the narcotics contained in the jewelry that will keep any sonofabitch away from her if she's forced to use them."

Donovan's words brought me to a halt. "During *Cinderella,* you told Oxford you didn't want to put me in the kind of danger I ended up in. As if a woman can't hold her own." I cocked my head as I studied him. "And now you're ready to let a junior female agent throw herself into a pack of wolves?"

Irritation flashed across Donovan's features. "You know I think all of RED's agents, female or male, are equally capable." He was quiet for a moment as his eyes held mine and his tone softened. "But *Cinderella*— from the beginning I had a bad feeling about that op."

"Yeah, yeah." I held my palm to my T-shirt, over the Chinese symbol meaning "dragon" tattooed around my belly button.

That op had gone bad. Real bad.

"We came up lucky with what Rublev got through to us." I figured I'd change the subject super-fast since thinking about what was beneath that dragon tat wasn't something I liked. "What she's doing isn't pretty. And it's dangerous for her to be taking chances like she did to get that intel."

Jenika Rublev had been a willing prostitute in a cat-house in Nevada, but I still didn't like the fact that she was having sex with men—and sometimes women— to feed us intel from the inside. Even though I'd been the one to go to her and offer her the assignment and the cash.

"Rublev made the choice, Steele. She jumped at the hundred grand to put aside for her twins' college education," Donovan said. "Not to mention part of it will help her get out of that Nevada shithole. Once this op is over, RED will make sure the job they land for her in the private sector will be damned good paying, too."

I sighed. "She was a lucky find."

When Donovan came up with the idea of searching for a Russian prostitute to work as a cooperative, I hadn't been crazy about it. But I'd still contacted some of RED's branch offices until I hit pay dirt in Nevada. I should have started there instead of LA and New York City since prostitution was legal in some parts of Nevada. One of the Las Vegas agents recommended Rublev. Wasn't sure exactly how the agent was familiar with the prostitute, but from the way he talked about her, I had my suspicions.

"Rublev can take care of herself." Nick leaned back in his seat. "She's been doing that since she emigrated from Russia."

"I suppose." I rested one forearm on the desk and glanced at the monitor, which had the beautiful prostitute's dossier next to Kerrison's. "She did say that the madame at her Nevada cathouse made sure her working girls knew how to de-ball any man who tried to get rough."

If I wasn't mistaken, Donovan winced at the *de-ball* comment. Men.

Rublev had turned to prostitution when she came to America and couldn't find a job in the sinking economy. She brought in good money in the cathouse, so she had stayed with it for the past two years to care for her twins and to be able to set some money aside.

Fortunately for this op, Rublev looked barely seventeen even though she was twenty-two. These bastards liked their girls young. We'd shipped her to Russia with her own fictitious background—using our Moscow contacts—hopefully to be chosen as one of a group of girls to be taken to a New York "modeling agency."

It had been close, but Rublev had made the "modeling agency"'s cut. She'd been sent with a group of nineteen other girls to a so-called gentleman's club. We just hadn't known which one until two months ago when she'd gotten word to us that she was at the Elite Gentleman's Club in Manhattan.

Pay dirt.

"Instead of going with everyone tomorrow, Saturday, you'll head out at nine PM on Sunday," Donovan was saying, drawing my attention fully to him. My skin prickled like a porcupine starting to bristle. He was giving me an order? "You need to be with your family for Sunday supper," he continued. "Zane said Ryan is in port. It might be a while before you see all of them again."

Heat crept from my body to my neck and to my face. There I was, barreling through life as usual and Donovan had been the one to remind me of the most important day of the week for my parents as well as the rest of us. With Ryan on leave from the Marines, all five of my brothers would be here as well as my sister.

"Thank you," I said quietly.

We spent the next forty-five minutes laying out plans for our backup team, surveillance, and every detail down to making sure our fictitious personal rap sheets were perfect.

We added a rap sheet for Kerrison that included being busted with me for her part in running the club. She'd managed the finances for that part of the business, which included taking cash from the customers paying for sex.

When it was time to head to the conference room, both Donovan and I stood, and I walked toward him. He wrapped me in his strong embrace and gave me one of his amazing kisses before we left my office.

No doubt about it. I was addicted to Nick Donovan.

CHAPTER TWO

Dasha

Beneath Dasha's palms, the clear plastic pole burned hot as glass heated in a forge. While she pole-danced, thundering techno music in the main floor of the club made her head pound from the inside out. Her mouth hurt, her lips quivering from forcing herself to smile so she wouldn't be punched by her handler.

Dasha, Yulia, and the blond girl, Jenika, who had become Dasha's friend, were onstage. The three of them writhed around the poles mounted along a narrow raised strip of the stage in the middle of the "gentleman's club."

A whorehouse, a prison, was what Dasha called it. Two months of being in the depths of hell. But she had learned to never say anything loud enough for one of the handlers to hear. The harsh man had punched her the one and only time she had referred to her life as it now was. What she was.

ПросТИТуТка. Prostitute.

Strobe lights flashed in the smoke-hazed room, making the glitter inside the clear pole sparkle in the colored lights. Jenika said it looked like fairy dust. Dasha thought it looked like poison ready to seep through the plastic and kill her. Maybe death would be better than this.

But if she killed herself, Matushka and Otets would be murdered. If she tried to escape, if she tried to talk to anyone, they would murder her parents. First one. Then the other left alive in case she tried something else.

The handlers had either beaten or abused each girl, making it clear that someone they cared for would be killed if the girl tried to escape, contact the police, tell a client, or kill herself. Each girl had been presented with photos of their loved ones to prove to the girls that they had no choice but to obey.

Dasha barely kept back tears as she tried to do what Madame Cherie instructed the girls to do—act like she was having sex while rubbing herself up against the pole. "Be sensual," the madame would say.

Be a good whore, Dasha always thought.

"Show us those tits, girly!" came a slurred, drunken man's voice.

Dasha raised her head and saw that the man was staring at her. His bald scalp shone beneath the lights as he raised a fistful of cash. Shame crept through her like a thousand Russian ratsnakes. From the leer on the man's face, she feared he would be the one crawling on top of her in a back room after this song was over. A shudder racked her body hard, but she tried to make it look like part of her dance.

More men shouted at her to take off what little she had on—the strip of cloth covering her nipples and her G-string.

Jenika could act like she enjoyed being a prostitute while Dasha struggled to wear a fake smile. Jenika always met several men's gazes as she danced, her blue eyes giving the invitation for something more, something erotic. She danced like the madame had constantly worked to teach all of the girls over the past two months. Jenika had tried to help Dasha with her performance, but Eddie always interfered.

Eddie was Dasha's handler, and he acted as a bouncer when the girls danced. Dasha glanced his way. His muscles flexed as he crossed his arms over his huge chest.

When Dasha slowly started to take off the thin material, revulsion crawled up her body to her throat and threatened to make her throw up on the stage. It didn't matter how many times she had stripped in front of leering men over the past weeks, she always had the desire to puke.

Sometimes women watched them dance, too. Sometimes women went with her to the back rooms and made her do things that made her as sick as when she was with a man.

Dasha tipped her head back so that she wouldn't have to look any man in the eye as she swallowed down the frothing sensation in her throat along with the taste of bile. She flung the bra onto the stage while men whistled and shouted horrid things they wanted to do to her.

"Come 'ere girly," came the same man's voice as

her nipples hardened from the cool air being pushed down from the fans above the stage. How she hated her body's natural reactions. "I've got somethin' for ya," the man called out louder.

"Show us that fuck-me look, Jewell baby," another man said.

Jewell was her stage name. Jewell was her whore name.

Dasha forced herself to look at the man, hold his gaze, and dance toward him as he rubbed his crotch with his free hand. She almost stumbled in the high, thin heels she had to wear every night. Her movements were stiff, awkward, but the men in the room didn't seem to care. Man after man called out for her to take off the G-string, too.

When she reached the side of the stage, the man with the handful of money stuck a few of the bills in the front of her G-string. He shoved his fingers down hard enough that his fingers brushed her trimmed pubic hair.

"That's it, baby," he said as more men pushed dollar bills through whatever spot on her G-string would hold the cash.

The stench of male sweat, sour beer, and cigar smoke nearly gagged her now that she was so close to the men.

Someone gave a hard jerk on one of the ties on her G-string and Dasha gasped. The tiny bit of cloth started to fall away. Dasha stumbled back and the men shouted louder and louder as the last barrier dropped from her body and the cash floated across the stage.

Shame made her insides sick, like she was filled

with slick crude oil. The shame and horror would never end. This nightmare would never end. If she tried to escape, the men promised they would kill Mother and Father.

Dasha's legs trembled as she turned, bent over, and grabbed her ankles, completely exposing the part of her womanhood that she now despised.

The pulsing beat of the song ended and Dasha's whole body felt like she was bleeding from every pore. She could almost feel blood coating her skin.

She straightened, completely nude, soon to be forced into acts that sickened her even more. As she walked toward the three stairs that led down from the stage, she swayed her hips like the madame had taught her. Why couldn't she ignore the men who continued to whistle at her and shout horrible things?

"I'd like a piece of that."

"I'll fuck her right here. Just spread your pussy, baby."

Dasha held her hand to her belly as if that could settle the sickness inside.

Why couldn't she leave her body and visit someplace in her mind like Yulia did? Where did Yulia go when she traveled outside her body with her mind?

Dasha glanced over her shoulder and saw her pretty friend whose brown eyes looked blank, empty. Yulia followed Dasha off the stage, but was the girl even aware of her own movements?

When Dasha stepped onto the floor, which was sticky beneath her heels from spilled alcohol, steel fingers grabbed her upper arm and jerked her sideways. Dasha let out a small cry as she tripped and fell against the handler, who forced her to her feet again while almost dragging her across the room to the madame who scheduled all of the girls' *appointments*.

"I'm going to let you have it good if you don't pick it up during the show," Eddie said close to her ear, his breath hot and foul with beer. Dasha flinched. "I think I'll have to teach you a lesson anyway. How much depends on how you behave the rest of the night." He stroked her hair away from her ear. "Maybe you screw up so much because you like what I do to you, slut."

The man's touch and his words made the ratsnakes in her belly squirm and push their way into her chest. He was one of the men who forced himself on her, sometimes in front of other men or the girls. Sometimes in front of everyone. And sometimes alone where he would hurt her in ways that no one would see. Make her scream and cry and beg.

Which was worse?

Dasha tried to pretend Eddie was nothing but a stranger she had never seen before as he took her to the madame. *Block him out like Yulia does. Force him out of your thoughts.*

They were almost to the madame, who was speaking with the horrid man who had waved the handful of American dollars. Madame Cherie was a beautiful but sharp-tongued woman who constantly trained the girls to dance and please men. It seemed strange, though, that she never treated the girls like wares for sale. Sometimes Dasha thought the madame might not know that none of the girls had chosen to be whores.

Was that possible?

One of Dasha's stilettos skidded when she stepped

into a puddle of spilled alcohol and she almost fell, but Eddie had a tight hold on her. She cringed and flinched as, at the same time her handler steadied her, a man bumped into her. The man tugged her bare nipple and another man slapped her naked backside hard enough that she knew there would be a mark.

Because of threats against their families and friends, none of the girls ever said anything aloud about being taken from their homes, their country. Nothing about the fact that they did not choose to be whores with ten, or even more, men a night. Could the madame not know because a word was never spoken about it? Always the cruel handlers were close.

Yet couldn't the madame see from the girls' expressions, their lack of pleasure in their task, that they did not belong in this place?

Sometimes Dasha thought she saw something in the madame's eyes. As if she suspected something was not right. Dasha prayed that Madame Cherie would learn the truth and find a way out for them all and for all of their families and friends to remain safe.

It was the only hope Dasha had.

CHAPTER THREE

I would sell my soul

"It's so good to have every one of my ducklings around me." Mama gave a broad smile like she always did when the seven of us joined her and Daddy around the family supper table.

She reached over and squeezed Willow's hand. "And my newest girl." Mama looked around at the bunch of us. "Who can kick all of your arses at basketball."

We laughed. It was true. Willow was five-eleven and had been such a good point guard at NYU that the WNBA had even tried to recruit her out of college. Instead she'd gone on to get her doctorate in education and married my formerly bachelor-for-life oldest brother, Zane.

Zane smiled and squeezed Willow's hand and winked at her. The grin she gave him was naughty, and I almost grinned myself.

"Is anyone up to the challenge of a little three-on-three?" Willow asked with a wicked smile.

Noise around the table broke out with the guys insisting this time they were going to beat her, Zane, and me. Picture five-four me next to five-eleven Willow and my over-six-foot-tall brothers. I could still kick major ass, though. I was quick and hard to block and had a mean layup. My younger sister, Rori, was shaking her head. She never joined us—might break a nail.

Zane also worked for RED, only no one in our family or any of our friends could know. Their lives would be in danger because of our line of work, and neither of us was willing to take that chance. Family and friends thought Zane was still Secret Service.

They also believed that after my time in Army Special Forces, I went on to work for an interpreter service. I speak nine languages, so no one has ever had a problem believing that.

The people around me—even at RED—never knew I'd been an assassin in the past, and they never would.

The exceptions were Karen Oxford and Nick Donovan. Nick had drawn every bit of my horrible history out of me. Over strawberry crêpes one morning during our last op I told him everything. Well, almost everything. Donovan must have put something into those crêpes to make me talk so much—other than making them orgasmically good.

Yet even after I'd let it all hang out, he still wouldn't tell me much about his own past.

It was starting to piss me off.

I turned my focus back to my family.

"You sure went all-out for supper, Mama." I sighed with my hand on my full belly and slumped in my seat where I sat between my brothers Zane and Evan.

Nettle soup, roast stuffed loin of lamb, celery with cream, and cauliflower in cheese sauce for dinner. Yum. Mama made the best Irish dishes in Boston.

I grinned at Mama and caught what I thought was a hint of wistfulness in her gaze. That one look made my thoughts pause before Troy spoke.

"Mama likes to spoil the Marine," Troy said with a snort as he gestured with his fork to Ryan, back from his latest tour with the Marines. Ryan was Special Forces and built like a tank.

Ryan didn't have any kind of witty comeback like he normally did. Instead he concentrated on his food. He was putting away as much of Mama's good cooking as he could shove into the gut of his huge six-two frame.

"Someone's in a bad mood," Evan said as he pointed at Ryan with his butter knife. Evan, Troy, and Sean laughed. I frowned.

Daddy leaned back and stretched his arms before clasping his fingers behind his head as his green eyes met Mama's. "That's my Molly," he said. "Perfect supper as usual."

"You just want your sweets, Keegan." They smiled at each other, and as always love was there—except something was different.

My supper started to sour in my stomach. What was wrong? It must have had to do with Ryan, since he was acting even more strange. Not to mention he was back from his last tour so soon. He'd only been gone around seven months.

Mama stood, her large bosoms stretching the fabric of her flower-print dress. "I'll need two of you to help me carry out the dessert."

"I'm there!" Sean pushed back his chair.

Troy beat the rest of us, too. "On your tail, kid," he said as the pair headed to the kitchen with Mama.

I glanced at Ryan, who was decimating a perfectly good piece of cauliflower. It almost looked like mashed potatoes. His jaw was tight as he pressed the tines of his fork into the cauliflower. Whatever it was had to be serious for him to act this way. It was going to drive me nuts if I didn't find out what it was. Soon.

Mama, Sean, and Troy emerged from the kitchen each carrying a plate with our desserts. "Porter cake," she said with a cheery smile. "Made with Guinness, of course."

"Porter cake's the best." Sean thought every dessert Mama made was the best. He plopped himself down in his seat and set the cake he'd been carrying directly in front of him on the table.

Evan reached across the table and snatched the cake plate that had been in front of Sean. "You're not hogging the whole thing, brat," Evan said.

"Hey." Sean scowled. "Give it back."

Evan cut himself an enormous piece. "When I get mine, kid."

I shook my head. Over the summer my twelve-year-old brother, Sean, had suddenly gone from a kid to a gangly almost-teenager on the cusp of "the dark side" as Daddy liked to say.

It wasn't long at all before the three cakes had been devoured. Mostly by my five brothers, even though Willow and I had healthy appetites, too. Rori just picked at hers as usual.

When we were finished, Daddy insisted on a round of single-malt Irish whiskey. That was different. He usually only brought out the whiskey on Christmas and on New Year's Day.

Daddy finished pouring us each a glass two fingers high with whiskey. Even for Rori who tried to protest that she didn't want any.

When he'd made his way around the table, Daddy set the bottle down. It clunked on the plaid tablecloth that covered the aged maple wood table. He raised his own glass. "Here's to the Steele family, together in body, soul, and heart."

Everyone looked as puzzled as I felt but murmured back, "To the Steele family," before we followed Daddy and slammed back the contents of our glasses.

I drank mine in one swallow and felt the harsh burn of whiskey hit my throat. Having been a sniper in the Army's Special Forces, surrounded by males, I'd learned how to drink my whiskey without choking. The alcohol rushed to my stomach harsh and hot.

Rori and Sean both coughed. Daddy had even given my twelve-year-old brother a small shot? Definitely something was up.

My heart started to drop as Daddy set his empty glass on the table as hard as a judge hitting his mallet to bring the court to order. Everyone at the table went quiet as Daddy moved to Mama's chair and he gripped the high spindles that rose to either side of her.

Ice crawled over my skin and in the silence I glanced at each member of my family, all with an expression of confusion, concern, maybe even fear. Ryan didn't look up. He just stared into his empty whiskey glass.

Daddy cleared his throat, and I looked at him. I took in his face, rough with whiskers, and the skin around his eyes lined with age. His skin was tan and weathered from a life of hard labor as a mason, and his hair gray, streaked with white, but his eyes were still as glass green as my own.

I clenched my hand around my whiskey glass and brought my gaze to Mama's. Her throat worked, and my body grew colder still as I realized she was trying to put up a brave display so that we would all be okay with whatever news they had. Her cheeks that normally had a rose hue seemed pale. Was she thinner? She was. Mama had always been robust, slightly plump from her cheeks to her ankles. Why hadn't I noticed earlier?

Daddy cleared his throat again. His Boston Irish brogue was strong as he spoke. "I guess there's no beatin' around the bush. I can tell from your faces you have your suspicions that we've not-so-good news to tell."

Everyone else remained silent. I was so cold my teeth started to chatter.

"Molly . . ." He paused and patted Mama's arm with one hand while gripping her opposite shoulder tight with his other hand. "Your mama has breast cancer."

Pressure squeezed my head as if all the air in the room pressed against it while stealing my breath at the same time. Muffled silence. My blood throbbing in my ears. Heart in my throat.

Mama, breast cancer? I started to shake. No. God, no.

"Come now." Mama's words and her own light Irish accented words barely made it through my nearly deaf ears. She gave us her normal no-nonsense look, as if she was pushing away any emotion that might be inside her right now. "No sense in you all looking like it's the end of the world."

"Mama!" Rori flung herself from her chair to our mother. Her sobs were loud as she wrapped her arms around Mama's neck and cried against her large bosoms.

I stared at those bosoms as voices started reverberating in my muffled head. She had cancer. There. Strange thoughts went through my mind as I sat in my chair. Her thick gray hair might be gone soon. Her breasts, too.

What if the cancer had progressed farther? What if—

I squeezed my fists on the checkered tablecloth. A strangled sound tried to come from my throat but didn't make it out.

Everyone but Ryan and I had gone to Mama to hug her. Daddy must have told Ryan about the cancer to bring him home, to be with us when he told the rest of the family the gut-wrenching news.

My big, hulking brothers didn't bother to hide the tears that trickled down their cheeks. I caught a glimpse of Rori's blotched red face and swollen eyes.

And still I sat.

My skin numb. My face numb. My eyes as dry and painful to blink as my dry throat hurt to swallow.

Daddy gripped the spindles on the back of Mama's chair, and his fingers were bloodless. He bent his head, his chin touching his chest, his eyes closed.

"Everything's going to be fine." Mama's voice wavered yet at the same time sounded strong and determined. She shooed everyone away. "Go on now. Sit down."

Rori was the last to release Mama and force herself away, tears slipping down her blotchy face.

Still I sat.

I couldn't move. My muscles didn't want to work. Didn't want to obey me as I told myself I should go to my mother. Hug her. And let loose the tears that burned behind my eyes. Tears backed up from countless years of being unable to cry. Even now at the most important time of all.

Shame burned my cheeks as my brothers and sister returned to their chairs and sat. Mama met my gaze and smiled, like she knew what emotions were building inside me that wanted to spew like a volcano, my body shaking me with the force of it all. Her eyes said it was okay. Everything would be okay.

It wasn't okay.

Mama turned her gaze to Daddy as she looked up at him and patted one of his hands gripping the chair spindle. When he raised his head he was tight-lipped, his normally tanned face pale and drawn.

Daddy started to talk, but nothing came out. He cleared his throat then managed to speak. "The biopsy report showed the cancer is invasive." The sound his throat made when he tried to clear it again was strangled.

Mama patted his hand and she said what he couldn't. "The doctors started me on chemotherapy last week." She spoke easily, as if this were a simple thing. "The cancer is far enough along that the docs need to shrink it before they perform surgery."

Her words didn't seem real. None of what she and Daddy said felt real.

Ryan finally took his gaze from his plate and focused on our mother. His voice was rough, serious. "You're too goddamned tough to let it win, Mama." He looked around the table. "She's going to beat it. She raised us, didn't she?"

"Do not take the Lord's name in vain, child," she said, as she always did if we strayed over that line.

She then moved her gaze to each of us, and there was strength and determination in her eyes as she spoke. "Be strong and courageous. Do not be afraid or terrified because of them, for the Lord your God goes with you; He will never leave you nor forsake you."

"Deuteronomy thirty-one, six," I found myself saying in a whisper, the words coming to my mind automatically from my Irish Catholic upbringing. I had long ago turned away from the faith I had grown up with. But at that moment I found myself praying that there really was a God and that Mama's faith in Him would eradicate every bit of cancer from her body.

I finally found that I had the ability to move my

body. The chair legs scraped against the wood floor as I pushed my chair back. The ache in my legs was as if my muscles still wanted to refuse me, but I made it to Mama. The wood was hard beneath my knees as I knelt beside her chair and wrapped my arms around her waist. I pressed my cheek against her bosom and squeezed my eyes tight.

"I love you, Mama," I said as I breathed in her scent, which reminded me of love and home and precious memories. "I love you."

Her lips were soft against my head as she pressed her lips to my hair. "I know you do, child. Everything is going to be fine."

I wanted to believe her, but I said nothing and just pressed myself closer to her and held her tight, as if that would anchor her to earth forever.

CHAPTER FOUR

Nick

Nick Donovan clenched his hand around his cell phone before he shoved it into the clip on his belt. He braced his forearm against the wall beside the window of the third-floor Manhattan apartment and stared at the Elite Gentleman's Club through the gap in the dingy but thick gauze curtains. He, Steele, and Kerrison had gone over the Elite's building schematics before they left so they knew the layout well.

The phone conversation he'd just had with Lexi played over in his mind. It wasn't like her to let the smallest amount of personal pain into her voice. At one time she'd shared some of her dark past with him. In that moment he'd known that what she'd been through had hardened her to the point where she thought showing any kind of emotional weakness was a flaw.

Like his own past had hardened him. A past he couldn't let die. Or wouldn't.

In the background, Jensen and Weiss argued about

the best surveillance tactics to use as they kept an eye on the Elite Gentleman's Club on East Sixtieth Street, between First and Second Avenues.

Nick and Steele's team were camped out above a camera shop. It hadn't been easy renting the apartment and getting their gear in without attracting attention once the place was cleared.

Weiss had posed as a cable TV worker who was installing cable in the apartment Jensen had just rented with Smithe. She'd refused to room with Weiss. If it wasn't for the fact Lexi's behavior had set his gut to roiling, Nick would have found the memory of Weiss and Jensen's last op during *Cinderella* amusing.

Getting the former occupants out of this apartment had been an even harder job, but Takamoto and Weiss had found the couple new digs and made sure they would keep their mouths shut.

A seasoned RED agent, Weiss had an uncanny ability to change into multiple personas, each distinct from the others—more so than any operative Nick had known. Weiss even looked damned brutal and deadly when he wanted, and no doubt he had scared the shit out of the couple in one way or another.

"Something up?" Kerrison said from behind Nick, her southern accent light.

Nick tried to relax his clenched his jaw as he thought about the slight tremor in Lexi's voice while she'd told him her operational status.

"Steele just called in." Donovan glanced away from the window to look at Kerrison. "She'll arrive at JFK tomorrow instead of tonight." That fact alone had been enough to send off alarm bells in his head. Lexi was never late on an op, much less not giving some kind of explanation for a change in plans. "You and Steele will move into your place in Brooklyn Tuesday instead of tomorrow afternoon."

"Works for me." Kerrison smirked as she inclined her head to Weiss and Jensen. "If those two can shut up long enough for us all to roll out our sleeping bags and get some rest tonight." Kerrison tilted her head and studied Nick. "Something's definitely up with you."

The new agent was too damned observant. *Save it for the op.* "Just thinking about the setup," Nick said.

Kerrison gave a slow nod before she left and walked toward the small apartment's grungy kitchen. Nick couldn't hear her, but she said something to Smithe, who hooked his thumbs in the belt loops of his jeans and grinned at her.

Nick focused his attention on the window and stared at the Elite. His gut churned as the memory of his own sister being auctioned as a sex slave and the fucking hell she'd been put through. Even killing the sonofabitch who'd bought and sexually abused Kristin hadn't given Nick one goddamned ounce of satisfaction.

Maybe bringing down Hagstedt, the man ultimately behind the auction ring that had emotionally devastated his sister, would.

Nick barely kept from ramming his fist into the wall.

Hagstedt was a dead man.

Nick's thoughts turned back to Lexi. He didn't know how it happened, but he'd started caring for her far more than he'd expected to. Hell, he wasn't the relationship type. He had too much darkness in his past.

But then again, so did Lexi.

Now he knew what the expression meant when someone had "gotten under your skin," because that was how he felt when he was around Lexi, or when he thought about her. Like she'd become a part of him that he couldn't separate from himself.

"Shit." Nick rubbed his eyes with his thumb and forefinger. "Way too deep, Donovan." Not to mention dangerous territory. Letting Lexi Steele have that kind of effect on him was just asking for trouble. "Because that's what the little shit is," he mumbled under his breath. "Trouble."

CHAPTER FIVE

Guinness and Pecan Sandies

Seeing Donovan when I walked into baggage claim shot heat through my chest. I almost came to a stop on the grungy terminal floor.

Donovan being there, waiting for me when I wasn't expecting it, set me off balance—probably because I'd been so preoccupied with thoughts of Mama.

One feeling after another shot through me, including my sudden desire to be comforted in his strong arms. I'd never allowed myself to need any person except for my family. I needed them.

As much as I hated to admit it, right now I needed Donovan.

I managed to keep one foot moving in front of the other until I reached him. "You shouldn't be here." I barely kept from throwing myself against him. I tilted my head to meet his gaze. "It's not a good idea to be seen in public together."

Considering how different I'd look once I was

undercover, that was a pretty lame statement, but I intended to stick with it.

"Tell me what happened, Steele." Donovan's blue eyes stared at me with such intensity I wanted to look away but didn't. I wouldn't. "Don't give me any bullshit that everything's okay with you. I know something's wrong."

For some reason I wanted anger. I wanted to tell him to fuck off, mind his own goddamned business, or tell him that nothing was wrong and I didn't know what the hell he was talking about.

Instead I couldn't speak, and I closed my eyes without meaning to. Every bit of the pain centered in my chest wanted to explode. I wanted to scream, to shout, to let that pain echo throughout the entire terminal.

I don't know how I ended up in Donovan's arms, my face against his hard chest. His musky scent was usually sensual and sexual. Now it was just comforting.

"Tell me what happened." His warm breath ruffled my hair as he spoke, and I tried not to tremble in his arms as I thought about Mama.

My eyes were still shut tight, aching, burning. I didn't realize until then that I'd released the handle of my carry-on bag and wrapped my arms around his waist.

He moved his hand up and down my spine. "Don't hold back."

"Mama has breast cancer," I said, so dazed the words came out before I realized I had spoken them.

"Jesus Christ." Donovan held me tighter. "I'm sorry,

Lex." He pressed his cheek against the top of my head. "How bad is it?"

"Bad." My voice was scratchy. "Mammy's acting like it's not a big deal, but it is. The cancer is advanced enough that it could spread through her entire body if the surgery doesn't get it all after she goes through chemo."

"Jesus," he repeated. I would have felt crushed from how tight he was holding me now if I didn't need it so much.

"Let's get your things," he said after he'd held me for God knew how long. "Before someone makes off with them."

I nodded, opened my eyes, and drew away as he released me. My eyes felt as if they were red and swollen even though I hadn't shed a tear. I turned away without looking at him and faced the baggage carousel. Three of the four pieces of red luggage that I'd purchased for this op were forlornly making the loop with no other suitcases left from other passengers.

Donovan headed toward the carousel before the luggage could complete the circuit and disappear behind the rubber flaps. For the first time since finding him waiting for me, I really looked at Donovan.

And swallowed at the sense of familiarity of every movement he made. His long legs were firm and muscular within his snug faded Levi's. He wore a blue turtleneck beneath a loose shirt where he no doubt had holstered his Beretta.

His shirtsleeves were rolled up with only a hint of the turtleneck's sleeves showing. His broad shoulders

dipped when he grabbed the first suitcase off the carousel, and his forearm flexed as he picked up the
piece of luggage and set it beside him.

He grasped the handle of the second suitcase, and
an image of his hands on my body slipped through my
mind. Hands that were capable of such incredible violence were so gentle and erotic on my skin when he
caressed my body with his callused fingers. No matter
how wild and rough our sex had been at times, he still
managed to touch me in ways I didn't think any other
man ever could.

With a large red bag tucked under one arm and a
big suitcase in each hand, Donovan returned to where
I waited. He carried the bags as easily as if they were
empty cases rather than stuffed with clothing, makeup,
and other things I'd need as a madame for the *Little
Red* op.

I like to travel light, but this op called for a hell of a
lot of props, including the dozen pairs of stilettos that
Georgina had been certain I needed to match each and
every outfit. And then there were the six white-blond
genuine-hair wigs in different styles stashed in one of
the cases. I'd never gone undercover as a blond who
could've been Norwegian. The wigs were so pale, they
were almost silvery.

It seemed like ages since Georgina and I had gone on
my "madame" shopping extravaganza the day before—
before my brothers, sister, and I learned Mama's news.

My gut churned again and my whole body hurt as
I thought of my mother. I was going to make sure this
op went smooth and fast. I had to get back to Boston
before Mama's surgery.

Without looking at Donovan, I bent and gripped the handle of the wheeled red carry-on before I stood and met his gaze.

"I didn't bring one of the rental cars, so we'll grab a taxi." He waited for me to walk beside him and head through the sliding glass doors that led to the curb outside the terminal.

The icy November breeze caused me to shiver. Having been so preoccupied, I hadn't thought to put on one of the sweaters in the suitcases. I only had my red button-up blouse, which let the wind through to my skin as if it were mesh instead of cotton. When I left Boston, the sky had been crystal blue, the weather fair in comparison with New York—unusual for Boston considering the season. Here the sky brooded with thick gray clouds that threatened rain.

Once the luggage was stowed in the trunk of a taxi and Donovan and I were in the backseat, my body slowly warmed. It was entirely due to the fact that he was sitting so close to me. It wasn't just the heat of his body. No, it was the instant reaction I always had to him whenever he was close.

Donovan gave the Arab driver an address. The man's red-and-white-checked headcloth, bound by a black band, moved as he nodded. He glanced back, revealing more of his strong features and thick mustache. As soon as he pulled from the front of the cabs waiting for fares, his cell phone rang and he answered in an Arabic dialect that I was familiar with, but I didn't attempt to listen to his conversation.

Actually, I didn't really pay attention to much of anything. Normally little would have escaped my awareness, but right then I didn't care. Instead, I stared out the window, barely registering the city decked out for the holidays. My thoughts traveled back to yesterday evening, and Daddy and Mama's announcement.

Because of my current career, and especially because of my past—which included massive amounts of both wanted and unwanted training—I was usually on constant guard. Donovan's presence and my complete confidence in him allowed me to let go while I tried to come to terms with Mama's diagnosis.

Not that I really thought I would.

Donovan paid the driver and thanked him in Arabic before he led me up a set of stairs of a brownstone. My mind had cleared and I'd gathered my wits enough to know we were on a really nice Boerum Hill street in Brooklyn.

The red-brick exterior of the building we were about to go into was brighter, cleaner looking than most brownstones I'd seen, as if someone had scrubbed it with a giant Brillo pad. Two medium-size pine trees grew in huge planters to either side of the shining brass-and-wood double doors leading into the brownstone. Hundreds of white Christmas lights twinkled on the branches of the trees. Big gold bows were tied to the end of every branch.

Donovan set a red suitcase on the landing and used a key to open one of the doors that led into the brownstone. He gave a nod for me to go in.

"You and Kerrison have the third-floor apartment. Two bedrooms, two baths." The door latch clicked shut behind us. "Living in such nice digs will back up your story to Hagstedt's men when you tell them you've had plenty of cash that you've kept in a Zurich bank from the cathouse you owned, then sold."

"Yeah, yeah." I sighed. "And I've been living on those funds since I was busted and put out of business and now I'm running out of cash thanks to my bad habit of spending too much money. Got it."

He glanced down at me. "I don't think the real Lexi has that particular problem."

True. That was easy to see by the modest triple-decker apartment in Southie that I lived in. Nothing special. I stashed and invested most of my money. Material things weren't high on my priority list.

A big portion of my accumulated funds was blood money, though, from when I'd been an assassin. It still made me gut-sick to know the cash was in an account in the Cayman Islands. I hadn't wanted to acknowledge it, much less figure out what to do with it. The rest was in legit U.S. bank accounts, IRAs, and conservative stocks.

My mind churned as we skipped the elevator and I followed Donovan up the well-maintained wood stairs that didn't even creak as we climbed. Mama's medical bills would be massive, and my parents didn't have enough insurance to cover close to the amount that would accumulate. If it took everything I'd saved, I'd help pay every dime of the bills. But I'd use only what I'd earned and saved over the years from working for RED. I wasn't going to use tainted money for anything related to my family.

My brothers and sister would help, too, of course.

We were a tight-knit family. Even though some of us had our differences, we were always there for one another and always had been. No matter what. No one messed with the Steele family.

When we reached a heavy oak door on the second floor, Donovan set one suitcase down, dug in a front pocket, and tossed me a key.

The metal was warm in my fingers as I unlocked and opened the door. Lemon oil was the first scent I caught—along with cinnamon and pine—when I took a quick glimpse of the gorgeous interior and a small Christmas tree. "*Nice,* Donovan."

He looked like he was hiding one of his adorable grins. I tilted my head, wondering what he was up to. "Fridge is stocked with Mountain Dew and Guinness," he said. "Plenty of Pecan Sandies and Doritos are packed in one of the cabinets."

"Thank God." I dropped my carry-on, and it thunked on the hardwood floor as I headed straight for the fridge. "You are one incredibly smart man."

Cool air flowed over my face when I opened the door and grabbed two brown bottles from one of the four six-packs of beer that sat next to no less than five two-liters of Mountain Dew. The fridge was loaded with other foodstuffs, but who cared about that when a Guinness was waiting?

The bottles of beer chilled my palms as I faced Donovan and handed him one after he picked up an opener off the counter. "Not just smart but brilliant," I added. "You even thought to buy the most important utensil known to man."

He winked. "I didn't want you to break a tooth in your hurry to crack one open."

I had already raised my bottle to my lips and almost snorted Guinness up my nose when I laughed. Would have been a waste of good beer.

A little of the heaviness I'd been feeling rose off my shoulders as I grinned at him. The easy camaraderie we had known the summer relaxed me a bit. I took a healthy swig of beer and glanced away from him to look at the furnished apartment.

My gaze skimmed the richly polished wood floor, the burgundy draperies pulled to the sides of wood blinds that matched the floor and the kitchen cabinets. A stuffed taupe couch and loveseat were in the living room along with a burgundy recliner.

"You really went all-out." I had a hard time imagining my apartment in the egg-yolk-yellow South Boston building looking anything like this place. No, this was more like the bottom floor of the brownstone Donovan had purchased for himself and his sister in Back Bay. "How'd you get something so nice so fast?"

"Plenty of apartments were available." Donovan shrugged. "Just picked one I thought you'd like."

I set my empty beer bottle on the granite counter and smirked. "And you chose this one after seeing my apartment in Southie?"

As he winked at me, he was probably picturing some of my clothing scattered on my carpet with an empty pizza box on the coffee table. I'd pegged Donovan for a neat-freak considering how spotless he always kept his place, but he never said a word when he'd been in my apartment in the triple-decker building, known locally as a trip.

"Is Kerrison already unpacked?" I leaned a little to the side to get a better view of the hallway. All I could see was one open doorway with a large four-poster bed covered with a chocolate-brown satin comforter and turquoise satin pillows. "Is she here?"

Donovan placed his own bottle on the counter and moved close to me.

He caught me off guard, but if he had been a criminal coming at me I would have had my Glock pressed against his forehead before he knew it. Or I would have taken him down to the floor in one smooth jujitsu move.

But this was Donovan.

Every bit of me went still. I couldn't step away from him for the life of me as he placed his hands on my hips. Was my heart pounding anymore? I wasn't sure at all as he brought our bodies so close my breasts almost touched his.

The headiness that overcame me certainly wasn't from one Guinness. I could easily put away a six-pack during a party. Or the amount of beer I drank whenever the Red Sox played and I was sitting on my back balcony while my neighbors were on theirs, and we were all yelling at our televisions with every play made.

Champagne—that was another story. Right now I felt like I'd had an entire bottle all to myself, my mind nearly spinning from his closeness.

"You need to lie down." He skimmed his lips over my forehead and I shivered, desire speeding through me like a well-aimed shot with a handgun. "You're tired. It's in your eyes. In your voice. I bet you didn't get one damned bit of sleep last night."

That was true, but having Donovan tuck me in wasn't going lead to rest—for now. That I could guarantee.

His hand felt warm and firm, comforting as he led me to the hallway. He bypassed the first bedroom and took me into one that might have been a little larger, but I could barely concentrate. It was hard to pay attention to details with a big brass bed only five feet away. When we stood beside the bed, he brought me around to face him and cupped my cheeks with his warm palms and stroked them with his thumbs. My whole body was going to get all rubbery if he didn't stop.

"Rest," he said and kissed the top of my head. "Now."

I swallowed. "I think you and I have very different ideas about the *best* use for a bed."

"No." Donovan's features grew taut, intense, as he pushed my hair away from my face. "Not one damned bit different at all."

CHAPTER SIX

Where's my Glock?

Donovan and I reached for each other at the same time and I groaned against his lips when they met mine. He slipped his tongue into my mouth and kissed me slow and gentle. I'd expected hard, fast, urgent.

The kiss was breathtaking, and he was in complete control. I couldn't have changed his dominance at that moment if I'd tried.

God, he tasted good. A familiar rumble rose in his chest, his sound of need making mine stronger than ever. Heat bolted from my belly button to the wetness between my thighs. I ached so much, I wanted to strip, climb him, wrap my thighs around his hips, and have him take me right where we stood. Forget slow and easy sex. I wanted him inside me *now*.

His cock felt solid as he pressed it to my belly, his jeans rough through my thin blouse. I moaned again and wrapped my arms around his neck. His musky scent enveloped me, intoxicated me to the point my mind felt like it might really start spinning. Who needed champagne?

Donovan moved his lips from mine to the side of my mouth before laying more soft kisses along my jawline. I started to say something—I'm not sure what—when he bit my nipple through the cotton blouse. I gasped then clenched my fists in his hair as he moved his mouth to my other breast and gave that nipple a soft bite, too.

"Donovan." I almost stuttered his name as he licked and sucked my nipples until my blouse was wet where his mouth teased me. "I—"

The strength he used when he pressed his fingers between my thighs caused me to cry out. I swear I could feel him already sliding his fingers through my slick folds even though I was wearing jeans.

I clenched Donovan's shoulders as I tipped my head back while he rubbed his cock against my belly and stroked his fingers between my thighs. Did I smell my own musk even though my clothes were still on?

The buttons on my shirt felt slippery as I fumbled with them, trying to hurry and get it off. Donovan wasn't any help as he nuzzled my neck and made me gasp and cry out at every one of his erotic touches, which caused my fingers to fumble even more.

Had to breathe. Had to get my shirt off. Had to get Donovan inside me.

It took too long as far as I was concerned, but I finally unbuttoned my blouse all the way. Now how was I going to get my bra off without him letting go of me? I really had to make sure I was always wearing one of my front-clasp bras.

Donovan made low growling noises while I shrugged off my blouse then tried to bring my breathing to a normal level as I squirmed in his arms. He moved his fingers to the back clasp of my bra and then I was flinging it across the room.

His palms were flat on my back as I met his gaze. Both amusement and dark desire was in his eyes.

"Payback, Donovan," I said, my voice husky, as I reached between us and grasped the hard ridge of his cock, so big and long against his jeans.

"You've always liked to live dangerously." He narrowed his gaze as he grabbed my ass again. I gripped his shoulders as he carried me to the bed.

Yeah, with Donovan the more dangerous, the better.

The mattress barely gave when he laid me on my back on the soft comforter, but it dipped from his weight when he got on. He moved between my thighs, which he pushed as far apart as he could.

"If you haven't noticed, we still have our clothes on." I reached for the fly of his jeans, but he pushed my hands away.

He lowered himself so that his palms were braced on the bed, his shirt almost brushing my nipples, while he captured my gaze. "You have the most beautiful green eyes." He bent to brush his lips over my cheek. "I love seeing how they look when you're aroused."

Something hot exploded in my chest and I caught my breath because of the way he was looking at me.

Donovan kissed me again.

Exit rational thought.

When he took my mouth with such slow and deliberate dominance, I gave in to every sensation I was experiencing. Just feeling and going with what my body wanted.

He moved his mouth to my nipples again, licking and sucking, and biting. Each moan and cry I made came out with such unexpected force that my voice seemed to bounce off the bedroom's walls as the sounds reverberated through my body.

Wonder if the neighbors could hear?

Forget that. Who could give a damn when having sex with Donovan?

A shudder ran through me as Donovan licked my nipple with a long stroke. "I've always loved your breasts," he murmured between flicks of his tongue. "The salty taste of your skin."

Donovan moved lower and unbuttoned my jeans. Every word he said sent pulsing sensations through my body, and all I could do was fall into what he was doing to me.

He pulled my socks off before he tugged down my jeans along with my panties. He dragged them past my hips to my knees, and then my jeans fell to my ankles as he pushed my thighs apart. I squirmed and kicked my jeans the rest of the way off as he took a deep, audible breath.

"God, but I love your scent and tasting you here." He plunged two fingers into my core at the same time he buried his face in my folds.

I gasped then cried out as his long fingers found my G-spot and almost sent me off the edge with his first stroke. His stubble scraped my skin between my thighs, the feeling rough and erotic. He licked my clit and thrust his fingers in and out of my core. Then he pressed hard against my G-spot at the same time he sucked hard on my clit.

My body burned as if fire rushed over my skin the instant I climaxed. I fisted the comforter with my hands as my orgasm flamed hotter and hotter. So hot. God, so wild and hot. I arched my back, feeling like I was going to self-combust. Heat blazed from inside my body and it felt almost uncontainable.

Donovan kept licking and sucking, driving me crazy even as I thrashed against his face and became almost too sensitized to stand one more lick of his tongue or thrust of his fingers. I was crying out. I was whimpering. Then I was calling him names telling him the pleasure was too much. He didn't let up until I kicked his shoulder with my heel hard enough to get his attention.

His dark hair was tousled as he raised his head from between my legs, amusement in his blue eyes. "Can't handle it, Steele?"

"Screw you." I wiped the back of my hand across my sweaty forehead as my core continued to spasm. I rubbed away more droplets of sweat rolling down the sides of my face from my now damp hair. "Better yet, screw me."

Amusement remained in his gaze. "The way you were whimpering, I think anything else might be too much for you to handle."

"Are you *nuts*?" I lightly kicked his shoulder again. "You are so dead if you don't get up here and get inside me right this second."

"Maybe." He caught my ankle in his hand before I could plant it on his shoulder. "Maybe not."

I stared at him. "Where's my Glock?"

Donovan moved so that he was right over me, the hardness of his erection pressed against my folds, the feel of his shirt against my breasts rough and erotic, and the scrape of his jeans sensitizing me even more.

His scent alone was enough to make me want him, much less everything else that made up Nick Donovan. Goddamnit, I didn't know if I'd ever stop wanting him. He reached between us, unbuttoned his jeans, and freed his erection.

Donovan drove his cock into my core in one hard, fast thrust. I gasped with pleasure that sent my head spinning. Our sex had always been incredible, but it had been utterly, unbelievably better to have him inside me without a condom after we'd had our blood tests together this summer. I could feel every hard inch of him inside me, his bare cock stroking the inside of my core.

"Christ." I sucked in my breath as he held himself still, his cock stretching and filling me so perfectly. I arched my hips, pressing our bodies even closer together. "Get moving already, Donovan."

His eyes met mine as he started fucking me in deep strokes, his jeans scraping the inside of my thighs with every motion. Sweat already beaded his forehead, and he set his jaws like he was trying to control himself and hold back his orgasm.

The increased sensations were almost too much as I let them sweep me away. My eyes practically rolled back in my head with every thrust as he stretched me and touched me so deep it caused me to gasp stroke by stroke.

"I don't think I can hold back." The strain in his voice made his words sound almost guttural.

"Then come." I made indescribable sounds of pleasure. Nothing was better than having Donovan inside me. Every time we were together it seemed even more so. "I had mine and this feels so good it might be too much for me to handle another orgasm." God, wasn't that the truth.

"Lex—"

I reached between our bodies and fondled his balls and what I could grasp of his erection.

"Christ!" His cock throbbed as I tightened my grip at the base while he came.

I squeezed his cock and rubbed my hand on the inch or two that wasn't inside me. I didn't let up during his last several strokes and the big man shuddered when he stopped thrusting. I moved my hand away as he pressed his groin to mine, his cock still pulsing inside me.

Donovan let some of his weight pin me to the bed as he braced his forearms on the mattress and met my eyes. "Goddamnit, Steele. What am I going to do with you?"

I wrapped my arms around his neck and smiled. "Make me one of your gourmet dinners. I'm starved."

He gave me his quirky little grin and kissed me. "Demanding, but you're easy to please."

"Ha." I grinned back. "Just wait till it's time for dessert."

Donovan brushed his lips against mine. "Can't wait."

For a long time we lay together and I enjoyed the feel of being in his strong arms. It was a comfort that blocked out the real world.

But my past wasn't like the real world. At least I didn't want it to be. It had been mine, though. Every bloody inch by inch.

Christ. I moved away from Donovan, suddenly feeling unclean inside. I *was* unclean inside, no matter how hard I worked to accept what I'd done in the past, who I'd been.

"What's wrong, Steele?" Donovan caressed my shoulder as I rolled onto my back and stared at the ceiling.

"It ruins everything." I shook my head back and forth on my pillow. "Why can't I make it stop?"

Donovan raised himself on his elbow and I met his concerned eyes. "Hey." He stroked his fingers up and down my belly. "We've talked about this. You weren't given any choice." Trust him to know exactly what was bothering me. "You've got to accept the fact that you did what you had to."

I closed my eyes for a moment, blocking out his handsome image. "I can see the faces of every man or woman I assassinated." I opened my eyes and met his. "Sometimes I want them to blur, to fade away. But then I realize I deserve to remember, to see them in my dreams. It's only right since I took their lives."

Donovan stroked the side of my face. "Try, Lexi. You don't deserve to feel like this all of the time. It wasn't your fault. None of it was."

I pictured the bastards at FAS. After what they'd done to me and forced me to do to others—theirs were dead faces I could live with. With satisfaction, even.

My thoughts turned to the fact that Donovan would never talk about his own past, yet he knew just about every dark secret I had.

I frowned. "When are you going to tell me what happened to make you so hard inside? Whatever it is holds you back from all of us. Not just me, but your sister, too."

Donovan settled onto his back and I rolled onto my side to look at him. He clasped his hands behind his head, and stared up at the ceiling. The way his muscles moved and flexed beneath his shirt, and the hard look on his features, showed his power and strength. The tenseness of his jaw told me he didn't want to discuss his past. Like always.

"I told you about what eats at my insides every single day of my life, Donovan." I grabbed his chin in my hand and forced him to look at me. "There's no reason why you can't tell me what's wrapped up so tight inside you." His blue eyes darkened as I spoke. "It can't be any worse than what I've done."

Donovan pulled away from me as he pushed himself up in bed. "It's different, Steele." He didn't look at me as he swung his legs off the bed, stood, then tucked himself in and fastened his Levi's. "It's a lot worse."

"This is total bullshit." Heat caused my skin to burn as I climbed out of bed, but this time the heat was from anger. "You need to let me inside that little black box you keep locked away so tight that I'd need at least a dozen keys to open it."

He said nothing, which pissed me off even more.

"I'm sure it has something to do with Manning, Lloyd, Harrison, and Freeman." I stood beside Donovan. I was naked, he wasn't, but I didn't feel vulnerable in the least. "Black ops? Was that it? Some mission gone bad?"

Donovan made a low growling sound in his throat as his eyes met mine. "Forget it, Steele."

"No." I kept my tone firm and even. "I won't."

"I'm going to fix dinner," he said before he turned away.

I picked up my running shoe and almost nailed him in the ass as he walked out the bedroom door.

CHAPTER SEVEN

Belgian waffle interrogation

"The madame's fixin' to be late," Weiss said in our earpieces in a perfect southern drawl. He could nail any accent. Five of nine languages I speak perfectly, but I never could get down a southern drawl. Weiss was stationed at the observation apartment watching the entrance to the Elite Gentleman's Club. "I could use forty winks. She'd better waddle that lardass out of the cathouse soon, y'all."

Lardass. Smithe laughed over the comm and I almost snorted. In the recon vids I'd been shown before we put our plan into action, Madame Cherie was so skinny she could compete with any emaciated Hollywood actress. Her huge boobs were large enough to make her look like she should topple forward with just a step. Hollywood plastic all the way.

Donovan sat in the utility van's driver's seat while I was in the passenger seat. The silence between us had been thick, dark from his secrets, ever since he'd left the bedroom earlier.

"Four thirty-six." I glanced from the darkened sky—as dark as Manhattan could get at night—to the van's dim dashboard clock. Donovan had taken a spot next to the corner curb on this side of the stoplight. Perry and Takamoto's rented Olds snugged up against the curb behind us on the corner on the other side of the stoplight.

"Takamoto." The irritation in my voice wasn't really due to the fact the madame hadn't shown up yet. Or my disagreement with Donovan. It was more due to the fact that I was trapped, unable to get home when I felt I was needed more than ever. "Your surveillance notes show she's never been later than three forty-five AM. Fifty minutes is a hell of a discrepancy."

Takamoto had seen me lose my cool plenty of times before, so he didn't miss a beat as he replied from the Olds. "This is a first since we started observing the Elite this weekend."

"Strange," Jensen said into her earpiece from where she and Kerrison had parked their Buick illegally three cars up.

"I damned sure hope that Giger dick hasn't decided she knows too much and is taking care of her himself," Kerrison said.

"Dick?" Obvious amusement was in Smithe's voice. "Since when did the lovely new Agent Kerrison stop speaking like a lady?"

Kerrison sounded like she needed her sleep as she snapped back at him. "Fuck you, Smithe."

Immediately Jensen jumped in with, "Don't even give the jerk an opening."

"We're all getting a little edgy." I shifted in my seat and rolled my shoulders. "Cut the crap."

Donovan studied me, and I turned away. Thoughts of Mama kept burning in my brain. We had to make this op a fast one, because I needed to be there for her. I *needed* to be there for her.

"Yes, ma'am." Weiss's drawl was thicker and exaggerated this time. Almost at once he added, "Hang on. The hag's on her broomstick. She just flew right out of the shithole."

Hag was another word that didn't go with Madame Cherie, who was anything but. Sexy clothing showed off her big boobs and skinny ass. She had long, sleek black hair and an oval face piled with enough makeup to hide any flaw that came with age. The woman had to be close to forty, but she did a great job of looking closer to thirty.

My blood started stirring as I mentally prepared myself for the job. Finally, some action. "Anyone following her?"

"Nope." The connection crackled as Weiss spoke. "She's headed straight down Sixtieth Street toward Second Avenue like usual. Three minutes and she'll be yours."

I huffed out a breath. A one, two, three easy op. Still, we worked the job with backup to make sure there weren't any snags. I peered out the black utility van's passenger-side window and at the streetlight-illuminated sidewalk. No one spoke over the comm as we waited.

Perry broke the silence as he spoke from the car on

the other side of the stoplight behind us. "Madame is just about in your lap."

I jerked down my black wool balaclava over my head so that only my eyes and nose were exposed. I glanced at Donovan whose face mask was already in place, exposing only his blue eyes and the lightly lined skin around them. His gaze had a sharpness to it that made me wonder what he was thinking about. But I wasn't the kind of chick to ask what was on a guy's mind every time his attention was focused on anything but me. That was for insecure women, and I'm anything but.

"All yours, sweetheart," Smithe added. "And Steele, I'm talking to Donovan. If there was ever anything sweet about you, the polar ice caps might melt."

I would have rolled my eyes but I was too intent on watching for Madame Cherie. I stared at the side-view mirror and saw her round the corner. She tottered on the four-inch heels she wore despite the fact she was at least five-ten, six inches taller than me without her shoes. What with the heaviness of her boobs, her thin frame, and the heels she wobbled on—all up against my extensive training—she ought to be easy enough to grab in a hurry.

Donovan climbed into the windowless back of the utility van and prepared to open the sliding door. I grasped the passenger-door handle. When the madame was directly in front of the sliding door, I gave a quick nod to Donovan.

He slammed open the door at the same time I bolted out of the front seat. It was his job to help throw her in once I grabbed her.

I sprinted the six or seven feet between her and the van.

The bitch pulled a can of pepper spray out of her small purse—and nailed me full in the face.

"Fuck!" I was blinded as brutal pain burned my eyes, forcing wetness down my cheeks, soaking my balaclava. The spray set flame to my lungs, and my upper body spasmed as I started choking. My eyes, nose, and throat were burning too bad to even smell it.

I tore off my balaclava but gulped in more pepper through my mouth and coughed even harder. I could barely open my eyelids a slit but saw her blurry figure turn to run. In Special Forces and during RED training I'd been sprayed while being forced to finish off my assailant. I hadn't lost either hand-to-hand combat exercise.

This bitch was so not getting away. I was beyond pissed as I tackled her skinny ass and brought her down hard.

She landed with a harsh cry and I heard a *thump* that was probably her head against the concrete sidewalk. A metallic sound skittered away. The pepper spray can, probably.

I was ready to slug her just to make myself feel better, but someone jerked me away from behind. Through the blur in my eyes I saw Donovan grab the kicking and now screaming woman and literally toss her into the van.

"I'll drive," Kerrison said from behind me—she must have been the one who pulled me off the madame. "You two take care of her. And please shut her the hell up."

I was gritting my teeth too hard from pain to answer. Instead, I dove into the van and slammed the sliding door into place.

Kerrison swung the van onto the street with tires squealing in a good imitation of a movie car chase. I stumbled before I went after the madame as she bucked and thrashed against Donovan.

When I looked at the woman—the best I could considering that my sight wasn't any better yet—I saw that Donovan had not only cuffed her wrists but put plastic cuffs on her ankles as well.

The language the madame used as she screeched was so expressive she might have embarrassed my commanding officer in the Army. Well, hardly, but damn could she let it out.

Pepper spray straight in one's eyes isn't always followed by reason. But I managed not to slug her as I dropped beside her and Donovan. Can't hit a bitch when she's down.

"The gag and the blindfold are by her head." Blood rolled down Donovan's cheekbone. Looked like the madame had nailed him with her pointy stiletto heel.

I kept coughing, but I was blocking most of the pain now, like I'd blocked just about any kind of pain countless times over the years.

My sight was less bleary as I was rocked back and forth while trying to crawl toward the gag. "Jesus," I shouted at Kerrison between coughs. "We've got her. Let up on the NASCAR driving."

Kerrison said something that I couldn't hear and I realized my earpiece had fallen out. The madame jerked her head forward and nearly bit my arm as I reached for the black strips of cloth.

"Knock her out or something," I said to Donovan. "Punch her." He shook his head in amusement as the woman stilled.

"That's better." I gave the madame a sweet smile. Ha! Tell Smithe I couldn't be sweet. Well, act sweet at least. Another cough spoiled my attempt at keeping my smile. "But I might punch you myself, just for fun."

Madame Cherie's look of bewilderment would have made me laugh if I wasn't still so ticked about being pepper-sprayed.

And if thoughts of Mama hadn't been heavy on my mind at the same time we were getting ready to interrogate the madame. We needed to get this over with, damnit.

We'd tied the madame to a kitchen chair in the middle of the living room in the snazzy apartment Kerrison and I would start sharing tonight. Or this morning, rather. Kerrison had sent all her stuff over during the day with Donovan. She and I hadn't been in the apartment together until now.

As Madame Cherie scanned the room with frantic-looking brown eyes, I sprawled in a big comfy leather chair that had an ottoman. I put my feet up while feeling like I had a bad sunburn on my cheeks and I'd smoked a pack of cayenne peppers. Unfortunately the stuff smelled more like ant and roach spray, which in turn made me smell like one big well-sprayed roach.

On the other hand, the smell of something heavenly was coming from the kitchen. God it was good having Donovan around.

"What's for breakfast?" I shouted as I thought about getting my butt off the chair and taking a shower. Kerrison was already taking hers.

Donovan walked the few feet from the kitchen area and looked at me. "You look like hell."

I flipped him the bird. "Nice shiner," I said as I looked at his cheek and the round cut from the madame's heel and the purpling skin around it. "So what smells so good that I'm tempted to skip a shower just to stuff my face with whatever it is?"

"Belgian waffles."

"With strawberries and whipped cream?" I sighed as he gave a nod. I placed my palm on my growling belly. "You're the best."

He shook his head with amusement before heading back into the kitchen. I glanced at the woman cuffed to the chair in the middle of the room. She might have been frowning if a person could frown with a gag in her mouth.

"Be a good girl and you might get some, Madame Cherie," I said. "Believe me, his waffles are worth spilling your guts for."

Kerrison walked in, her red hair damp and her cheeks pink from the shower. Her feet were bare, she wore an orange University of Tennessee T-shirt, and faded blue jeans. She looked just like one of those fresh-scrubbed girls from next door. Or whatever.

"So that's the latest in torture techniques?" Kerrison plopped onto the couch across from me so that the madame was between us. She jerked her thumb to the kitchen. "Let them get a whiff of his cooking and start salivating until they talk?"

"Oh, yeah." I nodded emphatically, keeping an entirely serious expression on my face. "Wait until you try them. His waffles have the prisoners telling us everything from the time they lost their first binky to the last time they had a bowel movement."

Kerrison tucked her long legs beneath her on the couch. She grinned as she looked at Madame Cherie, who had just rolled her eyes to the ceiling and shook her head in an *I can't believe these idiots* motion.

I almost laughed. "If you have any idea how this bunch probably saved your skinny ass, you'd be a little happier right now."

"Let's take her gag off and see if she screams." Kerrison had an evil-witch kinda light in her pale green eyes as she glanced from me to the madame. A hint of a southern accent was in her voice that I hadn't heard before. She uncurled her legs and got up from the couch. "Hey, you want to grab the bat out of the closet just in case she does?"

Kerrison was really starting to grow on me.

"You betcha." I stood, too. I really was going to hit the madame if she screamed. "But I'd rather use my fist to knock her out."

The madame didn't look even the tiniest bit scared. She just had an exasperated expression on her features.

"The woman in front of you has been trained in jujitsu since she was eight years old." Kerrison got behind the madame. "Twenty-three years is it?" Kerrison said to me.

"You do your homework." I nodded at Kerrison, a little impressed that a new junior agent had that info on me already.

Kerrison shrugged. "Some of the guys in the gym said they wouldn't take you on for anything. And jeez, a couple of those bastards are built like trucks."

I almost grinned, but I was trying to look mean-serious at the madame. Kerrison was right—a few of the big bad agents at RED said hell no to sparring with me, but it was good-natured. They'd seen me break a bad guy's neck using just my thighs.

Kerrison started untying the madame's gag. The woman was still cuffed at her ankles as well as her wrists. We'd taken her stilettos off in the van. Stilettos were lethal weapons—I should know since I'd once tried to kill a man while wearing a pair of my own. Donovan was lucky she hadn't planted one of her heels in his eye instead of on his cheekbone.

I pushed up the sleeves of the black turtleneck I'd worn for tonight. "Ready when you are."

"Sonofabitch" was the first thing Madame Cherie said after her gag was removed. She glared over her shoulder at Kerrison and then at me. "Get me out of these fucking cuffs."

Kerrison glanced at me, and I shrugged. "Go for it."

She went to a medium-size denim backpack that had been tossed on the living room's love seat. When she returned, she was carrying a pocketknife and a handcuff key. It took her a couple of seconds to slice the plastic cuffs off the madame's ankles then unlock the metal cuffs on her wrists. Kerrison shoved the folded knife in one of her front pockets and the cuffs in her back pocket.

The madame shook out her arms as she looked from me to Kerrison. She rubbed her red, chafed wrists as she studied us. "Want to tell me why the fuck you kidnapped me and what you want?" Her voice was harsh and angry. Not that I could blame her.

"Not really." I started toward the master bathroom to hurry and take my shower. "I'd rather let you sit there and wonder."

Behind me, Kerrison said, "She's the boss."

It took me ten minutes to take my shower and change into the clean crop-top T-shirt and a pair of workout shorts I'd grabbed before heading into the bathroom. I like to wear crop tops so that my dragon tatt symbol shows along with my diamond navel piercing. The apartment was nice and warm from the central heating.

"Breakfast is going to get cold," Kerrison shouted from the living room and down the short hall. "Hurry. I'm starving and I need some sleep."

Well, she sure wasn't a shy one. Yeah, I definitely liked her.

When I reached the dining nook, I dropped into one of the six straight-backed chairs.

The madame, totally disheveled but alert, was sitting next to Donovan. "Tell me—"

"Shut up and eat, Cherie." I took one of the thick Belgian waffles from the plate Donovan handed me then passed the plate to Kerrison. "It might be your last meal."

She glared but didn't pull the I'm-not-eating-anything-you-bastards-give-me routine. She loaded her waffle with strawberries and whipped cream and took her first bite. I held back a grin when I saw her expression—it was like she could barely keep her eyes from rolling back in her head from ecstasy.

I did laugh when she finished her first mouthful. "Anything you want," she said with an almost orgasmic groan. "I'll kill for you after getting a taste of one of these."

"What did I tell you?" I smiled at the woman, who seemed intent on eating the rest of her waffle in world-record speed. "We know the best torture techniques in the trade."

She swallowed and did come up for air. "What trade is this?"

I finished stuffing my face. Let her stew.

It wasn't long before all of us had cleaned our plates. I wanted to lick mine. Kerrison had eaten two of the thick, giant waffles like me, and the skinny madame had put away three to rival Donovan.

He gave me an amused glance as he got up and started clearing the plates. "Why don't you two start?" Donovan said to me.

"A man who cooks and cleans." I looked at Kerrison. "Along with kicking major ass. What more could a woman ask for in a partner?"

Kerrison smiled before folding her forearms on the tabletop. "Ready when you are, boss."

I faced the madame. "We need to know everything, absolutely *everything* about the Elite Gentleman's Club." I kicked back in my chair, one elbow on an armrest, my hands clasped over my happy stomach.

"From the girls who have sex with the clientele for money to whatever you can tell us about the owner, Beeff Giger."

Red crept into the madame's cheeks, and she didn't look quite as composed anymore. "It's not that kind of club. We don't allow the girls to have sex with our patrons—"

"Cut the shit." Kerrison leaned forward, her eyes narrowed. "Don't push me."

Madame Cherie raised her chin. "It's the truth."

Kerrison scooted her chair back like she was about to get up, but she stayed in her seat.

I rubbed my forehead. "Listen, Madame. According to our intel, I don't think you know just how deep the shit is that you're wading in."

"How well do you know the girls you've been prostituting?" An angry gleam was in Kerrison's eyes as she dug into her front pocket.

"We don't—" The woman stopped and her eyes widened as soon as she saw Kerrison opening and closing the pocketknife she'd just taken out.

It was probably the hard expression on Kerrison's face that made a believer out of the madame. Along with the pocketknife and the *click-click-click* of Kerrison's steady opening and closing of the blade.

"Yes, the girls have sex for money and drugs." The woman's face was bright red. "Of course it's their choice."

"Choice . . . ," Kerrison repeated slowly.

"Do you know any of the girls personally?" I asked. "Have you spent any one-on-one time with them?"

"No time, really. The girls are usually only at the

club for three months or so." She shrugged. "And their handlers always deal with them."

"Handlers?" Kerrison left the blade open, and the woman stared at the knife. "Since when do prostitutes need *handlers*?"

"It's just the way Mr. G likes to run the club." The madame seemed unable to look away from the knife. "All I do is schedule time slots for each girl whenever a man wants a little extracurricular time with her."

"That's what you call it?" Kerrison's knuckles whitened as she clenched the pocketknife's grip and stared at the woman. "Extracurricular time?"

I frowned as I worked over the madame's words in my mind. Jenika Rublev. We couldn't let our cooperative disappear to God knew where if they took the girls somewhere else—we weren't sure we knew where all the clubs were or even how many. No, I wasn't going to lose another person I'd put into danger, like Agent Randolph who'd been murdered earlier in the year.

"Why are the girls only there for such a short time?" I asked. "When is he moving them again?"

"I think he's planning this exchange soon." Madame Cherie cleared her throat. "He thinks it's good to get in fresh meat by rotating the girls out and putting them into other clubs."

Fuck. Rublev.

Kerrison looked even angrier, nearly baring her teeth before she spoke. *"Fresh meat?"*

I cut in before she could say anything else. "Who calls the shots on this?"

"Mr. G." Clearing her throat again didn't do a damned thing for the madame's voice. Her words came out hard, scratchy. "I'm pretty sure he makes decisions for all the local clubs. I think he owns the lot of them, but I've never asked."

"Do you think she knows the truth and is just bullshitting us?" I asked Kerrison and Donovan as he walked into the room, pulled out his chair, and sat.

"Our cooperative communicated that she doesn't think the madame knows everything." Donovan crossed his arms over his broad chest and gave the woman a look so dark and dangerous that it probably made her just about pee her panties.

In a fast movement, Kerrison had the point of her pocketknife pressed against the madame's throat. "But The cooperative believes the madame suspects the truth about these girls and why they're in the club to begin with."

Madame Cherie's throat worked. Her face was no longer red. Instead the color had slowly drained away until she was so pale, her skin stood in stark contrast with her black hair. We all stared at her until she started to speak.

"I . . ." She swallowed again. "I don't think the girls are having sex with men out of choice. They're always drugged out of their minds and they're not happy. They act like they're only trying to learn pole-dancing and attracting men because they have to."

"And you haven't done anything about it?" Kerrison's southern accent ratcheted up. She sounded so angry, I thought she was going to slit the woman's throat. "You just let Giger and his men prostitute those girls?"

The madame looked at me as if I was the most reasonable out of the three of us. If she only had a clue, I'd have been the one she'd be most frightened of.

"Ever hear of human trafficking?" I managed to keep my tone even, letting her have her illusions that I was the rational one of the bunch. "Those young women are sex slaves. Trafficked directly from Moscow to New York City."

An expression of horror started to creep across the madame's face. "It's true?"

"You start telling us every detail you can think of and answer every fucking question we have." Kerrison leaned closer to the madame, who winced as a single tear of blood formed at the point of the knife that was still against her throat.

Kerrison's voice came out low, deadly as she spoke. "*I* am not nice enough to let you keep those waffles down."

CHAPTER EIGHT

Giger

"Where is that fucking bitch?" Beeff slammed his meaty fist on his glass-topped desk as he shouted at Jacques. The vibrations caused pens and pencils to rattle in their holder, which was shaped like a pair of woman's tits. "Bring her to me and I will make sure she is never late again."

Beeff leaned forward, his square-cut three-carat diamond ring reflecting the orange glow from the Jägermeister wall lamp. He glared at Jacques, who had flinched at his tone. The goddamned Frenchman was one of the tallest and most bulked-up handlers who worked for Beeff, but also the biggest pussy. "You fucking find Cherie," Beeff said. "Go to her apartment."

"Immediately, Mr. G." Jacques's French accent was stronger when Beeff shoved shit down his throat. "Madame Cherie is never late like this—two hours now, almost showtime." He started to turn toward the door but stopped. "Do you think it possible that she learned the truth about the girls and went to the local law enforcement?"

"Fuck no." Beeff clenched his fists on his desktop, the thick gold metal of his ring cutting into his index finger, his face hot. "She's fucking oblivious."

"You are right, of course." Jacques nodded as he spoke in clear English despite the depth of his French accent. "I will find Madame Cherie."

Of course he would. Jacques wouldn't dare wipe his ass without Beeff telling him when and how to do it.

Pussy.

A hard rap echoed in the room from a knock at the door to Beeff's office. *Better be that bitch,* he thought, yet at the same time knew the knock was too loud, too harsh for the madame.

Jacques opened the door, and Stalder rammed into him as he strode into Beeff's office. Jacques stumbled back a few steps.

"She's a corpse." Stalder was a big, blond Swede, but spoke English without any hint of an accent. "Cherie."

Beeff stared at Stalder, slow prickles of heat running up his body. "What the fuck?"

"It was on the news on the bar's TV." Stalder gave a nod in the direction of the bar, which was on the other side of the wall. As usual, Stalder had an expression that Beeff couldn't read. It pissed him off how the man always controlled his emotions and expressions, even if everything was going to hell.

"Cherie's been ID'd by her sister who lives in the Bronx," Stalder continued. "Someone slit her throat and raped her. I'm not sure what order."

"Who gives a fuck what order?" Beeff slammed his fist again on the desk so hard that this time he felt pain shoot all the way to his wrist. "All I give a shit about is that we're down a madame at Elite and I have a club that had better run smooth as shit even without the dead slut."

With a surprised look, Jacques snapped his attention from Stalder to Beeff, but said nothing. What, did the idiot Frenchman expect Beeff to have any remorse over a cadaver? With thirty-two years in the business of prostitution, Beeff didn't think one woman's life was worth shit, especially if she wasn't one of the girls being fucked every night and raking in the cash.

It had only been nine years since he'd hooked up with Hagstedt and really started making money. Sex slaves didn't make a fucking dime. They were just merchandise that he used until they were worthless to him.

Stalder's expression hadn't changed when Beeff failed to show any concern over Cherie's death. He almost casually waited for Beeff's next instructions.

Beeff clenched his fists on the cool glass top of his desk. He stared at the two men and felt his wire-rimmed glasses digging into his cheeks as he narrowed his eyes. "I want someone to replace Cherie immediately. You get the goods on every one of the madames you interview," he said to Stalder. "I want clean histories with a shitload of experience in the business."

Stalder said, "Of course, Mr. G."

Jacques kept his pussy mouth shut.

"Stalder, you hired Cherie, and you will be the one

to get someone in here." Beeff leaned back in his chair, his striped button-up shirt tightening across his chest. "Same salary. Experience scheduling whores for the back rooms and teaching them to hump those fucking poles."

Stalder gave a short nod.

"I want to meet the final candidates this time." Fury that his club was fucked until they found a new madame made Beeff's head feel like it was burning at the roots of his short gray hair, as if the top of his head was going to explode. "I had better start seeing fucking madames in here by tomorrow night."

Beeff wanted to smirk when he saw Stalder's eyebrows lift a fraction before he schooled his expression again. "Get the fuck out of here," Beeff said.

Jacques started to leave, too.

"Jacques." The name shot out of Beeff's mouth like a punch. Jacques came to a halt. Stalder left the door open as he walked through it and into the hall leading to the main floor of the club and the bar. "For tonight, pick one of the more experienced girls, one you know will keep her mouth shut and has half a fucking brain. Have her schedule the whores and put the cash in the box, and don't move your ass an inch from her side."

The muscle-bound man practically gave a bow. The pussy. "I will take care of it now and make sure she is trained for tonight, Mr. G." Jacques sounded like a goddamned robot as he responded.

"Get the fuck out of here." Beeff took off his glasses and resisted flinging them across the room. "Lock the door."

The French bastard damned near ran for Beeff's open office door, set the lock, then shut the door behind him with a firm click of the locking mechanism.

Beeff stared at the wall, his eyes still narrowed. He didn't have time for this shit. Losing a madame two hours before showtime was a fucking inconvenience.

He had five clubs to run in New York City for Hagstedt—or whatever the fuck the bastard's real name was—and Beeff made sure he hired the right men as handlers and the right madames to teach and schedule the whores.

The Russian or Chinese sluts brought into his clubs fucked ten to fifteen men a night. From five PM to two AM, non-stop, as long as enough dicks wanted pussy. Most of the time he had to have his handlers use the designer sex drug Lascivious. It made the girls horny little sluts and ensured they gave a good ride to every dickhead who handed over enough cash.

A knock at the door. "What?" Beeff shouted, annoyance at being disturbed causing him to curl his lips away from his teeth.

The door opened and Andreas, his accountant, stepped through the door and closed it behind him. "I think we have a problem, Mr. G."

Beeff scowled and narrowed his gaze. "What problem?"

Andreas adjusted his glasses and raised several black-and-white printouts from a surveillance videotape. In the first picture one of the Russian whores stood outside Beeff's door. In the next still, she was picking the lock. In the third, she was slipping into Beeff's office.

"What the fuck?" Beeff shouted. "Who is this?"

"Her name is Jenika," Andreas said.

"Get her away from the other girls and take her upstairs to my special room." Beeff sucked air through his teeth. "I'll deal with her."

He didn't have time for this shit. What if the whore had found something critical? Beeff mentally cataloged everything in his office. No, it should be safe. His computer files and messages were always in code or encrypted.

Questions started nagging at him. Why would she be sneaking into his office? Was she with some branch of law enforcement or a government agency?"

Shit.

He'd find out, and then he'd murder the bitch himself.

"Go." Beeff pointed to the door. "I want her fucking ass in there *now.*"

"Right away, Mr. G," Andreas said.

Beeff had never let his staff know his name. He paid his handlers and madames a shitload, but he had the goods on every person he hired. He made sure they knew it once they were in.

No one screwed him and lived.

CHAPTER NINE

Ground rules—kiss my Irish ass

"Got it." Perry snapped his cell phone shut and looked at me as he walked in the suite's door and closed it behind him. "You're on, Steele."

The suite in the hotel that we were using as a base was bigger than the stakeout apartment and a hell of a lot nicer. The hotel was only a few streets away from the Elite Gentleman's Club. While my team was in action, a pair of agents from the New York RED office covered the stakeout across the street from the club.

"Johnny came through." I let my breath out in a rush and some tension eased from my shoulders as I made sure—for at least the tenth time—that my long platinum-blond wig was secure. "I wasn't sure he could pull it off."

Thank God he had. I wanted this assignment over so that I could get back to Mammy. Just thinking about what she was going through made my heart hurt and my gut sick.

Perry nodded. "As soon as word was on the street that the club needed a madame, Johnny leaked enough info to hook them."

Threads of adrenaline tied themselves low in my belly in anticipation of starting the undercover op.

"Excellent." Kerrison's skirt hardly covered her backside while she bent to pick up her small gold purse after having just applied another coat of her "erotic red" lipstick. "Stop staring at my ass, Smithe," she said without looking over her shoulder.

"How does she do that?" Smithe grinned. "That's so hot."

"What time is the interview?" I smoothed the lines of my blue evening dress, which was sexy but on the conservative side compared with Kerrison's emerald-green miniskirt and low-cut blouse.

"Three, which is plenty of time before the club starts hopping." Perry looked at his watch. "You've got almost an hour."

Smithe managed to take his gaze from Kerrison's ass. "Weiss, Takamoto, and Jensen are in place and ready to make sure any other candidates either don't make it back to the club or won't want to."

"You're keyed in on how to use the jewelry?" Donovan asked Kerrison when she straightened and slipped the lipstick—which was also a mini camera—into her small purse.

Kerrison raised her arm. The elegant bracelet and stunning rings that Martinez had designed fit her perfectly. She pointed to what looked like a simple clasp on her gold bracelet. "Unfasten the catch and RED will swarm the joint thicker than flies on a horse's ass." Her southern humor and stronger accent would've made me smile if I weren't so keyed up.

She wiggled the fingers of her right hand, and the precious stones and gold—all real—sparkled in the suite's lighting. Especially the diamond-cut emerald. "Press the largest stone of one ring," she said, "and the focused release of narcotic will bring down even the biggest jackass that tries to lay his hands on me."

"Just don't knock yourself out by accident." I looked at my three rings. "I'll do my best not to end up on the floor, too." The genuine diamonds and gold on my right hand sparkled even more than Kerrison's. I didn't have a bracelet so that we weren't dressed the same. Of course, my rings were designed differently than Kerrison's.

"The ring on my middle finger is my link to RED, right?" I asked Donovan, who nodded. "Martinez said the other two have the same narcotic that Kerrison's rings have."

When I met Donovan's gaze, I didn't want to look away. I wanted to kiss him—somewhere private so I could jump his bones.

Jesus. My lust for him was freaking nuts.

I broke eye contact with Donovan and spoke to Perry. "Do Kerrison and I pass the madame-and-sexy-assistant test?"

Perry tilted his head as he examined us. "Kerrison—with that outfit and her thick wavy auburn hair—she's a go."

"And me?" I put my hand on my hip. Sometimes I couldn't tell if my agents were giving me a hard time or were serious.

Perry reached into our supply cabinet of makeup, jewelry, and other female—generally—items. "Let's try this." He took out a pair of Chinese chopstick hair ornaments. "This will go great with that Mandarin-collared dress. You can use a sexier look."

"We're not trying out for the floor show," I grumbled, but I let Perry sweep up the long genuine hair of my wig, knot it, and secure it all with the chopsticks. Trust Perry to be able to fix hair. It wasn't bad having a metrosexual around.

Kerrison glanced at Donovan. "Any luck on coming closer to getting in with this Giger dick as a handler?"

He shook his head, his lips tight. "Still working on it. But I'll figure out a way to get in there if I have to kill every one of his other handlers to do it."

I punched Donovan lightly on his upper arm with the fist that didn't have any narcotic-filled jewelry. "Yeah, like that wouldn't cause anyone to be suspicious."

After we'd spent a sufficient amount of time screwing around while waiting for our appointment time, Donovan said, "You two had better get out of here." I hoped I was the only one who noticed the faint hint of concern as his eyes met mine.

He knew better than to worry about me. I'd kick his ass for it the next time we were alone.

Kerrison and I shrugged on long, dressy coats so we wouldn't freeze in the unusually chilly November air. We left the suite and took the elevator down from the tenth floor of the hotel. The moment we were rolling, I was Madame Alexis Johansen and Kerrison was Chandra Elliot.

An agent from the New York branch of RED was acting as our driver and was waiting for us at the curb in a black Lincoln Town Car. After Kerrison and I slid onto the leather backseat of the plush vehicle and closed the door, I met the agent's eyes in the rearview mirror and gave him a slight nod.

The agent acknowledged by checking traffic and pulling in the moment the way was clear. Three minutes later he drew the car up to the Elite Gentleman's Club. Small white Christmas lights illuminated the awning, which rippled in cheerful waves in the afternoon air.

Our "chauffeur" exited the driver's seat and I had to remind myself to wait and allow him to open the door for us, rather than climbing out by myself. It was all about appearances.

The agent opened the door closest to the curb so that Kerrison and I could ease out—as ladylike and sexy as possible. Not fun when my damned dress was doing its best to hike its way up my hips to my waist. The four-inch heels were a bitch to stand on gracefully in this position, but the agent did a good job of helping me as he held my hand.

I kept a professional if not arrogant expression on my features. Kerrison looked confident, like a woman who knew that she was sexy, but also that she was in charge of herself and her body.

Good girl.

We walked beneath the red awning, which flapped continuously in the increasingly harsh breeze. The bouncer positioned at the front door was a typical big, beefy guy and he wore a small gold hoop earring in one ear. In the sunlight his dark skin shone like polished ebony and his bald head gleamed. He was freaking tall. The guy had to be at least six-eight.

I tilted my head to meet the bouncer's dark eyes. I kept my voice cool, and there wasn't a trace of my Bostonian accent in my words. Instead, I spoke English with a perfect Swedish accent. "Alexis Johansen and Chandra Elliot. We're here to see Stefan Stalder for an interview."

The big guy didn't show any kind of expression that let me know one way or another what our chances were of getting through the doors of that club.

He pressed a button on the wireless earpiece he was wearing. "Two women to see Stalder. A Johansen and an Elliot." The man spoke in a deep baritone.

"Yes, sir." He finished the connection by pressing the button on his comm. Still no expression as he held open one of the two large oak doors that had beautiful frosted, beveled glass panes.

Phew. Johnny had come through big-time.

I hadn't expected the second bouncer and another set of oak doors. This bouncer had hair as silver-blond as my wig, and it hung over his shoulders.

He held the door open and let us through without saying anything. We entered what looked like a very classy nightclub.

Sure. Classy for a place that had a floor show during business hours and sex in the back rooms with prostituted girls. Disgust put a taste like rotten eggs in my mouth as I thought about the trafficked Russian girls who had to be hidden somewhere in this building until it was time for them to get down to business. Probably in the apartments above.

"Ms. Johansen and Ms. Elliot?" A man with a French accent walked toward Kerrison and me as the second set of double doors closed behind us. He wore a wireless earpiece like the bouncers did.

The man's appearance didn't connect with his voice and manner. He was entirely out of place. Hell, I didn't know what kind of place a guy like that belonged in. With his smooth French accent and elegant manners inherent from a seductive country, you'd think he'd look like an aristocrat. He didn't.

The man was built like the two bouncers with a bodybuilder's physique and muscles that threatened the seams of his perfectly tailored Italian-made suit. His silk tie was pink with light black stripes running diagonally across it.

"I am called Jacques," the enigma of a man said with a slight bow. His scent was light but odd, like dry red wine.

"Alexis Johansen." I gestured toward Kerrison as I laid on the Swedish accent. "This is my assistant, Chandra Elliot."

The guy did that French thing, taking first my and then Kerrison's hand in his and placing a kiss the backs of our right hands.

Gross. I did manage not to wipe mine on my dress. Score one for me.

I kept the professional look on my face and my

disgust to myself. I glanced at Kerrison, and her expression was just as composed as I knew mine was.

The Frenchman gave a low bow. "I will take you to Mr. Stalder now."

"Thank you, Jacques," I said in a firm, clear tone.

He escorted us past a U-shaped bar where countless bottles of liquor were arranged on glass shelves against a mirror backdrop decorated with frosted scrolls around the edges. Martini, margarita, and wineglasses sparkled from where they hung upside down from a wooden holder.

The mahogany bar top gleamed, no doubt polished with lemon oil because the lemony scent of it was strong. The bar was padded with black leather around its U-shaped section, and black-leather-covered stools were spaced evenly around the bar.

When I saw the levers for the draft beer lined up with Guinness as one of the choices, my mouth watered. I personally could've used some of that Guinness on tap right then.

Four mahogany ceiling fans stirred the air, causing the loose strands of my wig to tickle the back of my neck. My hip brushed the back of one mahogany-brown chair as I followed Jacques with Kerrison right behind me. My heels clicked on the floor as my gaze traveled along a darkened stage that had what looked like three crystal dancing poles rather than metal poles.

The inside of the gentleman's club was large enough that the wall we headed toward seemed at least a mile away. Hey, those four-inch heels pinched my toes—right now everything seemed far away.

Classic, wood-framed, and tastefully erotic Bettie
Page prints hung on the forest-green walls, the prints
illuminated by individual art lights. The quality of the
prints, the size of the club, and the expensive-looking
wood tables that gleamed in the low lighting made it
clear the place earned some pretty healthy profits. No
doubt the trafficked girls and not the beer and admis-
sion charge kept this place looking sharp.

At least the men who ran the place didn't have the
gall to try to make it look cheery with holiday decorations on the inside.

After passing through the dozens of tables and high-
tops, we reached the opposite end of the club. It wasn't
the basic wall it had given the illusion of being. Instead,
part of the wall was a few feet in front of the other part,
leaving enough room for a hidden door with a gold
placard that read MANAGEMENT.

Jacques pushed open the door, let us in, then closed
it behind us before escorting us down a hallway. It was
carpeted, unlike the club itself, and the brown Berber
cushioned our footsteps.

Even the hallway was classy with more framed,
illuminated Bettie Page prints—although these pic-
tures were among her more kinky poses. I winced
when I saw a depiction of her in leather, weilding a
whip. That picture brought back a few too many better-
forgotten memories. The walls were forest green above
mahogany molding about halfway down the wall with
dark, rich wood paneling below.

Three mahogany wood doors lined the right of the
hallway, and a single door was at the end. We passed
the first two doors, one of which was open. It was a

small private restroom that appeared just as luxurious. Wonder if the toilet seat was real gold.

Jacques rapped on the third door, which was open about six inches.

"Yes." The word from the man inside the office was said in a matter-of-fact if not bored manner.

My gut tweaked a bit. Showtime.

Jacques opened the door all the way, which caused a small draft and let out the scent of leather and wood. He stood aside as he held it open for Kerrison and me before he introduced us. "Mr. Stalder, this is Alexis Johansen and Chandra Elliot."

Stalder stood. He was a tall, blond, muscular man who looked like he might be of Norwegian or Swedish descent. He, too, wore an earpiece, although his was hardly noticeable. "Leave us, Jacques."

The Frenchman looked vaguely irritated at being dismissed but gave a slight bow and shut the door with a solid *thunk* behind him. By both of their expressions, it was obvious those two weren't crazy about each other.

With easy masuline grace, Stalder walked around his desk toward us. We stood behind the two chairs in front of the mahogany desk and I forced myself to keep from shifting from one foot to the other.

The room matched the rest of the club with its forest-green and dark-paneled walls, this time with framed, erotic *Playboy* centerfold portraits. Otherwise, the office was a simple room with only a computer monitor; a beer mug with two pens, a Sharpie, and a pencil in it; and a page-a-day calendar propped next to the holder. A few stacks of paper were organized on the desk. The wood-bladed fan wasn't on, and the light through the mostly closed wood blinds was faint.

As he came toward us, I noted Stalder's appearance in a quick scan. Jeez. Did Giger only hire guys with muscles upon muscles?

Or was this actually Giger, posing as a Mr. Stalder?

His dark blue Levi's looked new and he wore a blue-striped collared shirt. Short blond hair, blue eyes, and smooth fair skin gave away the fact that he wasn't in the sunlight for long periods of time.

"Ms. Johansen." He greeted me first by clasping my hand in a firm, decisive grip. His handshake confirmed my first impression as his palm wasn't callused, but smooth. He took Kerrison's hand. "Ms. Elliot." Kerrison and I returned with some kind of inane greeting.

When he stepped away, Stalder gestured to the chairs in front of his desk. "Please."

Sure wasn't much of a hello-and-how-are-you. Stalder turned and walked around the desk to the black leather office chair and took his seat, which creaked as he leaned back in it. I settled in front of his desk in one of the comfortable cushioned chairs, also black leather. Kerrison sat to my right.

Stalder looked at me and didn't waste time getting down to business. My kind of criminal.

"If you're hired, you will have most of the traditional duties of a madame." The man didn't have even a trace of an accent, but he spoke with such clear precision that I was certain English wasn't his first language. "From my preliminary research I know you have experience with prostitution."

I intentionally hesitated before I said, "That is correct."

He eyed me as if taking in the fact that I'd missed a beat. "Then we can skip the games and I will get straight to the point."

I gave a brief nod. "Of course."

"We have different ground rules at the Elite, Madame Alexis. This club operates differently than most." Stalder held my gaze as if judging my reaction. "Our girls have handlers. The madame does not interact with these girls in any way other than to perform her job."

I raised my eyebrows in feigned surprise. "That's unusual."

"It is how *we* operate." A touch of irritation crackled in the air, but the irritation didn't show on his face.

My scalp grew hot beneath my wig. His reply when I asked about the handlers was definitely a sign to back off. "If we hire you, Madame Alexis, you'll be expected to follow orders without question."

I made myself speak as formally as he was, laying my Swedish accent on a little thicker. "I—" I glanced at Kerrison before looking at Stalder. "We will perform as expected."

"Most madames do not arrive with an assistant." Stalder steepled his fingers. "Why do you think you are qualified for this job?" He focused on me as his chair rocked slightly. "And why do you think I should hire your assistant?"

"We're an excellent team." My heart rate picked up a bit now that he was actually letting me talk and I was "on." I allowed an edge more of the Swedish accent. "Chandra handles booking the girls for their extracurricular activities with the clients, as well as accurately keeping track of the payments. In addition, she assists me in teaching the girls how to be more appealing to the clients."

"Makeup, hairstyles, and clothing are my specialty," Kerrison said when I turned my gaze on her, telling her with my eyes that it was time to start selling her own abilities. "I also aid Madame Alexis with instructing the girls in onstage sensuality . . ."

Kerrison glanced at me and I gave a staged nod before she turned back to Stalder with a look brimming with sexuality. "I also assist in instructing the girls in how to pleasure a man . . . in other ways." The last sentence came out throaty, seductive, and inviting.

With a slight twitch along one jaw, Stalder betrayed the fact that her words had affected him. She'd probably given him a hard-on, but he wore an otherwise unreadable expression.

Ha. Kerrison had gotten to him. Bastard.

"If for any reason I can't be here," I added, not giving him a chance to respond, "Chandra is trained to take my place." I folded my hands with my newly done acrylic nails digging into my palms. "I have extensive experience, including owning a club in Boston."

"Until you were put out of business for prostitution in your establishment." Stalder glanced at the papers spread across his desk. "There was a great deal of press at the time, which makes you more visible than I like."

"That is true about the publicity." I cleared my throat. "It is why Chandra and I moved to this area. To get away from the publicity and to lie low for a while until the opportunity arrived for us to return to our chosen occupation. We think this position is the right opportunity." I kept my words mostly free of slang and formal as many immigrants do when English is not their first language.

Stalder looked down and pushed aside a few pieces of paper from one neat pile with his long, elegant fingers. "I am not sure you would be the right candidate considering your controversial background."

"My background is extensive and exemplary." I straightened as if I had just bristled. "It has also been over a year and I am not in the same state."

He gave me a long look before doing the same to Kerrison. "We will contact you if we decide to extend a second interview."

Shit. This wasn't ending well. "With my and Chandra's experience in *educating* the young women, your clientele will be extremely satisfied. They will return often for their favorite *treat*."

Stalder got to his feet, and Kerrison and I did the same. He extended his hand again. "As I said, we may be in touch with you."

"Of course." I returned his grip with a firm one of my own. "I hope to hear from you."

He escorted us to the door, where he paused. "We can reach you on your cell?"

"I keep it with me at all times," I said.

"That will change if you are hired." His tone was authoritative, matter-of-fact.

I gave him a surprised look. "Why?"

"Cell phones are not allowed anywhere in our establishment." He tapped his earpiece. "We use wireless radios instead."

I shrugged. "As long as we have a way to communicate, that is fine with me."

"Good." Stalder kept his poker face in place, but I had a feeling that we had passed several tests, after all. "I will be in touch if we would like to call you in for a second interview. You would meet with Mr. G if that is the case."

Excellent. "I am looking forward to it," I said before Stalder closed the office door behind us.

CHAPTER TEN

He's lucky I didn't shove that pencil holder up his...

"How are you feeling, Mama?" Hard plastic dug into my palm as I clenched my personal cell phone to my ear. I paced the floor of the Brooklyn apartment, no doubt wearing a groove in the fine wood. It was the morning following my and Kerrison's afternoon interview with Stalder.

"The doctors are taking care of me." Then my mother added with a touch of amusement and exasperation, "Your daddy and all your pesky brothers and Rori won't let me be for five minutes." I could imagine her shaking her head. "Ryan insists he's leaving the Marines to stay close to home. He should be off serving his country instead of worrying about me, but Zane found him a job with one of those three-letter initials. FBI, CIA, NSA. He's being evasive and I don't like it." Mammy sounded miffed as she spoke. "He's probably going to be doing something more dangerous than the Marines. If that's possible."

That last bit caused me to blink. Had Zane gotten Ryan a position at RED? I'd have to find out. Of course he wouldn't have given out RED's three-letter acronym.

~~But that didn't matter and I let the thought slip~~ away. My chest ached like it constantly did when I thought of Mama. As if a wrecking ball had slammed into my ribs. "I wish I was there, too."

"Go on with you, child." Her tone was strong and certain. "I'm fine, and if you don't stop worrying I'm going to take a switch to your backside."

Mama almost made me smile despite the fact that she was facing the worst trial of her life. She and Daddy had never laid a hand or anything else on my brothers, sister, or me.

Although sometimes I wondered if they'd ever been tempted to with the stunts the seven of us kids pulled over the years. Our mama's tight lips and disapproving stare and the red flush to our daddy's face were enough to set us straight—until the next time we got into trouble.

But right now I was going to damage the floor with all of my pacing. Like I cared. In the kitchen Nick knocked something around while he started dinner.

Kerrison was glued to a University of Tennessee football game. UT was playing Vanderbilt. I think. I didn't get into college football. Now, the Boston Red Sox and baseball season—that was a different story altogether.

During the commercials, I heard Kerrison talking in French to someone on her cell phone, and what little I heard was surprisingly mushy. I'd never have guessed

Kerrison would have a guy she'd talk lovey-dovey with. It didn't seem her style. So much for my right-on instincts when it came to certain people.

When she had seen me press the speed-dial number on my cell phone to call Mama, Kerrison had lowered the volume on the TV and talked in a quieter voice to the guy on the other end of the line.

"How are you feeling?" I bit the inside of my cheek and focused fully on my mother. "The chemo—is it working?"

"I'm perfectly okay, pet." It was obvious, to me at least, that she was working hard to make herself sound positive while she was on the phone with me. "You stop yourself from worrying and concentrate on being an interpreter—where did you say you are?"

"Sweden." I put one hand on my hip. "Mama, tell me the truth or I'll be flying back from Stockholm on the next plane out so I can see for myself."

She sounded tired but also like she was trying not to let it show. "The doctors believe the chemotherapy is doing what it's supposed to and is shrinking the cancer. I've only been taking the treatments a short time, so it may be a little longer before they can perform the surgery."

I shut my eyes tight and asked a question I didn't want to. "Is the cancer only in your breasts?"

"They think so." Then she gave the first sign of weakness I'd seen from her since I'd learned she had breast cancer. The first sign of weakness I'd ever seen from her in my thirty-one years. "I need to lie down, pet. I'll talk with you longer the next time you call from wherever you end up."

Mama taking a nap? Never.

"I'll be home after this assignment." My stomach twisted and I pressed my free hand to my belly as I opened my eyes. "If you feel any worse, you call me, Mama." I put a stern note in my tone. "I'm going to check with Daddy and the rest of our family, too."

"Don't you worry about me," she repeated just as sternly.

As if she could see me, I raised my chin at a stubborn angle. "I will if I want to."

Her voice held a smile as she said, "I love you, child."

"I love you, Mama," I whispered before she said good bye and I heard a click in my ear.

I stopped pacing and for a moment held my flip phone open without pressing the off button. On the screen I saw that Mama had disconnected the call, and I felt as if the invisible cord connecting us had frayed. As if she was slipping away from me.

Christ, I was being melodramatic. She was going to be okay. Mama was too tough to let anything take her away from us.

It would only be a couple of weeks at the most. I would finish this goddamned op—bring down this New York prostitution circle and, most importantly, get Hagstedt. And I would go home and be there for Mama.

"Steele." Donovan jerked me out of my thoughts as he called to me from the kitchen. "Could use a hand here."

"Yeah. Sure." Since when did Donovan need the slightest bit of help from me when it came to anything relating to the kitchen? Delicious smells were coming my way now. Something sautéed like beef and vegetables.

When I reached the kitchen, he grabbed me by my shoulders and pulled me aside, out of view of the living room. He wrapped me in his arms and held me tight. How did he know I needed this so much? He was the most alpha male I knew, and I knew a lot of alphas in my line of work. But he was also one of the most intuitive people I'd ever met.

I hugged Donovan back, needing to feel his arms around me and the comfort of his body against mine as long as possible. He felt and smelled so good. So warm. Male. Spicy. I drank in that incredible scent, and it comforted me almost as much as his embrace did.

He pressed his lips to the top of my head and I felt his warm breath. "Is your mom doing any better?"

"I don't think so." I placed my forehead against his chest, his navy-blue T-shirt soft against my skin.

"Do you want to go home?" he said, his voice low, concerned.

"Yes, but I'm the only one who can pull this job off, especially the part of being a madame." I gave a sigh. "Months of preparation trying to find this bastard—if we don't get Hagstedt on this op, who knows how long it will take. We've got to get him *now*."

"We will." The determination in Donovan's words and in his voice matched my own. "We're going to get you home as soon as possible." He gave me another long comforting squeeze.

"What smells so—" Kerrison said from behind me, then added, "Oops. Sorry to butt in."

If I had jerked away from Donovan, it would have made both of us look guiltier than hell. Instead, I slowly stepped back and tried to smile at Kerrison as Donovan's arms slipped away from me. "Not at all. Donovan was being a good friend and comforting me."

Kerrison frowned. She'd scrubbed her face clean of makeup, revealing a smattering of light freckles that weren't normally visible. She'd put her long red hair into a ponytail and pulled it through the rear opening of her UT ball cap, allowing the thick ponytail to fall down her back.

"Is everything all right?" She had a genuine, concerned expression. "Is something wrong?"

"To be honest? Things aren't fine." I pushed my hair out of my face, the strands suddenly irritating me. "It's a family issue."

"Okay." Kerrison shoved her hands into the front pockets of her faded Levi's, and I was glad she didn't try to pry about the subject. "I can't offer a big shoulder to cry on like Donovan can, but if you need help with something, name it."

"Thank you." I didn't know what else to say and started to feel uncomfortable, like I was going to squirm beneath her gaze, but only for a moment.

"Fajitas, right?" Kerrison seemed to understand my need for privacy by going to the stove and paying attention to Donovan's dinner preparations instead of me and my issues. "Mmmm. Beef, sautéed onions, and sweet peppers. This smells almost as good as my aunt's cooking."

She looked at the small bowls to the side and

grinned. "Oooh, and sour cream, guacamole, along with a bowl of cheese and a stack of tortillas." She glanced at Donovan. "I'm impressed. And starving."

"Those tortillas are homemade, too. Donovan's are wicked good." I allowed a little smile as I moved next to Kerrison at the stove. "His cooking is pretty darned close to being as good as my mammy's." I glanced up at him, ignoring the twinge in my chest at the mention of my mother. "But not quite."

Kerrison wasn't looking. He tugged at the end of my French braid, then leaned close to speak in my ear low enough that Kerrison would have needed supersonic hearing to catch it. Although with her remarkable skills, maybe I shouldn't have doubted the possibility.

"I can cook up something special just for you, Steele," Donovan said in a low rumble.

My nipples ached at the sensuality in his sexy voice, the promise of good things to come. Real good.

The ring of my work cell phone jarred me out of my desire for Donovan. I'd taken it off vibrate while I wasn't on duty in case any important calls came through. I stepped away from Donovan and checked the phone number on the caller screen. I didn't recognize it, but the area code was one of New York City's exchanges. Stalder?

I glanced at Donovan. "I think it's the club," I said before answering the phone and saying "Hello," in a throaty, sensual voice.

"Madame Alexis?" Stalder, definitely. "You're to come in for a second interview with Mr. G."

I pumped my fist and elbow in a *yes!* motion as I looked at Kerrison and Donovan. "Of course," I said in a calm tone. "When?"

"A driver will meet you outside your apartment building in fifteen minutes."

Christ.

"Fifteen minutes," I repeated for Kerrison's benefit. "Chandra and I will be ready for the appointment with Mr. G."

Kerrison raised her hands and looked down at her jeans and T-shirt before looking at me and mouthing, "What the fuck?"

"We look forward to seeing you soon," I said before I closed the phone and added, *"Shit."*

"You have got to be kidding me." Kerrison shook her head. "What do they think? That we're dressed to the nines the whole day, just waiting for their call?"

I rushed straight for my bedroom. "How can I possibly do my makeup and put on the damned wig, not to mention getting dressed, in fifteen friggin' minutes?" And miss Donovan's fajitas, damnit.

Kerrison muttered what had to be a curse word beneath her breath by the anger in her tone. *"And* this means no fajitas." She sounded madder at that than at having to leave so fast as she echoed my thought.

The silvery-blond wig had to go on first so that I could make sure every strand of my dark hair was tucked in place. Thank goodness I'd put my hair in the French braid this morning in preparation for when I'd be going undercover. I chose the wig with long, loose hair to make it easier to cover any of my natural hair that might stray in the back. Then I performed what must have been the sloppiest makeup job in history.

As soon as I finished making the mascara as thick as possible in that short amount of time, I spritzed on some perfume. I slipped a cell phone the size of a credit card into a pocket built into my bra on the outside of my left breast.

I'd tucked my miniature lock-picking tools into an even smaller pocket on the right side of my bra. I grabbed the black purse that was pre-stashed with my fake driver's license, a couple of credit cards, another cell phone, and some cash. Despite the fact it was fall, I also had a dark pair of Prada sunglasses that Oxford would probably read me the riot act over buying.

Well, she might not notice that three-hundred-dollar receipt for the sunglasses when she got a look at the bills for the clothing and shoes. Normally I was happy in jeans and T-shirts. But as a classy madame, I had to look the part, didn't I?

Kerrison and I almost ran into each other as we came out of our rooms at the same time. She gave me a critical look. "Steele, you have mascara tracks under your eyes."

"Damn." I rubbed my fingers over the skin beneath my eyes.

"Better." Kerrison held her brown handbag in one hand while she brushed her long red hair over one of her shoulders with her other hand.

The motion revealed the spaghetti strap of her cocoa-brown half top, and the light caught the glimmer and sparkles from the bead fringes along the hem of her top and around the hem of her miniskirt. That skirt showed off her perfect figure and her toned, fit thighs and calves.

"You're supposed to be my assistant, not one of the girls," I said with mock-seriousness as I glanced down at my elegant black sheath dress.

Kerrison grinned. "Can't hurt with the big boss man to look like I'd be happy to do him."

We reached the living room. "Uh, what if he comes on to you and does want you to do him?"

She shrugged, and her RED-issued gold bracelet winked in the brighter living room light. "I'll think of something."

"Damn, damn. Ten seconds." I whirled and ran back to my bedroom. "Forgot my jewelry."

I scooped the rings off the vanity dresser and slipped them on as I hurried as fast as I could while wearing my black strappy four-inch sandals. Kerrison's heels were only two inches high, so I was only two inches shorter, rather than the usual four.

Donovan appeared from out of the kitchen, grabbed my upper arm, and dragged me two steps behind the door before I could follow Kerrison out of the apartment. "Be careful," he said as he brushed his lips over mine.

I grinned as he pulled away, some of my thickly applied red lipstick smeared across his lips. "Give it up, Donovan. I'm always careful."

Sort of.

He closed the door behind me as I ran the six or so steps to the elevator Kerrison was in. An annoying buzzing sound started when the elevator doors couldn't close because she was standing between them.

When I stepped inside it, the elevator smelled of brass polish that made the brass handrails gleam in the elegant lighting. The closed-in space also smelled like an orchid hothouse where the orchids had been fed massive amounts of steroids.

"What did you do?" I wrinkled my nose. "Pour perfume on every inch of your body?"

"Too much, huh?"

I nodded and she shrugged.

As the elevator started down, Kerrison pulled a tube out of her purse, unscrewed the wand, and drew it out. Lip gloss. "Stand still. Your lipstick doesn't look right," she said before running the spongy part of the wand over my lips. "There."

"Everything else on straight?" I pointed at my wig.

"Looks fine, Goldilocks."

I made a face. " 'Silverlocks.' I don't think there's a strand of gold in this wig."

She smiled. It was a casual smile of camaraderie and it was easy to smile back at her.

We walked out of the elevator at a sedate pace, the beads on Kerrison's skirt and top making soft clinking sounds as we walked. An average-looking guy—who dressed like he was trying to look not so average— was in the small lobby. He wore a black suit, black polished shoes, and black sunglasses. His dark skin was smooth, unblemished, and unlined, and I'd have bet he was barely in his twenties.

"Ms. Johansen and Ms. Elliot." He said it in a way

that was a statement as opposed to a question. Like he already knew what we looked like. He'd probably been shown a still of us made from vids from the cameras located around the club floor.

I gave him a nod before I slipped on the pair of sunglasses from my purse. After a slight bow, he turned and held open the door for Kerrison and me to pass through.

The blast of New York's November chill instantly caused goose bumps to rise on my skin.

"Our coats," Kerrison said with a groan. "We were in such a rush."

"No time to go back." I paused a moment so that the man in the suit could open the door to the waiting black Lincoln Town Car. I swear, everyone in New York drove black cars.

Kerrison followed me as we slid across the black leather and settled into the posh seats. We looked at each other when the man shut the car door behind us. "You're stinking up the car with that perfume," I said before the driver got in his seat on the other side of the car. "You smell like orchids gone rogue."

She gave an evil grin. "At least I didn't just leave half my lipstick on a man's face."

My cheeks burned, and I forced myself to meet her gaze with my best *what the hell are you talking about* expression. "You're delusional."

Kerrison snorted. I looked away as the driver settled himself in his seat and shut the door. We were all silent as we drove from Brooklyn to Manhattan.

During the drive, my thoughts wandered from Kerrison's keen observation, to Donovan, to the op, and to

Mama. She never left my thoughts, but like any part of life, no matter how much we want things to go our way, we have to continue on with what we're given.

Daddy and Mama had drilled that into the seven of us from the time we were young, when we didn't have a lot of money. Those were the years we lived on cabbage and whatever else Mama grew in the garden in the back of the house, including potatoes. Like the original settlers did, we had potato bread instead of bread made from white flour.

Mama's cooking was every bit as wonderful then as it came to be once they'd saved and built up a good living for all of us. As far as growing up not having much money—my brothers, sister, and I never knew the difference. It was a part of our lives, and for the most part we were a happy bunch.

Well, when we weren't getting into trouble in one way or another or fighting like brothers and sisters do. Yeah, we were a bit of a challenge to Mama and Daddy. Putting it mildly.

My focus returned to the op as the car pulled up to the Elite Gentleman's Club and of course the driver aided us in getting out of the car. Again we were under the club's red awning decorated with white holiday lights. And again we were facing the same large, tall, muscled bouncer who'd been there yesterday.

This time he held the door open as soon as we approached him, apparently expecting us. Still, he said something over his wireless communication device, no doubt informing someone we'd arrived.

I slipped my sunglasses into my purse as we met up with another muscled guy who waited at the second door, a different one this time. This behemoth was bald and had a small diamond earring high up in the cartilage of his right ear.

Mr. Frenchy wasn't waiting for us once we passed through that door, either.

Stalder was. He had that no-expression look down pat. "If you meet Mr. G's approval, you'll begin working today," he said.

The fact he'd just stated we'd be put to work immediately, without the option of choosing when we would start, set me on edge. It was what our team wanted, but I've never liked not having a choice.

But in undercover work, I wasn't always given much choice.

We followed Stalder to the back of the club and into the hallway. This time we headed for the closed doorway at the end of that long hallway. Stalder rapped on the dark wood twice then opened the door without waiting for an answer. Probably because he was expected.

"Mr. G." Stalder motioned for Kerrison and me to go in before him. When we stood before a man seated behind a huge desk made of dark wood, Stalder gestured to the two of us. "Madame Alexis Johansen on the left and her assistant, Ms. Chandra Elliot."

The barrel-chested, fifty-something man behind the desk didn't stand. He pointed to the chairs with his thick index finger as if we were a pair of truants there to see the principal. "Sit down."

I resisted the urge to look at Kerrison and instead made myself walk with confidence. I sat with as much grace as I could and relaxed my grip on my purse as I settled into the green and maroon-striped high-backed chair in front of his desk.

Stalder stood to the side of us with an almost military stance, but with his hands folded in front of him. Perhaps he had been in the military at one time.

The man behind the desk didn't waste time with any niceties. He said in Swedish to me, "I read in the report you're from Sweden."

"Stockholm is where I was raised," I replied, also in Swedish. "Although it has been many years since I moved to America."

"I've taken a look at your records." He switched to English and thumped a folder on his desk. "Paper doesn't mean a fucking thing. Give it to me in your own goddamned words."

No problem. I launched into our cover story, sticking tight to what we'd established. Kerrison and I had it down so well that it came easily to both of us. When it was her turn, Kerrison's additions to my story were as smooth as what I had told "Mr. G."

After we'd finished, he observed us for a long time. "Hopefully the dickheads who work for me didn't screw this up," he said. "I'll hire you with a thirty-day probation to make sure you're not a couple of fuckups."

Yes, I thought, but I kept my expression composed, doing my best to look like I'd never even questioned the possibility of not being taken on as madame at the Elite.

"I'll hire both of you, Alexis and Chandra." He used our first names as a way to make it clear we were his underlings while he remained Mr. G. No doubt about that.

His features became almost dark as he looked directly at me and continued. "Your salary will be smaller because I'm paying more for your assistant. You're fucking lucky I'm taking her on, too." He named a figure that was ridiculously low for a madame and one even lower for Kerrison. "Depending on how the girls do onstage and how much they bring in upstairs, you might earn bonuses. I expect you to work your asses off."

The way he looked at me made me feel like I'd better keep my mouth shut and not even pretend to haggle over salary with him. "I understand, Mr. G." I added the *Mr. G* to make him feel important, so that he would think we knew our places just as clear as those dancing poles were. Gag. "We'll teach these girls so well that the club will be busier than ever."

His eyes looked like they contained jagged shards of gray flint as his gaze roved over Kerrison and me. "Anyone you have ties to is in our records now. If you think you want to leave, think twice and *discuss* it with me first."

He spoke in a way that sent a chill down my spine even though I'd expected it.

What few contacts were listed in my history were cooperatives paid to say they knew me in whatever fashion we needed them to. They were carefully chosen and didn't know who the hell who Kerrison or I really was. But they liked the cash, and RED paid them well. Very, very well.

The cooperatives weren't in danger. This Beeff Giger would be roadkill before he had a chance to hurt anyone else. We had no doubt we'd be bringing him down before he could touch any of our "friends" from our fictitious pasts. Not to mention we kept an eye on our cooperatives in case they did need our protection.

As for his veiled threat—which pissed me off even though I knew our cooperatives were safe—I acted the part of a madame who didn't know how to respond. So I sat without moving and waited for him to speak.

Giger took his time letting his gaze rove over my body, especially my Victoria's-enhanced breasts. Then he took in Kerrison's appearance. Of course her choice of attire made her look a lot more like eye candy than mine did. Plus she was a complete knockout to begin with, and she was playing it full-tilt.

He moved his gaze back to mine, his eyes somehow darker and dangerous enough that I almost sucked in my breath. "Get to work. *Now.*"

Yes, I thought again, only this time with a feeling of triumph. *We're in.*

I'd expected Giger's tone and his demand that we start tonight thanks to Stalder's earlier comment, so I handled my expression with no problem. Kerrison sat next to me with an equally calm look on her face.

"What would you like us to start doing first?" I asked.

"The handlers will bring the girls to you on the floor." Giger gestured toward Stalder. I'd almost forgotten the big blond guy was there. "Work on having the whores damned near fuck the poles. Make them look like they're fucking the clients just by looking at them."

"We're very good at that," I said, trying on a seductive smile when what I really wanted was to shove that titty pencil holder on his desk right up his ass.

"You fucking damned well better be." Giger's expression told me he'd have no compunction about taking out our "friends" if we didn't come through.

All right. We were ready to play his game. *And* we'd beat him at it.

CHAPTER ELEVEN

Bachmann, alias Hagstedt

The view of Lake Geneva from his home not far from Château d'Oex pleased Karl Bachmann. Cool satisfaction settled in his chest as he smiled.

As he'd built his empire, he had purchased this seventeenth-century mansion with its extensive and prosperous summer vineyard. In the winter, when the ground was covered with snow as it was now, his ski chalet thrived. Downhill skiing on the Alpine glaciers of the canton of Vaud brought tourists from all over the world.

After touching a call button, he put his hands behind his back, his stance wide, and surveyed the Alps. He imagined that he could see the passengers being transported in the ski lifts operating from his extensive and luxurious ski chalet. He insisted on only the best for his guests at his lodge, which catered to and allowed only the most exclusive clientele.

Karl's reflection in the glass caught his attention,

and he smoothed one side of the sleek hair that his stylist maintained a healthy dark brown, keeping him looking closer to his early forties than just over fifty.

That and his model-fine but mature features, as well as his fit body, kept him popular with the socialites. He maintained his physique by working out in the large gym in his mansion and had earned his black belt in karate by bringing in a private martial arts instructor.

His wealth no doubt added to the attraction women felt toward him. That was fine with him. Whatever it took to catch the attention of the sexiest and richest women in Switzerland.

He had decided on occasion that he needed to own a couple of the young women he had met and had orchestrated their disappearances. After he tired of them in his private home, he had arranged for the beautiful women to be sold in private auctions, another part of his lucrative business.

One of the girls he had introduced to the men who frequented one of the most popular amenities at his ski chalet. Many elite members were aware of the maze of fetish rooms below the lodge. Those who were allowed to know about that exclusive recreation paid well for the women Karl's men had stolen from their homes across the globe, brought to Switzerland, and forced to be high-priced whores. Slaves, really.

The men especially enjoyed the socialites. Sometimes Karl would arrange to secure a particular woman whom a client had brought to Karl's attention. Almost always a very young woman whom the client believed would be a fine addition to Karl's stable of sex slaves—and the man implied he would pay well to enjoy that particular woman. Frequently.

It was easy enough to arrange for the kidnapping of almost any woman.

His extraordinary business abilities, his eye for the best moneymaking opportunities, and his keen sense of enterprise and ambition had made him a billionaire.

Too bad he had business to attend to today or he would now be enjoying fine skiing from last night's snow. He could almost see his skis flashing in the cold sunlight, snow spraying in high arcs as he wove his way down the slope through the fresh powder.

A man cleared his throat from behind him. He turned to face his butler, an aging man wearing black who had liver spots on his hands and lines on the paperlike skin on his face. Was the butler now in his midseventies?

What did it matter? The old man was just a servant.

The butler's back was stiff, his posture rigid, his chin high. "You rang, Mr. Bachmann?"

The butler referred to him by his real name, of course. Karl was only known as Anders Hagstedt in his most profitable enterprises, which included any number of ways to traffic humans. Bachmann was easily one of the most powerful men in the industry.

Karl had taken a big risk by having the prostitutes available at the ski club when his real name was attached to the business.

However, it was beyond profitable, and he made sure

not one man would cross him. Every man allowed to indulge in his fantasies at the lodge resort was well aware that his own reputation could be damaged if word got out that he was screwing sex slaves.

Karl only allowed the elite as well as easily bought men know about his special amenities. Local heads of law enforcement, government officials, famous actors, singers, even billionaires.

Karl chose men with power and money—and usually men with wives—to be introduced to the delicious girls he rotated in and out of his personal businesses. Any man whose reputation could be easily smeared if word got out about his activities at the club was seduced in one way or another into the downstairs pleasure arena.

"Have my Lamborghini prepared and brought up to the front door," Karl finally said to the butler. "Bring me my driving coat. I will not need the chauffeur." *I have very important business contacts to meet.*

"Immediately, sir." The butler bowed his way out of the room.

Eighteen years ago, when he was thirty-three, Karl had purchased his mansion in his Swiss homeland with earnings from the ski lodge and chocolate factory his parents had owned. The hefty insurance payment and inheritance courtesy of his dead parents had been an excellend bonus.

How convenient it was that they had died in the car accident in Zurich. His parents had been so . . . tight with their money that they hadn't shared their wealth with him. He hadn't been able to touch it until the mysterious accident, when their brakes failed on an icy road in the middle of a snowstorm. What a shame.

Karl smiled as he moved toward the opposite end of his glass-walled suite. The enormous windows were always kept open during the day, the glass allowing him incredible views.

His ski lodge and chocolate factory now served to launder money he made from his most brilliant enterprises. The beyond-lucrative business that he ran under the name Anders Hagstedt.

Now at fifty-one, as Hagstedt, his human trafficking rings had made him a billionaire several times over. He preferred forced prostitution of females over trafficking children, women, and men for manual labor. However, both industries had their places, and both earned him not only millions but also respect throughout the world of men and women in the business.

Along with that respect, he had cultivated a deep-seated sense of fear within anyone who might try to fuck with him.

Karl preferred to be as hands-on as possible with his enterprise and traveled the world. His key sex trafficking operations were in Beijing, Moscow, Stockholm, New York City, and Daytona, Florida. He'd chosen Daytona for the sheer enjoyment of it. He enjoyed the climate, the atmosphere that was so unlike any other place he conducted business in.

His business primarily prostituted girls, but occasionally young men. Although most of his clients preferred females, some of his buyers' sexual proclivities included young males.

He glanced toward the paddocks and smiled when he saw his own boy slave busy combing down Hagstedt's most prized Lipizzaner stallion. He kept the boy busy with chores when he wasn't in the mood for the male to suck him off or literally be his piece of ass.

Karl's penis hardened, and he rubbed it through the fine wool of his tailored slacks. Perhaps he would call the boy to one of his private rooms before his drive. Maybe the two females he owned as well.

His slaves didn't have names. They were material items among his belongings that included his collections of ancient Roman artifacts and his stable full of champion Lipizzaner stallions and mares. His stallions gave the most magnificent Airs Above the Ground performance, an incredible work of art.

He didn't have to worry about his human possessions trying to escape. Karl had ordered his men to murder the boy's father when the boy attempted to escape, shortly after Hagstedt had first chosen him from a fine crop of newly acquired males. The boy's mother and five sisters would be next . . . one at a time . . . if he tried to escape again.

Karl had forced his female slaves to witness the execution. He had brought the Russian boy's father to the mansion and used him as an example. His slant-eyed Chinese academically brilliant schoolgirl and his blond American high school cheerleader, and of course the boy, had been suitably terrified by the example.

As he slipped his hands into his slacks, Karl continued to stare through the window at the boy who was brushing down Karl's mare. Right there, behind the boy, was where the snow had turned brilliant red with his father's blood only weeks ago. He had made the boy clean the mess and he'd had him haul his father's body to the incinerator.

Of course it was the same incinerator where Karl had disposed of his last three slaves when he grew tired of them after a year. And the slaves before that.

"Your coat, sir." The butler stood in the doorway holding Karl's favorite driving coat. It was extremely fine, and very illegal gorilla fur, and had cost more than one of the classic vehicles from his extensive collection. The coat he owned from the endangered clouded leopard had been an even greater expense.

Karl slipped his arms into the coat with the aid of the butler. "Is the Lamborghini ready?"

"It awaits you at the front door." The butler's voice was formal and unreadable as always. He had been with the family since Karl had been a boy, and he still couldn't remember the butler's name. Perhaps soon it would be time to get rid of the old man. As they say, out with the old and in with the new. Karl almost smiled at the thought of a naked slave as his new butler.

"May I be of further assistance?" the butler asked.

"Not now." Karl gave the man a dismissive nod toward the door.

The butler bowed himself out again.

Karl thought one more time about fucking the girls and the boy before taking his drive. Unfortunately that would have to wait. The anticipation would be better, anyway. Late tonight when he returned, he might use the riding crop on all three. It had been a while since he had enjoyed that particular pleasure.

He smiled as he walked from his personal suite, down the grand staircase, and to the foyer. Prisms of light from the chandelier glittered off the walls and wood flooring. Every teardrop on the chandelier was made from exquisite Swarovski crystal. At least a thousand individual pieces.

After the doorman opened the door, Karl walked out into the cool late-November day. The doorman closed the door behind him while Karl drew butter-soft driving gloves from his coat pockets. He headed down the white marble steps leading from the mansion to his circular driveway.

His customized pearl Lamborghini Gallardo LP560-4 purred as it idled and released a steady stream of fogged exhaust into the cold air. Bachman's fingers were already nearly numb as he tugged on his gloves, walked around the car to the driver's side, and used his remote to raise the driver's-side door that had been left closed to keep the warm air inside the vehicle.

He climbed in, and the door eased shut with a fluid movement before he flexed and unflexed his fingers and grasped the driver's wheel. The interior of the car was suitably warm.

Key men from China, Russia, Sweden, and the United States would be waiting at the exclusive restaurant in Geneva for Anders Hagstedt, not Karl Bachmann. It was time to see how his enterprises as Hagstedt were progressing.

Then in two days he'd make a personal trip to New York City to observe how his Manhattan business was doing. He was in the mood to sample the choicest treats from the next shipment due to arrive in the city from China.

CHAPTER TWELVE

Dasha

Something about the new madame, Alexis, and her assistant, Ms. Chandra, was different. They had just started this afternoon, and Dasha wondered what happened to Madame Cherie.

Dasha shivered in the sheer top and skirt she wore, and her legs felt colder yet in the netting she was forced to wear for tonight. Every night they wore something different. Scraps of cloth were all they had.

The club was empty now except for the girls and their handlers. Soon the tables would be packed with men who smelled of sweat and beer, and the girls would all face another night of hell.

She looked at the other girls, who were mostly waxy-faced and so drugged they had a hard time standing. Eddie still liked to keep Dasha from being too doped up, because he wanted her to know he had control over her, and wanted her to feel the pain he caused her. He was sick.

Would it be better to be drugged and not know what was happening to her every single night since she'd been brought to this country?

Dasha studied the two new women. She couldn't quite place the difference she felt in the presence of Madame Alexis and Ms. Chandra, but she couldn't say it looked to be worse working with them than it had been with Madame Cherie. What had happened to her?

The other madame had been a bitter, demanding woman with a rough voice and even rougher vocabulary. These women seemed almost nice in comparison.

"Again." Madame Alexis with her pale blond hair and fair skin had a strict, almost angry voice as she spoke, but the anger didn't seem to be directed at the girls. Dasha didn't know how she'd come to that conclusion, but there it was. "Watch Ms. Chandra closer," Madame Alexis ordered. "Follow her lead and you'll have every man in the building wanting you."

The madame said those words like they were distasteful and she wanted to spit them out and wash her mouth with a cake of soap.

Strange.

Ms. Chandra, on the other hand, smiled a lot and seemed patient in teaching every girl she brought up on stage. "Klara, you've almost got it," Ms. Chandra said as she started to undulate against the pole again. "Follow my example a little more and you'll have it down perfectly."

Dasha cocked her head. Ms. Chandra said the words with a smile, yet Dasha was sure she saw an angry glint in her pale green eyes. She wondered what caused the spark that Ms. Chandra tried so hard to keep from showing. It couldn't be that she was keeping it from the girls—what would be the point?

Both Madame Alexis and Ms. Chandra were trying to hide anger. Why?

Dasha waited with most of the girls to the side of the empty club where she smelled cigar smoke. It was still strong despite the staff's daily attempt at freshening the air and cleaning the leather seats. The lemon oil used to polish the wood barely helped to mask the smell.

Ms. Chandra invited two more girls up onto the stage, gesturing to Olga and Vera while she also kept Klara beside her. "Now we'll work on the fine art of the striptease."

The woman began demonstrating how the girls should slowly strip clothing from their bodies to entice and tease clients enough to want a lap dance.

"Once you get the client in the booth for a lap dance," Ms. Chandra said, "it's up to each of you to encourage the men—or women—into paying to join you in the upstairs rooms."

Of course the girls had no choice in that regard, either. There were always cameras. Always someone who would punish them if they didn't do as they were told.

Another sick feeling gripped Dasha as if raw sewage churned in her belly. *Why can't I be numb to everything that is happening to us like Yulia appears to be?* Dasha asked herself yet again as she glanced at her friend, who had a dull look on her face that went beyond being plied with drugs. *Or why can't I go into another world that makes it look as if I like sex in the same way Jenika manages to do it?*

Dasha frowned as she looked around the room. Where was Jenika? Dasha couldn't remember seeing the older girl since last night when she had left with one of the handlers.

Before she had been taken away, Jenika had been in the girls' common room that was on the top floor of the building where they lived when they weren't being prostituted. Dasha had just assumed the handler assigned to Jenika had taken her for a short *visit,* like the handlers frequently did with any girl of his choice.

"Got an early one for you." Eddie's coarse palms gripped Dasha's upper arms as he shook her hard from behind. Dasha clenched her teeth to keep from gasping aloud and shuddered from his touch and even more when the handler leaned close to her ear. "Looks like you are a lucky little girl, since the dickhead knows Mr. G."

Dear God, no. Dasha bit back words she wanted to spew out to him. Words that would only earn her slaps and punches in places not easily seen by paying customers or other handlers.

If she could only go back to that day when she had seen the advertisement for the modeling agency competition. At that moment, part of her had thought it might not be a good idea to leave her homeland and her family.

The other part, the vain and stupid half of her, had brought her to this place, this hell.

Yes, she had wanted to help Matushka and Otets by sending them money so that they no longer lived in poverty.

But she had also imagined herself in the spotlight, people admiring her for her long, pale blond hair and her silver-blue eyes. Her picture on magazines, televisions, advertisements.

Pain shot through Dasha's scalp as Eddie jerked her braid and caused her to stumble backward, against him. "You've definitely earned what your favorite client is going to give you. You're a sorry-assed dancer and shitty at doing a striptease. Yeah, you need some personal attention."

Eddie gave a laugh. "Maybe you need some of the same treatment that whore Jenika is getting. I hear she fucked up bad enough to have the shit beat out of her and she's been locked up. I think she tried to get to the cops. Now, you wouldn't want that, would you—have the fucking shit beat out of you?"

Dasha's heart dropped at the thought of Jenika being beaten for trying to escape.

At the same time, knowing she was headed for some sick surprise Eddie had for her made Dasha want to claw off the flimsy miniskirt and bra. Claw off her skin. And wash herself inside and out while swallowing enough of the water that she would drown. If not for her parents, death would be better than this.

Eddie drew her out of the crowd of girls and forced her ahead of him, out of the main club floor, behind the curtain, and into the dank, musty hallway. Then he pushed her up the stairs, causing her to trip and fall.

She hit her elbow so hard, pain shot through it. He jerked her up by her hair, and more pain splintered through her scalp.

When they reached the landing of the second floor, Dasha heard a scream that was so loud her entire body chilled. She came to a complete stop. Goose bumps rolled over her skin, prickling her entire body. Another scream followed by loud sobs. Then what sounded like a hard slap and more crying, then a woman begging someone to stop. It was muffled through the room's door, but Dasha thought she heard a woman shout, "I've told you everything. I don't know anything else."

Another scream.

Dasha held one hand to her belly. Jenika. The voice had sounded like Jenika. Had she been given to some man who liked to beat up women? Some men did and sometimes the handlers would laugh about it.

But then what would she mean by what she'd been shouting about telling everything she knew? Did they want to know why she had tried to go to the cops, like Eddie said she had been doing?

"Third floor, bitch." Eddie shoved Dasha to the next flight of stairs. "Looks like you've got room four with the dickhead who's got such a hard-on for you. Parkerson. More like Peckerson. Skinny-assed pervert."

Not Mr. Parkerson.

Dasha felt hot and cold and let the memory of Jenika's screams slip away as they reached the third floor landing. She once again started down the too-familiar hallway toward the room where she would be handcuffed to the bed. Mr. Parkerson always liked

her bound while he did things to her that made her
impossibly more ill than anything else that was done
to her by other men.

When Eddie shoved her into room four she almost
screamed at the sight of Mr. Parkerson, who had a bat-
tery on a chair next to the bed. He was holding a clamp
with long red grips in his right hand, another clamp
with long black grips in his left.

Dearest God, she thought as tears rolled down her
cheeks before she could stop them. She started to
shake, her whole body trembling like she was going
to come undone. What was the man going to do to her
this time?

Dasha hardened inside for the briefest of moments
as she visualized Mr. Parkerson handcuffed to the bed
instead of her. Eddie handcuffed right next to him.
Both men naked, that hideous part of them bare.

She saw the image of herself holding a handgun.

In that brief daydream, she squeezed the trigger and
shot the abusive Mr. Parkerson where it would hurt the
most, his groin, before she shot him in the head.

Then, in her mind, she killed Eddie.

CHAPTER THIRTEEN

Jenika

Icy water splashed hard against the side of Jenika's head, jerking her back to consciousness.

"Wake up, bitch," came a hard, angry voice. "Open your fucking eyes."

What? Her thoughts wavered in and out, spotty, confused. *Open my eyes?*

Jenika tried to obey the voice as water rolled from her hair and face, down her neck, and between her breasts. Her head lolled forward, and she didn't know how she even managed to sit up. Her face felt like her skin was stretched tight, so swollen it would split if she opened her mouth.

Somehow she knew she had to open her eyes or it would mean something bad. Really bad. But they were swollen shut. The lids felt like they were glued together with tree sap.

An acidic stench mixed with a dusty smell from a heater that must not have been used in a long time. Its heat was focused on her and despite the ice water that had been splashed on her face, the intensity of the heat made her feel like she was burning, her face on fire. A coppery taste was in her mouth along with the taste of stomach acid.

Her mind wouldn't let her focus long enough to remember where she was. Why did her head feel like it had been used as a soccer ball? And her body felt stripped raw, as if she'd been mauled by those great white tigers in Las Vegas.

More water slammed into her face, this time directly in front of her, and she gasped, sucked in water, and sputtered. It tasted dirty, vile. Like water squeezed from a mop after being used on a floor. She spit it out and coughed again as it rolled down her body.

"Open your eyes," the voice said in an almost deadly, quiet tone. "Or I'll start cutting you."

Jenika's heart slammed into her ribs, and she finally managed to pry her eyelids open a slit. A well-lit shabby room. A steel table. Metal folding chairs. A door with its peeling white paint showing the aged wood beneath.

A man with buzzed gray hair stared at her with eyes that were gray like the dirty mop water she thought had been thrown at her. He was holding a glass of white wine and was casually sipping it as he studied her. She looked at the huge diamond ring on one of the fingers gripping the wineglass and she sucked in her breath.

Images pounded at her head as hard as she remembered the fists that had been pounding her body. Three men, including the one staring at her with narrowed eyes—the men punching her. Kicking her. Everywhere on her body.

And that huge stone being driven into the side of her head when the gray-haired man had punched her, right before she blacked out. The coppery taste in her mouth was blood from the inside of her mouth splitting open from the power of his punch.

Bile rushed up Jenika's throat, and she tried to move to spew it out to her side. She couldn't. Her upper chest and shoulders were bound to the top of a high-backed chair, her hands cuffed behind her, and her ankles strapped to the chair legs.

She couldn't stop what little was left in her stomach from coming up. She puked onto her chest, then saw what had been dried, crusted vomit, now wet from the water. Vomit from when she had thrown up earlier. The sight of her own puke and the stench of it caused her to heave more, even after she no longer had anything left.

"Tell me," the man said slowly as he set his wineglass on the metal table. He came to her, bent, and placed his hands on his thighs so that he was at her eye level. "Who do you work for?"

"Please don't hit me." Jenika tried to shake her head but it hurt too much. "I-I don't know. That's the truth."

The huge diamond glinted on the man's ring as he raised his fist. "One. More. Time." He bared his teeth. "You *will* die if you don't tell me." Then he tried to turn his lips up in some semblance of a smile. "On the other hand, if you give me the information I need, you can walk out of here."

Tears flooded Jenika's eyes as she thought about her twins and saw their pretty faces in her mind. The girls would be three in just a few weeks. Her precious babies had been born on New Year's Day. A new year, new life, new start.

The woman who had paid her so much money had promised she would have the twins taken care of while Jenika worked for her. And she had promised that the girls would lack for nothing if anything happened to her.

If anything happened to me.

The woman had told her it could be dangerous, but Jenika had only seen the money that would help her get away from the life she led as a prostitute in Nevada. No matter how much the woman tried to impress upon her the danger she might face, Jenika had pictured herself in a career where her children could be proud of their mother as they grew up.

She should have known then, when the woman offered her the money. She should have listened, *really listened* to the woman. Maybe then she would have realized that she was being asked to do something so dangerous it was possible she might never see her girls again. So dangerous she might not survive. Was it worth all that money for her twins to never see their mother again?

"I asked you a question," the man said in a snarl.

"All of what I have said to you is true, I swear to it." Jenika coughed and her chest burned as tears flooded her cheeks, which were fiery hot from the heater focused on her face. "A-a woman. She came to me. Gave me money."

"Who?" the man said his words in what sounded like short, sharp barks. "What does she look like?"

"She had dark brown hair that was cut all the way to the nape of her neck." Jenika tried to concentrate on the image of the woman who'd come to her at the cathouse in Las Vegas. "She was petite, shorter than me. Like a pixie."

It was so hard to see the man through the slits of her puffy eyes, but she heard him speak as if the volume of her hearing had been turned all the way up. "What's this fucking pixie's name?"

Jenika sucked in a breath. Her chest hurt from one of the men kicking her before. "She didn't tell me."

He brought his face closer to hers. "Why did she come to you?"

Jenika wanted to draw away, but her head was already against the seatback. She started sobbing and hiccuping. "I don't know. Please. I don't know."

"Why would this woman come to you?" the man said. "Out of nowhere? If you're telling the truth, which I don't think you are, where did she find you?"

Jenika froze. If she told him that the woman contacted her at the cathouse in Nevada, they would question people who worked there. Ultimately he would find out about her daughters.

No. No, no, no. She would die before letting that happen.

"It was in Moscow." Jenika's voice shook as she hurried to get out every bit of her lie that she could. "I had no money. What she offered was a way for me to start a new life. She said she would make sure I wouldn't be here for long. She just wanted me to see if I could get pieces of information to her."

The man leaned forward, his face in hers, blocking the heat but forcing her to smell his sour breath. "What information have you given this woman?"

Jenika again tried to shake her head and felt like her brain was going to fall into pieces. "I only found some kind of paper that didn't make any sense. I still gave it to the man I was told to once I found something."

His face reddened. "What man? You didn't mention any fucking man."

Jenika's heart slammed against her chest harder. "He never came back. I gave him the paper one night while men stuffed dollars into my G-string and I never saw him again."

"You're a lying bitch." Through her puffy eyelids as she saw him draw his fist back. "We'll just keep doing this until I beat the information out of you."

The huge diamond ring on the man's fist was the last thing she saw before pain splintered through her head and her world spun into a shattered void.

CHAPTER FOURTEEN

Killer Ant hills and scrotums

It was one of the hardest things I'd ever faced in my career as a RED special agent. I could almost feel the cool metal of my Glock in my hands as I squared off and one at a time took out all the bastards who were prostituting these girls. My body was flushed with heat, but my mind was focused on doing what I had to do to end this.

Watching what these girls were forced to do was like razors slicing my intestines into ribbons. I couldn't do anything yet for those innocent young women dancing half naked on the stage to screaming, pulsating music. For that one moment as I watched the girls, I felt impotent. Helpless to be unable to do what needed to be done so badly, fast enough. Like now.

Screw helpless or impotent. I was going to make this happen and get the girls safely out of here.

I looked at my watch. I couldn't call Mama again until tomorrow morning. I didn't know if I could even sleep between the time I got home from the Elite until I talked with her.

The girls were so drugged they probably didn't even know what they were doing. I imagined all that went through their heads were refrains of threats against themselves and their families if they didn't do what they'd been told. A program looping through their confused brains.

Maybe it was better for them that way.

Kerrison stood at a podium in a darker part of the room, to the left of the stage, close to the curtain that hid several lap-dance booths behind it. The bead fringes along her half top and miniskirt sparkled, reflecting the colored lights that flashed throughout the club.

Men had started approaching Kerrison at the podium and handing her credit cards or enough cash for a lap dance with the girl of their choice. Stalder mentioned that some of the men in the club would pay for two or more girls at once. Not only for lap dances, but for a group get-together in a private room upstairs.

Somehow I had to get my anger, the tension in my body, under control. I wasn't going to do anyone a damned bit of good if I didn't maintain.

"Not much of an improvement." Stalder's voice came low and even from behind me but hair prickled at the nape of my neck. "The girls still look as if they do not know what they are doing."

I turned to face him and gave him a cool stare. "Two hours to work with the girls before showtime is not enough time to make true progress." I gestured to the three girls who were pole-dancing onstage and stripping off what little clothing they had on. "And they are drugged terribly. How can they dance when they are like this?"

His stare remained cool, and I tried to pretend that I assumed they were junkies by choice. "Is there a way you can get the girls to stop the drugs until after they are finished working for the night?"

Stalder gripped my upper arm so hard and so unexpectedly that he was lucky he didn't end up in a heap on the floor. Two moves and I would have had him there.

"You ensure these girls make the clients *very* happy." He leaned close, and his Tiffany Sport Cologne made me want to sneeze as I caught its scent that on him was like pepper and some kind of herbs. His breath brushed the hair around my ear, and I had to resist the urge to ram my elbow into his solar plexus. "Mr. G will not be pleased if you do not improve their performances."

I turned so that I could meet his gaze head-on even though I had to tip my head back. "I will do my job and Ms. Chandra will do hers."

He studied me for a long moment before he turned and vanished into the crowd. Jeez but the guy gave me the creeps.

My gaze returned to the girls onstage as men now pawed at them. Sticking bills into their G-strings, but touching other places on the women that they weren't supposed to.

The power of my anger was just as intense as it had

been when Donovan's sister and other young women had been kidnapped and sold in online auctions. Men from around the world bid on them and considered them merchandise—the women were shipped mostly ~~to foreign countries as sex slaves. Sometimes they~~ were taken by U.S. buyers, as Kristin had been.

My and Donovan's team of RED agents had had to find and stop the next auction, and take down the local ringleader, a masochistic sonofabitch. We'd been almost too late for the latest group of women who had been kidnapped from local dance clubs.

It *had* been too late for Kristin Donovan. A fact she had to live with every single day of her life, even after her recovery by Donovan and RED.

Rage twisted my insides until I thought I might not be able to hide my fury. Thank God I have a good poker face or the depth of my anger would have been flaming in my eyes. Here, at the so-called Elite Gentleman's Club . . . worse than watching the girls dance mostly naked was knowing that they would be taken into rooms and prostituted as soon as they came off that stage.

And this was only the start of my and Kerrison's first evening on the op.

My thoughts raced as my anger made my head ache while I watched the girls undulate and thrust their breasts out as they'd been taught. I wanted to eliminate Hagstedt's New York City ring as fast as possible and bring down the bastard himself, which would help dismember and destroy his international operations.

I had to help these girls.

It could take days before we got our claws into Hagstedt. Or weeks. Depending on whether or not Hagstedt came like we thought he would, according to the encrypted note Jenika had intercepted and Kerrison had deciphered.

What would Hagstedt look like when I finally faced him? How would I know it was him?

Whatever the case, I could easily picture a bullet hole in a generic man's forehead. Knowing that man would be Hagstedt.

The music blaring over the speakers was coming to an end, a disgusting song when tied to these girls. It was a woman who shrieked about men going down on her and then screwing her brains out. Yeah, that set the mood real good for these assholes in the club.

I backed away from the place where I'd been watching the stage, and I went to the podium to join Kerrison. I wanted to reach her before this first trio of girls and their handlers. The men would take strips of paper with each of the girls' assignments.

Kerrison was putting on a brilliant and most definitely fake smile for a man who paid her with a thick stack of bills. All hundreds if my sight was as good as usual despite the dim light. The rotund man, who was wearing a clearly expensive business suit, was obviously a regular who wanted to go straight for the goodies.

What would he think if he knew he was in fact raping a woman who'd been kidnapped into forced prostitution, sexual slavery?

Did he know? Was he among the men who were

fully aware that these women were unwilling prostitutes, like the handlers knew? Whatever the case, I'd have been glad to make it so that he'd never screw another woman again.

"How's it going?" I said low and close to Kerrison's ear.

"As well as it can considering the situation." She still wore her fake smile. Damn, she was good at that. I might have to take lessons from her.

My gut twisted for another reason, and my heart thrummed as I let my gaze drift over the room that was blurred by cigar smoke. "Have you seen Jenika anywhere?" I asked, keeping my mouth close to her ear. "She wasn't there during our first lesson with the girls this afternoon."

"No." Kerrison still smiled but anger tinged her voice. "And we can't even ask about her because we're not supposed to know she's here. We're not supposed to know *anyone* here."

Fire continued to simmer under my skin. "And that bastard, Giger, sure made it clear that questions aren't allowed." I tried on a fake smile of my own as I looked at Kerrison. "You can bet I'll find a way."

As thoughts of Jenika rushed through my mind, fear for her made my hands shake. I'd been the one to go to Jenika at the cathouse in Nevada. I'd offered her the money and the deal. I'd taken her from her children and promised their safety and Jenika's safe return.

I'd lost an agent on the last op—she'd been murdered. My stomach clenched hard. The bastards had raped and slit Randolph's throat when they discovered she was an undercover agent.

Later in the op I'd been taken by the same men who'd killed Randolph. I'd been interrogated. Beaten. Humiliated in a way that I'd never forget.

I held my hand to my belly and felt the diamond piercing beneath my dress. I tried to concentrate on the Chinese symbol for dragon around my belly button rather than what had been carved there.

Something was definitely wrong. Jenika should be here. I had to find her and make sure she was all right.

I sucked in a deep breath and regretted it as I coughed out cigar smoke.

"Maybe she's ill," Kerrison said as she finished accepting cash from another john. "Hell, maybe they moved her to a different club."

"I'm going to find out." I *wouldn't* lose another person on my watch. Jenika was an innocent, too. She wasn't trained to be a spy. She was a working girl whom we'd ultimately exploited to get inside this trafficking ring. I'd allowed her to be put in the line of danger. I'd been the one to make it happen.

Christ.

The three now topless girls who'd been onstage swayed as they walked toward the steps. Their individual handlers waited at the stairs to help them—as drugged out as the girls were, there was no way they wouldn't fall flat on their faces without help down the steps.

The first two handlers reached for a paper Kerrison handed one, then the other. I studied each young woman. The third one had been taken away early from the lesson Kerrison and I had given earlier today.

Out of all of the girls, this one looked the most lucid. Jewell. That was the name the DJ had called her by when he'd announced her. Maybe she would know where Jenika was. If I could just talk with her.

"Ask this girl," I said to Kerrison. "She doesn't seem as strung out as the others. I'll get you as much time as I can."

"You've got it." She smiled as the girl and man approached.

I made a quick turn from behind the podium as if I was headed back to the floor. I ran straight into Jewell's handler, putting myself between the pair and separating him from the girl.

I stumbled back then grabbed his wrist as if to steady myself. "I do not appreciate being trampled over." I kept my tone haughty as I looked at the thickset, muscular guy with crooked teeth stained yellow from smoking too many cigarettes. "Watch where you are going next time."

"Get out of the way, bitch." The handler started to push me out of the way but I released his wrist, reached down, and grabbed his balls. I squeezed, hard. His face paled, and he came to a complete stop.

"Fuck with me again and you might lose something precious to you." I kept my tone pleasant. "That includes how you address me. *Madame Alexis* is the only way you will refer to me."

His voice pitched higher. "Mr. G won't put up with this shit."

I laid on the Swedish accent, smirked, and squeezed

even more. "A strong man like you is going to go to your boss and tell him that a wee girl like me had you by the balls?" I squeezed tighter, and he looked even paler. "That should give him a good laugh."

I didn't think he could get a word out, as good a grip as I had on him, but I still asked, "What's your name?"

Sweat dripped down the side of his face. "Eddie."

"You do not mess with me or my assistant." I added in a sweet tone as I lessened my hold on his scrotum. But not entirely.

"Yeah. Sure." His voice was even higher-pitched. "Just let go of my fucking balls."

"There you go." I patted his crotch. "I am pleased we got that out of the way."

This time Eddie walked around me. With a furious scowl, he yanked the piece of paper from Kerrison's hand as he gripped Jewell's arm and jerked the girl behind the curtains to the private booths.

When I went back to Kerrison, this time her smile was both genuine and on the verge of being angry. In other words, I think she'd been successful in obtaining some information, but she wasn't happy about it.

I waited while Kerrison took another john's credit card and swiped it while he told her he wanted Starlight again, who was one of the next three girls on the stage pole-dancing now.

"Full course," he added with a grin.

I looked down at his balls.

Fortunately he didn't notice the maniac light that was probably glinting in my eyes at that moment.

When the future to-be-de-balled man left—one among many men who took advantage of the girls in this club to face de-balling—Kerrison met my gaze. "Her real name is Dasha," she said. "And you're right, her handler thinks it's fun if she's more aware of what's going on. Really likes to humiliate her."

I pictured *Eddie's* balls on the end of stakes driven into the ground. Man, I could have some fun figuring out different neutering methods. Darts, anyone? How about pellet guns? Fishhooks. Ice picks. Knitting needles. Rottweilers.

Spread-eagle on a killer ant mound, the scrotum coated in honey. The carcass would be reduced to polished bone in a week or two. Yeah, killer ants were the ticket.

Okay. So I have a thing about rapists deserving ant hills and dick stockades. So sue me.

Kerrison glanced toward the next man coming toward the podium before looking at me again. "Today her handler told her she'd better not screw up like the girl called Jenika who tried to go to the cops. He said Dasha might be beaten like Jenika, maybe to death." Kerrison's jaw was tight even as she tried to keep her fake smile on. "When Eddie made Dasha leave the rehearsal early for a client, she swears she heard Jenika screaming. Things about already telling whoever everything she knew."

"Shit." I gripped an angled part of the top of the podium and closed my eyes for a moment, trying to hold on to my composure. I opened them and looking at Kerrison again. "Where?"

She glanced up at the ceiling as if we could see

through it to the floor above, and then she cut her gaze back to me. "The off-limits area."

I rubbed my eyes with my thumb and forefinger as fear for the young cooperative flowed through me. "Time to visit the second floor."

CHAPTER FIFTEEN

Gone

First thing on our initial and extremely brief tour, we'd been warned that we weren't allowed on the second floor. Of course I'd planned to examine every room there anyway, though not tonight.

But having just heard what the Russian girl had said to Kerrison, now was the time to move.

Kerrison shifted to speak even closer to my ear so the man couldn't hear—despite the fact that music was screaming so loudly, I doubt if he could have caught any of what she said. "Somewhere down the hall on the second floor, at the opposite end. She said she was sure that whatever room it was, it wasn't one that was close to the stairs."

"Cover for me." I glanced over my shoulder to make sure Stalder and the other handlers weren't looking my way. "Give me about ten to twelve minutes. Tell anyone who asks that I've got the runs."

She nodded at the same time she looked away from

me and processed the next man's bill, and I slipped behind the curtain. I stayed in the curtain folds to check the time on the slim cell phone—which was illegal according to Giger—that I'd tucked into my bra. I'd set the display to be as dim as possible.

Okay. Twelve minutes. That was probably all I'd get away with and not face questions or, worse yet, get caught.

The hallway behind the stage curtains had ten lap-dance booths on the left, each draped with a green velvet curtain and each girl's handler standing nearby. The hallway smelled like testosterone and male sweat along with the pine cleaner that had been used on the black-and-white-checkered linoleum floor.

On the opposite side of that wall was a hallway that led directly from a door into the club from the street. A filthy corridor that was used to take the girls inside and out that we'd logged during surveillance.

I tried to ignore the male voices behind the curtains. A couple saying things like, "Come on, sweetheart, give me a little more than a lap dance. Let me touch you . . ."

The female voices replied like automatons with words that had been drilled into each girl. "We can go upstairs and be alone, baby, and you can touch me all you want to. Ask Ms. Chandra . . ."

As I walked past the booths, I held my chin high and didn't look at the four handlers currently there, as if they weren't important to me at all. I did notice Eddie's glare but pretended not to. Fortunately the restrooms were around the corner at the end of the hall, close to the stairs and out of the handlers' eyesight.

The moment I was around the corner, I pushed open the door to the women's restroom. The door squeaked loud enough that the handlers would be able to hear the sound from where they stood beside the lap-dance booths.

Instead of going into the restroom, I let the door swing shut, spun around, and jerked my stilettos off. I ran, then glided on my bare feet the rest of the way across the linoleum before I hid my stilettos in a little alcove by the bottom step. I jogged up the single flight of stairs to the second floor.

The metal staircase had been painted black multiple times, the layers showing through chips in the paint that were rough beneath my palms as I hurried upward.

We'd already known the building's schematics beforehand, but the territory is always different when you're on the inside. Chairs, tables, lamps—every little thing makes a difference.

The third through fifth floors we'd been shown, but we hadn't been allowed in any of the rooms, except for the common room on the fifth floor where the girls supposedly relaxed during their time off. The fifth floor was also where the twenty girls doubled or tripled up in the six rooms. Stalder had given us the line that room and board was part of the payment they received as employees at the Elite Gentleman's Club.

Yeah, right.

That left the third and fourth floors as the "working" floors. A total of twelve rooms, six per floor.

I came to a stop on the second-floor landing. Quiet. Absolutely quiet, just like it had been when we'd been given the brief tour and bypassed the floor. Checked my cell. Ten minutes left.

A yellow nylon rope was draped between a metal pole near the landing and attached to a metal hook on the wall across from the pole. A sign hung from the rope that read NO ENTRANCE. Which was an invitation to me to visit it just as soon as I could.

Yup. I'd decided I'd have to visit each room on the second floor even if each room was filled with only cotton candy or toxic waste. I'd figured I'd find things that would have nothing to do with anything as innocent as teddy bears and baby bottles.

I took a quick inventory of the walls and ceilings to make sure there were no cameras, no sensors. Fortunately, the hallway was lit by three bulbs strung from one end to the other in the same way all the other floors were illuminated.

The checkered linoleum floor was hard beneath my knees as I crawled under the rope. Based on my first impressions, I didn't think it was likely these guys were intelligent enough to have any sophisticated booby traps to worry about tripping. Or maybe it was the fact they were too confident of their power and control over everyone around them to believe anyone would disobey.

After I got to my feet, my pulse kicked up a notch in preparation for a little hunting. I headed for the end of the hallway that smelled of must and rat droppings.

The brass knob to room 2F was cold beneath my palm, but turned easily. I peeked into the dim room and let my eyes adjust since the only light was what came in from behind me in the hallway.

It looked like a supply room with large flattened cardboard boxes stacked high, piles of bubble wrap, as well as rolls of packing and duct tape. Lots of other things scattered around that weren't the least bit interesting right now.

Room 2E was also unlocked. It was filled with tables, chairs, and even mattresses and bed frames in disarray. A real mess.

Just like home sweet home.

I wasn't so lucky with 2D. I had to reach into my bra and take out the small lock-picking kit from the hidden pocket. Three seconds and I was in.

Now, this was more interesting. An office with a computer, file cabinets, and bookshelves. I'd have to find a time to slip away to get back to this room and do some investigating.

An excellent place to plant a bug, now. I hurried to the metal desk while I slipped my fingers into my bra again, this time in a small pocket under my armpit. I drew out a strip with four black disks stuck on it, each about the size of my pinky and thickness of a dime.

I peeled one off as I analyzed the desk. The fact that it was metal wasn't going to help a whole lot. For optimum reception, I needed this type of bug somewhere that wasn't on, under, or behind a lot of metal. The office chair on the opposite side of the desk would have to do. The back was hard plastic, the seat cushions fake leather.

I pressed the sticky side of the bug near one arm of the chair, hoping it wouldn't be noticed. The fact the bug was black like the chair would help. I pushed down and heard a soft click that told me the bug had engaged and would now show up on the surveillance team's grid.

Planting the bug had taken about twenty precious seconds. The cell phone showed that all I had was five minutes to find Jenika before it might be noticed I was missing. God, I hoped she was still alive.

I tucked the cell phone away as hurried out of the office. From under room 2D's door I saw a sliver of light. Someone might be there. I pressed my ear to the door but heard nothing. The doorknob refused to budge, and I had to use the lock pick again. The door squeaked as I opened it, and I winced. I stayed as far back away from the entrance as I could, just in case. I leaned in when I didn't hear anything.

My heart thumped hard. A powerful heat lamp that glowed red in the center of the well-lit room made sweat start dripping down my face.

But it was the folding chair in front of the heat lamp that caused my body to go cold despite the heat. Blood spotted the empty metal chair, a pair of handcuffs dangling from one side. Shredded flimsy clothing lay around the chair's legs.

Large chunks of hair had been dropped onto the floor.

Hair the same pale blond as Jenika's.

My heart dropped to my stomach.

"No, no, no." I ground my teeth as I stared at the mounds of what had once been long beautiful blond hair on a lovely young woman. "Not dead. Jenika *isn't* dead." I stomped my bare foot. "I will not accept that."

I reached into my bra for my cell phone again and checked the display. Three minutes. I raised the phone and used it to shoot several photos of the place Jenika may have been tortured.

After I tucked away the phone, I flipped up the hem of my dress and used a tool from my lock-pick set to remove a couple of stitches. Just enough to make a small pocket to tuck away several strands of the blond hair. That would be enough to test for her DNA.

I glanced around the mostly empty room, and my gaze landed on a steel table. And a wineglass on top of it. I hurried toward it and leaned close enough to see that it was covered with clear prints from whichever bastard had probably hurt Jenika. I couldn't exactly tuck the wineglass in my bra . . .

Tape.

I checked the hallway before I darted down to 2F, the first door I'd opened. I barely avoided tripping over a bag of packing peanuts before I reached the clear package tape.

Shit. One minute according to my cell phone. Stalder had probably already noticed I'd been gone awhile. Kerrison was a good enough liar—and flirt— to hold him off a little longer.

The hallway was still clear and I bolted into the room with the locks of what I was sure was Jenika's hair and ran for the wineglass. I tore two strips of the sticky clear packing tape and tagged them on the edge of the metal table. I took the wineglass by its stem and hoped I'd manage to do this right.

I took the first piece of tape and pressed it smoothly against the glass before removing it as slowly as I could. Three clean prints came away with it. Then I stuck that piece of tape to the nonsticky backside of the second piece. My hands trembled from adrenaline as I shoved up my skirt and pressed the sticky side of the second piece of tape to my bare upper thigh. The heat lamp was so hot, the hair beneath my wig was growing sweaty, and I began to feel like I was getting a sunburn.

Cell phone. Minus two minutes. Damn.

I peeked out of the doorway, then closed the door behind me when I saw the empty hallway. I listened for sounds of voices or footsteps but heard nothing until I reached the rope.

The hard *thump* of heavy boots banged against the stairs, causing the metal to ring, as someone walked up from the first floor.

Crap.

I slid on my bare feet straight for one of the support beams that helped brace the staircase and hoped I could do a good-enough job of hiding behind it. There are plenty of perks to being petite, including hiding behind things some people can't.

My lungs started to hurt as I held my breath. I let air out in a slow exhale, as quietly as I could. Then I heard the *tap-tap* of a woman's high heels. The sound was irregular, like the woman was stumbling.

"Come on, baby." The man's voice was surprisingly high-pitched considering the amount of noise his boots made on the staircase. Can't judge a man by his boots. "I'm going to fuck you twelve ways to dawn."

The girl whimpered and I clenched my jaws.

I leaned my head back against the support beam. Thank God it was a client and not a handler. At least the handlers didn't follow the girls upstairs with the clients.

A tall wiry man, who sported a goatee and wore a cowboy hat and boots, passed by. He gripped Jewell—Dasha's upper arm tight enough that his fingers made white prints against her already pale flesh.

For a brief second her tear-filled eyes met mine, and her silent plea nearly tore out my heart.

I tried to show in my eyes that I wanted to help her. That I would help her.

But the disbelief in her gaze was obvious before she turned her head away.

Killer ants eating flesh from the bodies of the traffickers, while the men were still alive, sounded better and better all the time.

When they had passed, I slipped under the rope and hurried down the stairs to the first floor. I barely skidded to a stop halfway between the bathroom and the landing when I remembered my stilettos. I ran back, slipped my feet into the pair, then walked as quietly as I could to the bathroom door and pushed it open.

It squeaked so loud I flinched, and I was met by a wave of lilac air freshener that mixed with the pine cleaner used to mop the floors earlier. I followed my instincts and checked my reflection in the mirror. Thank God I did. One strand of my dark hair had escaped from beneath the wig, and I adjusted it before I checked the cell phone.

Damn, damn, damn. Eighteen minutes. This would call for some serious acting on my part. But before I went anywhere I needed to let my team know about Jenika. The cell phone was powerful despite its tiny size. I sent Takamoto a quick text message in a shorthand code and explained everything I'd done, including snagging the fingerprint. I forwarded the photos I'd taken with the phone camera.

After I tucked away the cell phone, I took a tissue off the marble counter and rubbed the heavy blush off my cheeks, hoping to make myself look paler.

My face glistened from sweat thanks to that heat lamp in the room upstairs, which helped me look fairly bad. I started to wipe off the mascara that had smeared beneath my eyes thanks to the sweat.

Instead of wiping off the black smudges, I took my index finger and rubbed the black just enough to make me look like I had dark circles under my eyes.

Ha.

The sticky tape pulled against the skin of my thigh and I hoped I'd managed to secure the lock of blond hair well enough that it wouldn't fall out of my hem. My eyes were dry from the heat lamp, and they watered after I held them open as long as possible before blinking.

I clutched one hand tight to my belly as I grasped the door handle with the other. I caught my breath when I almost ran into Stalder. He was standing on the other side of the door, his arms folded across his chest.

"Ms. Chandra says you are ill," he said in a way that made it clear he hadn't believed Kerrison's story. "What have you been doing for the last twenty minutes, Madame Alexis?"

I blinked away the moisture in my eyes I'd managed to manufacture a minute ago, then held both of my arms across my abdomen and winced as credibly as I could. I followed all of that by a very convincing groan.

"I am sick. I cannot seem to stop vomiting." I wiped my fingers around my mouth while still clutching my belly with my other arm. I spoke in Swedish then English as if slightly out of it. "I ate from the bar menu. Nachos. I think they did not agree with me."

Stalder's expression remained in his usual ice-mask as he stepped out of my way. "Get back to work."

"That is what I intend to do." I raised my chin. Figured I needed to stay in character despite the fact I was supposed to be ill.

Brilliance prevailed. I clapped my hand over my mouth and bolted back to the bathroom door. I shoved it open with my free hand and ran for a stall, where I shut the door behind me before making retching sounds loud enough for the jerk to hear.

"Return to work," Stalder said from the doorway.

Bastard.

The door thumped shut behind him, and I took a deep breath. Mission accomplished.

Except Jenika was gone.

CHAPTER SIXTEEN

White sand beaches and cabana boys

At four AM Kerrison and I stumbled into our Brooklyn apartment from our first afternoon *and* night *and* morning at the Elite.

We were friggin' freezing since we'd forgotten our coats. Thank God for the car's heater and that the central heat was on in the apartment. My fingers and toes started tingling immediately as they began to thaw out.

I didn't know if I was going to collapse from sheer exhaustion or starvation, or if I'd explode from unadulterated fury before going on a killing spree at the Elite.

"All of the above," I grumbled as I flung my stilettos across the room, barely missing a vase on an end table with one while the other stiletto thumped the wall beneath one window. The rental deposit should cover the dent the heel made in the wall.

My feet screamed from being wedged into those

damned stilettos for so long. My toes had already started to swell after I jerked the heels off in the car. When I'd removed them, I'd contemplated going back to the Elite and using them to commit murder—those nice, pointy heels made perfect weapons.

"All of what above?" Kerrison seemed to process that I'd spoken aloud as she closed her eyes.

"Collapse, eat, explode, homicide." I jerked off my wig and tossed it onto the coffee table before massaging my scalp with my fingers. "And not necessarily in that order."

Kerrison sprawled on the love seat, her long hair looking like tangled red yarn on the leather. Her makeup was smudged, and she had dark circles beneath her eyes. Her beaded fringed brown skirt was hiked all the way up to her waist, showing pink panties. "If you're talking about going back to kill every man in that place, can we at least get an hour's sleep?"

I plopped into a padded chair. "I'll take a minute to think about it and get back to you."

"Food." Kerrison sat bolt upright on the love seat.

At the same time I caught the delicious smells and said, *"Breakfast."*

We both cut our gazes to the entrance of the kitchen, then looked at each other. Not even a second passed before we jumped to our feet and headed for the kitchen.

Donovan stepped into our path, and he was lucky we didn't run him down. He carried an oval serving platter filled with a breakfast that smelled so good I knew I'd orgasm from eating just one sausage link. If I wasn't so tired.

"Oh, God." Kerrison looked like she was going to faint when she closed her eyes and took a deep inhale of the delicious smells.

A mountain of buttermilk pancakes, a pile of crisp bacon, lots of sausage links, and a mound of scrambled eggs were on the platter. He carried a pitcher of maple syrup in the hand that wasn't carrying the platter.

"Get to the table, Agents Steele and Kerrison." Donovan hadn't shaven, and his two-day stubble made him look good enough to eat, too. He wore a gray T-shirt and Levi's, and his feet were bare. I might have cared about how completely sexy he looked if the breakfast he'd fixed hadn't been calling to me. "Your next two assignments are eating then bed," he added in a firm tone.

"Uh-huh." Kerrison followed him and dropped into the closest chair at the dining table. "Whatever you say, boss."

The table was already set with three china plates, three place settings of silverware, three crystal glasses, a crystal pitcher brimming with milk, along with a porcelain napkin holder in the middle of the table.

Kerrison didn't hold back when Donovan set the plate down. She'd speared two pancakes, two sausage links, and scooped up a bunch of scrambled eggs before I'd had a chance to pick up my fork.

"Jeez, save some for the rest of us, Kerrison." I gave her a mock-frown that she ignored as she snatched the small pitcher of maple syrup from Donovan and drowned her pancakes and sausages.

Donovan wore an amused expression as I filled my

plate almost as fast as Kerrison had. He loaded his own plate with what was left of the breakfast. Fortunately for him, he'd cooked enough to land healthy servings of his own.

While we shoveled food into our faces, we gave him the highlights and the lowlights of the evening, including that we'd learned Jenika was missing and what we thought happened to her. My stomach soured and I found myself not quite as hungry any longer. I told them about the evidence I had stuck to my thigh and in the hem of my dress, as well as the pics I'd forwarded to Takamoto. I'd been so exhausted on the way back that I'd forgotten to tell Kerrison.

When we finished eating, Kerrison slumped in her seat, leaned her head back against the high-backed chair, and placed her hands on her abdomen. "If I wasn't already taken, Donovan," she started with a satisfied sigh as she raised her head and looked at him. Exhaustion yet humor was in her eyes as she continued, "And if you weren't one of my bosses—not to mention if you were my type—I'd tell you I love you."

Not her type? I almost laughed. How could Donovan not be every woman's dream man?

"So you liked the breakfast," Donovan said with one of his rare, quirky little smiles.

I just gave a sated moan and looked at Donovan. Then every ache in my body started to make itself known again, and I winced.

"Bed." He stood and pointed toward the hallway with the two bedrooms.

"Most happily." Kerrison shoved back from the table, her chair scraping on the wood floor. She dropped her napkin onto the table and stood before she pushed her stringy hair over her shoulders. "Thank you for the incredible breakfast, King of All Men," she added before weaving down the hallway. Her door thumped shut behind her.

"King of All Men, huh?" I smiled at Donovan. "I might have to agree with Kerrison on this one. You've earned the title after that breakfast."

"I intend to take advantage of my new title." Donovan moved around the table to where I had just gotten to my feet. "I have an order for you, Steele."

I scrubbed my hand over my face, trying to force the exhaustion away. "I've got to figure out what to do about Jenika. I can't take time for sleep."

Donovan's jaw and his expression tightened. "You're not going to be worth anything if you don't get rest during the op."

Rest. Just the word brought on more exhaustion.

When he reached me, I fell forward against his chest and I let him bring me tight to him. I hooked my arms around his neck, and his delicious male scent seeped into my pores.

My mind turned entirely to him as if I had no control over my thoughts. Instead of wanting to sleep, I had the sudden desire for something altogether different. My nipples tingled, and my aching body wasn't aching in the same way it had been before.

He kissed the top of my head then settled his arm around my shoulders. I leaned against him and he partly supported me as he guided me to my bedroom. Before he opened the door, I smelled the vanilla candles that flickered in their holders on the bureau, the vanity, and a nightstand. When he closed the door, the room was dim except for the dancing candlelight.

"You're the best, Donovan." I must have said that to him a million times since the first time he'd taken care of me during *Cinderella*, and I meant it every time.

I turned into his embrace and rose up on my toes to meet him part of the way when he lowered his head to kiss me. He brushed his mouth over mine, back and forth a few times, then gently bit my lower lip. He parted his lips as I opened my own so that my tongue could meet his. He tasted of milk and maple syrup.

"Hold that position," I said as I stepped back.

He cocked his head and watched me as I pushed up my skirt and winced when I pulled off the clear packaging tape that had the fingerprints from the wineglass. Then I dug in the smaller suitcase for two small plastic evidence bags. Shoved the piece of fingerprinted tape into one, then flipped up the hem of my dress, drew the chunk of blond hair out, and slipped it into the other bag. I tried not to think of what those two pieces of evidence might mean as I stared at them.

"Later." Donovan took me by my shoulders, turned me around, and brought me back into his arms. "You need distraction and relaxation right now."

"Distraction? Is that what you're doing to me?" You bet he was. His hands rubbed up and down my back, massaging me at the same time we kissed. "You're going to have me feeling entirely boneless if you don't stop soon," I murmured. "Which means I won't be standing up much longer on my own and you're going to have to hold me up."

"That's the idea." Donovan's fingers found the zipper to my dress and eased it down to the base of my spine.

I shivered as cool air met my bare back. While our kisses grew more intense with every thrust of our tongues, he unfastened my bra. We separated and stared at each other as he pushed the dress and bra straps over my shoulders and I let them slide down my arms and drop around my feet.

When I was just in my thong underwear, I stumbled over my clothing as he guided me to the bed. The comforter had already been pulled down.

"On your belly and rest your head on your arms," he ordered as he lifted me onto the mattress. The sheet he laid me on was cool against my chest, abdomen, and thighs. I already started to feel more relaxed as I breathed in the smell of clean cotton sheets and vanilla candles.

"Whatever way you want it," I murmured as I settled my head, one cheek on my forearms, "I'll take it."

"You've always had a one-track mind, Steele." His voice was all deep and rumbly.

I wiggled on the bed. "When it comes to you."

My eyelids drifted closed and I heard the dull clipping sound of a cap opening then the slap of his palms as he rubbed his hands together. Entirely erotic-smelling Caribbean spices flowed through my senses and a tremor of anticipation ran down my spine.

With his strong fingers he began working in the

sensual oil, concentrating on my shoulders and neck. It was a warming massage oil that heated my skin the more he rubbed it in.

I gave a long contented sigh. "You are a god."

"Just remember you said that. As well as whatever it was Kerrison called me." His voice was husky as he gave me a deep-tissue massage. I moaned as he started to relax my tense muscles. "I'll remind you if you forget."

"Mmmm . . ." I fell into the incredible massage as the mattress dipped and Donovan straddled my thighs.

His jeans rubbed the outside of my legs, and I would have preferred his skin to be bare against mine. His hands were strong, his fingers loosening up my tired, tense muscles and drawing me away from a day filled with anger at horrors beyond some people's imaginations.

Countless people around the world were safe and comfortable in their homes. People ignorant of men like Hagstedt and their trafficking empires that needed to be destroyed. I hoped that none of them would wake up to reality and have a daughter or son suddenly missing.

Donovan's massage allowed me to slip away from reality. Caribbean scents of cinnamon, nutmeg, allspice, ginger, and thyme . . . All I needed was a cruise to the Bahamas, crystal blue water, white sand beaches, sunshine, a deck chair, a cabana boy, and a piña colada.

Make that an icy Bahama Mama, one of those fruity alcoholic things you're supposed to drink when in the

Bahamas. A drink made with rum, orange, pineapple juice, grenadine, and other froufrou stuff. I suppose I could possibly do without Guinness for a trip to the Caribbean. For one night, anyway.

And I could skip the cabana boy as long as Donovan was with me.

The Caribbean was one place I hadn't been to, one place in the world not tainted with memories of times I wished I could completely forget.

For now I could.

I allowed myself to escape into thoughts of hearing nothing but the sound of water lapping against sand, smelling sweet spices along with the salty scent of the Atlantic, feeling the sun's warmth on my back . . .

"Mmmm." Instead of becoming sleepy as I was sure Donovan had intended, sexual energy washed through me like a tide rushing in. My mind became fully alert, and so did my body—in ways only Donovan could address.

Talk about a second wind.

I gained a little leverage and pushed myself onto my back so that I could look up at Donovan. "There's no way you're going to tell me I'm too tired." I reached between us and ran my fingers along his thick erection. "And you certainly can't hide the fact that *you* are not the least bit sleepy right now."

It was easy to see he tried to keep the corner of his mouth from curving up into his sexy little smile, and failed. Instead he reached for the warming oil, poured some on his palm, then snapped the lid shut and set the bottle on the nightstand.

My nipples tingled as he rubbed his palms together

before grasping my breasts and massaging them. More Caribbean spices. More warmth.

I gasped and arched my back as he began tweaking and pinching each of my nipples then massaging my breasts again. He leaned down and pressed his lips against mine, and I bit his lower lip hard enough to make him smile against my mouth.

"Wildcat," he murmured. "Maybe you should save a little strength for tomorrow. I think you might need it."

"I don't care about tomorrow." Our lips, teeth, and tongues moved together, nipping, tasting, teasing. "Screw the real world. Right now is all that matters."

"If you say so." He rose up, his hands braced to either side of my shoulders. "You're the boss."

"Yeah, I'm the boss." His T-shirt was soft beneath my palms as I pushed against his chest. "And I say so."

Donovan adjusted his position and pushed my thighs wide so that he could settle himself on his knees between my legs. My thong was damp and my ache for him growing more and more intense. Especially as he drew his gray T-shirt over his head and I watched his muscles ripple and flex with his movements.

I sighed at the pleasure of seeing such male beauty and I stretched out my arms and reached for him. But he backed away and I frowned. The mattress squeaked and rose as he climbed off and unfastened his jeans and pushed them down before stepping out and returning to me.

He hooked the sides of my thong with his fingers

and tugged them over my hips and legs. I smiled again.

Donovan eased onto the bed, between my thighs again, and moved so that his cock was pressed against my folds. "We went too fast last time." He brushed the back of his hand over my cheek. "I want to take my time with you."

"When I haven't had any sleep for God knows how long?" I reached between us and wrapped my fingers around his erection. "We'll save slow for later."

"You're the boss," he said again as I placed the head of his cock against the opening to my core.

He definitely didn't hold back for slow.

Donovan thrust inside me and began taking me hard and fast with such intensity and fervor that my head was close to banging the headboard.

With every plunge of his cock, I cried out and arched up to meet him. My mind was gradually going blank. All I was doing was feeling Donovan. His thick girth and length inside me, his bare chest against mine, his groin slapping against mine.

I almost forgot to hold back a scream when I came. Instead I bit my lip and gave a loud moan.

At the last second I remembered that Kerrison's room was across the hall and what Donovan and I were doing wasn't likely to meet Oxford's approval considering he and I were co–Team Supervisors.

But with the waves of my most excellent orgasm washing over me, I really didn't give a damn right then.

My core spasmed again and again when Donovan

climaxed inside me. His cock was so big, I could feel every pulse of his orgasm. By the way he was baring his teeth, it was obvious he was holding back a shout of his own.

When both our orgasms subsided, Donovan rolled with me so that we were both on our sides, facing each other. The flickering candlelight showed the sheen of sweat on our skin and the rise and fall of our chests as we worked to catch our breath.

I put my forearm against Donovan's. He looked tan against my fair Irish skin.

"I've never asked you anything about your ancestry," I said as I hooked my arms around his neck. "With your darker skin and the angular lines of your face, you don't look Irish, but you have an Irish last name. Mine's an unusual Irish surname, not a Mc or an O'something or other, but *Steele* is still Irish."

"Steele was brought to Ireland by the English," he said with a teasing look.

I sniffed and gave him a haughty look. "One of my ancestors thought there were too many MacDonalds where he lived, so he adopted Steele as a last name." I rolled my eyes. "For that I thank God. I can just see my agents asking me for fries with all of the orders—assignments—I give them."

Donovan grinned. "Personally, I'd like a Big Mac."

I slugged his shoulder. "Our genealogy has been traced back to the dawn of time—more or less—and we're a hundred percent Irish." I slipped my hands into his hair. "The question is, Mr. Donovan, what about you?"

He circled one of my nipples with his fingertip.

"I can think of something we could be doing again, rather than discussing my ancestry."

"Uh." *Focus, Steele. And not on the way he's teasing me.* "Just tell me."

Donovan lowered his head and licked my other nipple and I gasped and arched my back without meaning to.

"You never fight fair," I said between gasps.

He met my gaze and gave me an amused look. "So that's what we're doing? Fighting?" He grabbed my ass and brought me so close to him that I felt the hard line of his erection.

"That was fast," I said as he pressed his cock against my belly. Losing my mind again was a distinct possibility. "Stop it. I want to know."

Donovan propped his head in one palm, his elbow on the mattress as he trailed the fingers of his opposite hand in lazy circles on my chest and around my breasts.

"I'm not sure." He brought his hand up to my forehead and drew his index finger down my nose, over my lips and chin, to the hollow of my throat. "I was adopted."

"Kristin isn't your biological sister?" I said.

"She's every bit my sister, just not by birth." His gaze was so intense, his voice almost harsh as he met my eyes. "She's my adoptive parents' biological child. Harry and Angie Donovan adopted me when they thought they couldn't have children, and they christened me with their last name. Then my mother got pregnant with Kristin."

"I know she's your sister." I gripped Donovan's

strong shoulders and searched his gaze as I remembered his fury, his terror, and most of all his pain when Kristen was abducted and auctioned as a sex slave. "Birth has nothing to do with that kind of bond."

Donovan pushed my hair from my face, and it was easy to see the pain from his helpless feeling in being unable to help Kristin mentally heal faster.

I wanted to draw away the ache. He lived with enough of that every day because of what his sister had gone through. "I bet your parents were proud of you when you were a Navy SEAL." I smiled. "And with your build and dexterity, I'd bet you were one of your high school's star varsity running backs."

"You got one out of two right. I was a running back on my football team." His sudden scowl after that surprised me. "My adoptive parents were another story altogether. I was seven when they took me in from the orphanage, and the stork brought Kristin a year later." His body tensed against mine and he looked away. "Once Kristin was born, they didn't need me anymore."

Then he gave a humorless laugh. "Not that I expected anything, but when Harry and Angie Donovan lost their lives in that small-plane crash, I was curious what their will would read. Just as I'd thought, they left everything to Kristin."

He shook his head and continued. "I didn't want a dime so I didn't care. It was simply a way they showed the depth of *their caring*."

Christ. I'd grown up with a huge loving family. We

weren't perfect, but our parents cared for every single one of us. So much for taking away Donovan's pain.

I took his face in my palms and forced him to meet my eyes. "You have a wonderful sister you love and that's all that matters."

He placed his forehead against mine. "You're right, Steele. Kristin is all that matters."

CHAPTER SEVENTEEN

Devastating secrets

Dogs bark and men crash through the Mexican jungle behind me, the men's shouting growing louder. Underbrush scratches my bare thighs and calves as I push and push myself to run and run and run.

I jump over fallen logs, dodge trees, shove brush out of my face. I never stop looking ahead for dangers in my path at the same time I try to escape even worse danger behind me.

My breath rushes in and out of my chest. My lungs feel scalded, like boiling water has been poured into them. How long have I been running? Almost two miles.

Goddamnit. That fucking dog. The sleeping powder in the treats I gave to the other huge beasts had done a great job in knocking them out. But I didn't know about the third dog. How could I make such a stupid mistake? This one is almost as big as a Mexican fighting bull and just as black.

My heart is going to explode from the combination of adrenaline and from running for so long.

And fear. I'm scared. I'll never shake the dog. Maybe the men, but not the dog.

Human scents can't be masked. The sweat on my skin, the oil from my glands . . . gases and skin cells. Like a fingerprint. There's no way to escape a trained dog.

I screwed up. I thought I got in undetected but I missed not only one dog, but the man handling the beast. Shit. He saw me assassinate the Mexican general.

Now his men are going to kill me. Or torture me. Probably both.

Large hands grab me from the side. Jerk me off my path. I bite back a scream as I kick at whoever has me. He grunts with pain.

"Stop. I'm saving your ass." It's a familiar voice. But I can't think of who the man is. He even smells familiar.

I'm thrown into the back of a Jeep. From the momentum I slide across the bench seat. Pain rockets through my head when my skull hits the metal door on the opposite side.

I try to sit up but I'm thrown to the floor as the Jeep lurches into gear.

"Stay down!" shouts the man who grabbed me.

I know that voice.

I trust him. Whoever he is.

Why? I don't trust anyone. I haven't since FAS forced me to work for them. To assassinate for them.

This man doesn't belong here. Why is he here?

The Jeep's engine rumbles. My ears are filled with the power of its roar.

I try to get up, but the man pins me to the floor. Which is soft now. Like a bed. "Calm down, Lexi," he says. His hands are gentle as he holds me. How does he know my name?

How can he be talking to me? He's driving the Jeep . . .

"You're having a nightmare." He shakes me by my shoulders. "Wake up."

My eyelids opened and I found myself looking into Donovan's vivid blue eyes. His expression was hard, his jaw tense. Both of my shoulders hurt, and I realized he was gripping me and probably had been shaking me before I woke up from the nightmare.

"Donovan." I sounded like I'd really been running through a jungle when I said his name.

"You had another nightmare." He released one of my shoulders to caress my hair from my face. My hair had been sticking to my cheek and felt damp when he pushed it away.

"You were there." I stared up at him and tried to shake off the strange sensations that were coursing through my body. "I was running through the Mexican jungle again. The same jungle I tried to escape in after I assassinated the Mexican general. Before the men caught me and took me back for interrogation and beat the shit out of me. Before I escaped."

Donovan frowned. "Your nightmares haven't been this bad for a while."

I felt my brow wrinkle as I frowned. "It was different this time," I said. "*You* were in my nightmare. You've never been in my nightmares before."

"In what way?" His expression turned dark enough that instinct made me want to recoil even though I knew, I had not a single doubt, that I would always be safe with him. "Did I hurt you?" The words came out in a harsh, guttural sound as he spoke them.

Where would he come up with that thought? I blinked, a feeling of confusion washing over me. "Of course not."

Donovan lowered his head. He relaxed his fingers on my one shoulder that he'd still been holding. It felt bruised and it ached. I didn't realize he'd been gripping me so hard.

"I don't get it." I put my hands on his biceps and stared at his bowed head. "How could you even begin to think that I'd dream about you hurting me? What's going on?"

"Nothing." His eyes were closed, and he didn't look up at me as he spoke. He breathed like his chest was tight and it hurt with every inhale and exhale. "I—" He was searching for something to say and I didn't believe him when he did speak. "I just don't want to be part of your nightmares."

"As a matter of fact, you rescued me." Not that I ever liked admitting I needed rescuing, but not everyone's perfect. And Donovan *had* rescued me during the last op. "Something else is going on here."

"No." He raised his head, still not looking at me, and started to pull away from my hold to get off the bed. "There's nothing."

"Bullshit!" I shouted loud enough that Kerrison

probably heard me all the way to her room. I barely realized I was digging my fingers into his biceps in an attempt to keep him from getting off the bed. "It's about something in your past as a SEAL, or some branch of the government that you served in later. Whatever it is, it's about what you've been refusing to tell me. Isn't it?"

"No," he said again, more emphatically as he met my gaze. I could see the truth, though. It didn't matter that to anyone else he was wearing a poker face. They wouldn't be able to see the emotion in his eyes. I could.

He was so big, so powerful, that I couldn't hold on to him, and he pulled away and got up from the bed. The muscles in his shoulders and back shifted and his large biceps and triceps flexed as he clenched and unclenched his hands, his back still to me. He was wearing black boxers and I wanted to ask since when had he started wearing anything to bed, but at that moment I didn't really give a damn.

I scrambled out of bed on the side I'd been lying on, opposite of where he'd gotten up. I was naked, having fallen asleep not long after talking about his last name. The scent of exotic spices from the massage oil was still in the air along with a slight whisper of perfume from the vanilla candles.

I practically marched to one of the unzipped suitcases I hadn't unpacked and let clothes fly as I dug through it for my favorite pair of worn jogging sweats, a faded Red Sox T-shirt, and a hooded Red Sox sweat jacket.

"I've had it, Donovan. I told you every dirty detail

about my past." I shoved one leg then the other into the sweatpants. "I told you about people I assassinated. I told you how I didn't even know why the Fucking Asshole Sonsofbitches forced me to kill those people. Those people I murdered could have been innocents instead of criminals. Maybe one of the FAS just didn't like the way someone looked on a bad hair day. So he ordered me to kill the man. Or woman."

A lacy black bra followed by a satin pink one went flying out of my suitcase before I found one of my sports bras and put it on. The cotton of my red T-shirt was so old I tore a hole in one of the armpits when I jerked it over my head and jammed my arms through the sleeves. "I told you about my fuckups. But you won't say one goddamned word about your past."

Donovan still faced away from me. He stood at the doorway of the master bathroom, grasping one side of the door frame, his head slightly bowed.

"You've never killed children," he said before he walked into the bathroom and shut the door behind him.

For a long time I couldn't move as I stared at the closed white bathroom door. How long did I stand there? My eyes were wide and I'd covered my mouth with my palm. Anger at him for keeping his past a secret vanished as horror washed over my skin in a chilling wave.

I couldn't imagine Donovan following any kind of assignment that involved killing children. There was more to the story. Had to be. No, Donovan wasn't going to get away with this. I'd leave him alone, but I wasn't about to let him say something like that and not explain.

Donovan's last words kept pounding at my head even as I finally looked away from the bathroom door. I jammed my feet into my jogging shoes after tugging on a thick pair of socks.

My sweat jacket should be warm enough to keep me from freezing while I went out for my run. Before I took off jogging in my Red Sox sweat jacket, I'd loosen up with a few stretching exercises in case I ran into any Yankees fans and had to kick their asses.

I zipped my jacket up, pulled my hair back in a ponytail with a red ponytail holder, and headed out the door of the bedroom.

When I entered the hallway, I heard Kerrison's voice coming from the living room. She spoke rapidly in perfectly accented French. She had on a pair of navy blue sweatpants with a matching sweat jacket and she was in some kind of yoga pose on the floor as she spoke.

"You knew when you married me that I'd likely be traveling around the world," she was saying as I walked into the living room. "Don't try to make me feel guilty for not being home with you."

Kerrison was married? I raised my eyebrows. I'd had no idea. That fact should have come up on the extensive background check we did on every individual we considered hiring as a RED agent. It would be public record.

I mentally shrugged. She could have gotten married after she signed on. It wouldn't have made a difference to RED unless her spouse or boyfriend was a convicted felon. She'd had a roommate at Vanderbilt, but no boyfriend that we'd come across.

Kerrison's back was to me. Her free hand gestured animatedly as if she'd completely fallen into the part of being French as she spoke the language while she sat in her yoga position. "I told you. I'm in Stockholm and I'll be back as soon as I can. I do not think this assignment will take long."

She paused, obviously listening to her apparently French husband on the other end of the call.

I was almost to the front door when she said in a softer voice, "You know I'm not ready for children yet."

I hesitated as I reached for the doorknob. Not because I wanted to eavesdrop. Well, maybe.

"We should wait to adopt, my darling." Kerrison spoke such beautiful French, and her voice sounded soothing. "You will make a wonderful mother. Just give us a little time."

Mother? She was telling her husband he'd make a wonderful mother?

"I will call you soon." Kerrison's tone was so low and soothing as she spoke. "I love you, Francesca."

Oh.

Ohhhh. Kerrison was a lesbian.

I didn't realize I was staring at her until she turned and saw me. She wore white-and-gray New Balance running shoes along with her sweatpants and sweat jacket.

She shoved her cell phone into her pocket and shook her head. "Women." She dug into the opposite pocket, drew out a lacy ponytail holder, and used it to pull her long red hair back. "The only thing worse than having a nagging wife is the entire population of men."

No wonder she'd said Donovan wasn't her type. He definitely qualified as a member of the male population.

Kerrison walked toward me and I couldn't think of a damned thing to say.

"Going jogging?" she asked when she reached me. I heard her slight southern accent and wondered how she had met and married a Frenchwoman.

I nodded. "Want to run with me?"

"You bet." The bones in her neck made popping sounds as she rotated her head back and forth before rolling her shoulders. "After talking with Francesca, I could use a good run."

"I know how you feel," I said as I thought about Donovan and the cryptic and horrifying way he'd ended our conversation.

Bastard. That hadn't been fair of him.

"Want some advice?" she said as we headed out the door.

I glanced at her and met her light green eyes. "Maybe."

"It's the best anyone will ever give you," she said.

I smiled. "Go for it." I shut the door behind us. "Let me hear this stellar advice."

"Never get married," she said as we walked to the elevator. "It changes everything."

"You don't have to tell me that." I pushed the down button. "No way am I getting married. Ever. My life is perfectly fine the way it is."

"Lucky you." She sighed as the elevator dinged at our floor and the doors opened. "The sex is lots better when you're not married."

Donovan was gone when Kerrison and I got back from our jog. Probably one of two things. No, one of three. He was headed off to work his end of the op; he hadn't wanted Kerrison to know he'd stayed the night; he was avoiding me and having to go any farther with our conversation.

I chose option number three.

Jerk.

He was not going to get off so easy. All he'd done was postpone the inevitable conversation between us, and he hadn't done it in a fair way at all.

Donovan had apparently taken the fingerprint sample back to our makeshift HQ because the plastic evidence bag containing it was gone, along with the bag with the blond hair.

Kerrison and I had discussed the op in-depth as we took a slow jog along streets decorated for the holidays, filled with holiday shoppers. One of the things we talked about was the need to get into Giger's office on the main floor as well as the office I'd come across on the second floor.

Where had Jenika come across the coded message to begin with? My bet was the office on the second floor. I didn't see how she could get into the other one.

Was Jenika hidden somewhere in the Elite building? Or had Giger's men taken her somewhere else?

We had to find Jenika. We had to help the trafficked girls. We had to get to Hagstedt. There was so much we needed to accomplish fast. Time wasn't on our side.

Always in the forefront of my thoughts was the fact that I had to get back to Mama as soon as possible. I needed to be there for her.

After Kerrison and I caught our breath, I grabbed my RED secure cell phone and called Takamoto to get a briefing from his end. No sign of Jenika and no word on her whereabouts.

Shit.

He didn't have any more information on Hagstedt other than what we'd already gathered before we came to New York City. All we knew from that deciphered note was that Hagstedt could be here any day.

I relayed the info to Kerrison.

"Damn." She pulled off the lacy ponytail holder and shook out her long red hair, tangled and sweaty from our run. "It's almost time to head off to the greatest job on earth. Working for scumbags and not being able to take a shotgun to every one of those men and blow their dicks off."

"I like you better and better," I said with a not-so-humorous laugh. "I have some ideas of my own that I'm working on. My current favorite is strapping the bastards down on killer ant hills and letting the ants swarm then eat them until their bones are shiny clean."

Kerrison gave an approving nod. "I heard you were tough, Steele. Can't wait to see you in action."

We both headed to our bedrooms for showers and the ordeal of caking on makeup and squeezing into gravity-defying push-up bras and sexy clothing. At least my wardrobe could be a little less revealing than Kerrison's was.

I just finished securing one of the silvery-blond wigs on my head when she knocked on the frame of the open door. I gave a low whistle at the sight of her black two-piece ensemble. Another tiny skirt—only this one was so short it barely covered the important parts. The top wasn't a whole lot more than a black bra. This time she wore four-inch heels and fishnet stockings.

"If I didn't know better, now," I said as I slipped on my rings, "I'd think you were hot for men."

She put one hand on her hip. "You think only men like women dressed like me?"

I shrugged. "Never really thought of it." But then again, on the last op there had been that Amazon who made it clear I turned her on . . .

Kerrison moved just enough that I could see the black line up the back of her stockings. She looked over her bare shoulder. "Gets them every time."

"If you say so," I replied while thinking at the same time that she did look friggin' hot.

This time we remembered our coats. As we stepped out into the cold, windy late-November day, I glanced at the afternoon sky. Gray, like my mood.

We'd better get somewhere with this case. We were all running out of time.

Helping every single girl who was trafficked. Grabbing Hagstedt and eliminating his personal human trafficking rings for good. And now Jenika. Everything in my gut told me we had to find her fast.

Or we wouldn't find her alive.

CHAPTER EIGHTEEN

Nick

Wearing all black, Nick blended in with the darkness as he stayed in the shadows next to a dive bar on Fifth Street, close to Avenue B.

The bar's holiday decorations looked tacky and sloppy, from the loopy way the colored lights had been strung around the door frame to the variety of faded depictions of Santas in the dirty windows. The picture with good ol' Claus mooning the street reminded Nick of the dropping-pants-Santa back in the Human Trafficking CC at RED.

Courtesy of Madame Cherie's well-planted heel, Nick's cheekbone burned in the cold. Hell, it was nothing but a mosquito bite compared with what he'd been through in his career in Navy Special Ops, then black ops.

A man stumbled out of the bar, and Nick tensed. When he got a good look at the man's face in the streetlight, he relaxed. It wasn't Mike or Jorge—two of

Giger's men whom Nick had tailed all the way from the back door of the Elite. He'd heard their names during their bullshitting back and forth on the way to the bar. From their conversation, he'd learned that they had the night off and apparently preferred a cheap shithole like this over a place as expensive as the Elite.

Nick ignored the stench of piss recently splattered on the side of the building. He also blocked out the odor of the nearby pile of garbage bags and boxes on the sidewalk. The refuse would be picked up by one of the city's sanitation trucks, probably in the morning.

He stomped his feet for the hundredth time in an effort to stay limber. To keep his fingers feeling loose, he flexed his grip on the Glock 10mm as well as clenching and unclenching his free hand.

Nick had already attached the suppressor. From the intel they'd gathered, Nick and Steele's team knew that Giger's boys carried heavy-duty firepower. Glock .45s and 10mms were high on the list for these guys.

He dragged his gloved hand down his face, over two days' worth of stubble he'd grown to help him look on the scruffy side. Not clean-cut, but not ragged, either. In keeping with what he and half the population of New York City generally wore, Nick had chosen a black T-shirt beneath a heavy black bomber jacket, and black Levi's. He'd added shitkickers, these particular ones being serious combat boots with steel toes.

Earlier today another lead hadn't panned out. He was sick of it and didn't really have a choice but to do what he was about to.

Goddamnit. He needed to snag a job as a handler at the Elite to back up Lexi and Kerrison, as well as find Jenika, *now*. So far every damned lead and informant had turned out to be bullshit or a dead end. Even Johnny hadn't come through.

Two men walked around the corner of Avenue A then toward the bar. They didn't so much walk as they wove their way down the sidewalk with drunken steps.

Three men strode from inside the bar at the same time the two other men reached the doorway and squeezed by to get in.

"Why don't you wait your fucking turn?" one of the men walking out said in a snarl to the men going into the bar.

"Fuck you," one of the pair heading in said, his words slurred.

The men traded insults, but fortunately none of five seemed in the mood to fight. Nick didn't have time for that kind of shit, which might throw off his game plan.

He stayed in the darkness and concentrated on the men who were leaving. Not one of the three had the gait or movements of either of the pair of Giger's boys whom Nick had followed to this goddamned bar six hours ago. As bad as he wanted Giger's men, it was good that none of the trio matched the pair he was after. He needed just the two men he'd stalked. And he needed them alone.

Soon, before he froze his ass off and couldn't follow through with his plan.

Nick's warm breath fogged in the icy air as he blew it out in a frustrated huff and stomped his boots again to loosen his legs. He'd had enough of waiting. To-night he'd create openings for two handlers at the Elite. Might as well give himself a little insurance while taking down two shithole trafficking scumbags at the same time.

His conversation with Steele yesterday morning kept intruding on his thoughts and had Nick grinding his teeth. He hadn't returned to the apartment yet. Call him chickenshit. He didn't give a fuck.

The sharp edge he'd balanced on for years was hard to keep stable now that Steele refused to give up on getting him to tell her about his past.

Christ. He had no desire to talk about the shit he'd gone through, the shit he'd done, when he'd been re-cruited into black ops. The years that had gone by since had never dulled the memories or pain. Hell, he deserved to remember and feel the pain of what he'd done. Nothing would change that.

Harsh laughter drew Nick's attention to the bar's doorway again. Giger's men. The blond was the one named Mike, the Hispanic was Jorge.

Now, as the pair left the bar, Nick recognized the sniggering laugh of the blond shithead, Mike. He said something Nick couldn't hear, but the inflection in his voice was unmistakable as he spoke to Jorge.

Nick waited until Mike and Jorge got at least thirty feet away, almost to the corner of Avenue B, before he stepped out of the darkness to follow. When they rounded the corner, Nick picked up his pace and guessed he was now within twenty-five feet of the men.

With a cautious look around the corner, he made sure Jorge and Mike hadn't spotted him.

Good. They were almost at the location Nick had selected. A dark stairwell that went down to a doorway secured with a heavy padlock. He was fifteen feet behind the men when they were positioned exactly where he wanted them.

He held the Glock with its silencer in a standard two-fisted grip. "Hey, dickheads!"

Giger's men turned just enough. Exactly like Nick had planned.

The Glock with the suppressor made an impotent sound as Nick put a bullet in the center of Jorge's forehead. The dead asshole dropped next to the stairwell.

Before Giger's other man registered that Nick had taken out his buddy, he was already running toward the asshole.

"What the fuck?" The man reached behind his back and brought out his own gun.

By the time Mike had the gun in his hand, Nick had already closed the fifteen feet between them.

Nick tackled him. Giger's man went down with a shout as his back hit the sidewalk. Mike's gun went clattering and made a skittering sound along the sidewalk.

Mike jerked Nick's ankle with his foot, causing Nick to drop harder to the sidewalk than he'd planned. Nick twisted, trying to protect himself and his own weapon.

The suppressor on his Glock hit the ground concrete hard. He didn't like the immediate difference in the gun's balance as he gripped it.

Fuck. The suppressor was probably hosed.

Giger's man reeked of sweat, alcohol, and cheap

cigarettes. Despite the fact he was clearly drunk, the man was quick and strong. Nick had to fight to keep the man down and keep him from going for his own gun.

Nick slugged Giger's man at just the right spot on his temple to knock him out. Mike instantly went limp. Nick had used a martial arts method that would make it impossible for anyone to tell the man had been hit in the head and knocked unconscious.

After checking around him with a quick sweep of his gaze to make sure everything was clear, Nick grabbed the still-alive asshole number two, Mike, and dragged him down the stairwell. He propped him up against the locked door.

With one of his gloved hands, Nick reached around the man's waist and took Mike's gun from the holster at his back. Nick pocketed it while he made sure the guy wasn't coming to. Mike was left-handed—he'd reached for his gun with his left hand, and the holster was made for a left-hander.

Nick checked the silencer. Shit. It was fucked-up like he'd thought. Gritting his teeth, he worked in quick, precise movements. He screwed the silencer off the 10mm. He'd already removed the serial number from the Glock he'd shot Jorge with. Nick shoved the suppressor into the opposite pocket of his bomber jacket. Then he pressed Mike's fingers against the barrel of the gun before he wrapped the man's palm around the 10mm's grip.

Nick took out the handgun's magazine and removed the bullet that had automatically slipped into the chamber. Mike stirred, but Nick wasn't worried the guy would have a chance to shoot—much less have any ammunition in the gun to shoot with. Still, he hit Mike again with the side of his hand, causing the guy to go slack.

He took the five steps in two strides as he returned to the dead man at the top of the stairs. Only a trickle of blood was on Jorge's forehead, but the back of his head had been blown away. Nick avoided blood and brain matter as he moved around corpse number one.

This part would be easier as long as no onlookers showed up.

And as long as no one placed the sound of a single shot.

Nick found Jorge's gun in a side holster. Good, a right-hander. He wrapped the dead man's right hand around the gun and aimed it at the throat of the very-much-alive man propped against the door at the end of the stairwell below.

Nick used the dead man's finger to pull the trigger. The handgun's retort echoed through the night, and its bullet blew a hole right through the hollow of Mike's throat. Nick's accuracy with any kind of handgun was so consistent, he was certain the spinal cord had been severed with that one shot.

Unfortunately, since the gun hadn't had a silencer, that shot would likely draw some attention.

Nick jogged down the steps to Mike's body. The bastard's eyes were now open and glassy. A surprised expression was on his face. Nick needed only a couple of precious moments to shove the magazine back into the 10mm and the one bullet into the gun's chamber.

From an inside pocket of his bomber jacket, he took a small plastic bag containing about two grams of crystal meth. He stuffed it in the man's right hand, the hand that soon would be immobile in the corpse's "death grip."

He was back up the stairs within ninety seconds. To complete the setup, he found the spent shell casing from his initial shot at Jorge. He tossed it down the stairwell and it rattled on the concrete until it came to a stop by Mike's corpse.

Nick had already disappeared into the night and into Tompkins Square Park barely minutes before he heard a woman's scream.

Nick headed back to HQ.

As long as no one put the pieces together, it would be slam-dunk case of one drunk killing the other over drugs.

Looked like Giger's stable of handlers had two new openings.

CHAPTER NINETEEN

Bachmann/Hagstedt and aliases three and four

Karl Bachmann gripped his martini glass as he looked out the limo's window at the gray, wet afternoon and the equally gray, dismal city. The driver guided the limo toward Columbus Circle at 1 Central Park West, to Trump Tower, his favorite hotel. The word *hotel* was far too modest for the finest and most luxurious accommodations in New York City.

Of course Karl was checking in under a third alias, Isak Alexandersson, and not as Anders Hagstedt or Karl Bachman, or even a fourth alias. He ensured nothing tied the names together. *Nothing.* He had exceptionally well-made fake passports for all three of his aliases, as well as having an original passport for his real name, Karl Bachmann.

However, through his extensive channels of information he knew he could no longer travel as Hagstedt. He clenched his jaw then forced himself to relax. That name was now on law enforcement radar, which meant there had been a leak.

The leak had probably happened when his Boston operation was taken down by an unknown organization. One day he would learn the identity of the organization that had ripped apart his extremely profitable Boston-based Internet sex slave auction rings.

He had seen footage of a man and woman who had broken into Benjamin Cabot's office and were likely agents or spies from that unknown organization. He would learn the names of the primary players responsible for destroying his perfect setup.

In turn, one day he would destroy them.

Karl tried to relax his grip on his martini glass as he adjusted his position to look in the direction the limo was going as it sliced its way through the sea of Yellow Cabs.

Unfortunately, due to Cabot's mediocre business skills, Karl had been unable to obtain other surveillance videos or photographs of those who had infiltrated his auction rings. Benjamin Cabot had been a mistake in every way as Karl's choice to run his Boston enterprise.

Raindrops splattered harder against the window, blurring images outside the limo. The people wearing primarily black trench coats and carrying black umbrellas looked like morbid figures painted in oils on a dirty canvas.

He averted his attention from the window and back to his dry martini, no olives. He took a sip, the gin rolling smoothly over his tongue and down his throat.

His private jet had arrived at JFK with precisely enough time for him to get to his hotel, check in, and wait for the untouched treats to be delivered to his room.

Karl shifted on the luxurious leather seat of the limo, his dick growing uncomfortably hard.

Yes, untouched delicacies only, and absolutely no drugs in their systems. Virgins were perfect because he didn't have to use a condom. He didn't have to worry about what might have been in that pussy before the girl was selected and brought to him.

Not to mention virgins screamed better.

Karl's limo pulled up to the Trump International Hotel and Tower. He was looking forward to relaxing in his room and looking even more forward to what would come not long after. The fabulous views of Central Park, along with Times Square, Rockefeller Center, and the Ford Center were a few of the choicest views from the Tower.

Most men didn't give a damn who'd fucked a slut before they got ahold of her. A shudder traveled Karl's spine at the thought of dirtying his own dick in a well-used prostitute who was doped up on the heavy doses of the opoids Giger liked to give his whores.

The driver came around to the side of the limo and opened the door. Karl tossed his martini glass on the leather seat, ignoring the remaining drops of liquid leaking onto the leather. He stepped out of the limo and into the covered area used for arriving and departing guests. He didn't acknowledge any of what might be considered helpful staff—his own, or the hotel's.

Karl's driver grabbed the light luggage to be taken directly to his room. The locally hired man had called ahead, and the room was already prepared and waiting for Karl. The driver would pick up the key from the concierge, give it to Karl, and follow behind him with his suitcase and dress bag.

Karl didn't need to worry about pregnancies and abortions with any of his girls around the world. That was thanks to the "morning after" pill and his ability to buy large, cheap quantities from a manufacturer in Mexico.

His men were required to force all of the girls who were trafficked as prostitutes to take the pill. Pregnancies and abortions were a waste of time and money, money that the girl could be earning on her back.

With the driver trailing him, Karl entered an elevator and was pleased no other person stepped into the car with them. It rose smoothly to the seventeenth floor, to his favorite luxurious suite. His extensive trafficking organization allowed him to enjoy the most pleasurable amenities.

He was a businessman. Easily one of the most intelligent and cunning in the world. He was also one of the richest, worth well over a billion. He controlled a multibillion-dollar trafficking organization that spanned the globe and was arguably the largest trafficking empire that existed.

Using humans was far better than dealing in narcotics. Once someone snorted a line of meth, that meth was gone, never to be used again.

A human, on the other hand, could be used repeatedly. One woman could easily bring in three times as much money in one night as it would cost to buy a single eight-ball of meth.

The driver opened the door to the suite and stepped back so that Karl could walk through. Immediately he was greeted with the clean scent of fresh flowers from the enormous bouquet on the table in the center of the suite. He ignored the card beside the floral arrangement. For now. It would contain the card key for his other room on the floor below.

He took off his suit jacket and handed it to his driver, a man of limited intelligence. In this man, Karl could easily see a resemblance to their Cro-Magnon ancestors.

"Go." Karl slipped the man a hundred-dollar tip and dismissed him by turning his back to look at the incredible view of Central Park through his floor-to-ceiling windows. He forgot the man almost immediately after the door closed behind him with the whisper-soft sound and movement that Karl preferred.

The cell phone in his pocket vibrated. Karl withdrew it and saw a text message from Giger.

The merchandise has been prepared.
Where would you like it delivered?

Karl glanced at the envelope by the flower vase, the envelope containing the other room card. One of Karl's associates had booked the extra room and had paid cash for it ahead of time, under Karl's fourth alias. Again, no name association.

Karl entered on the touch screen before he sent the return text:

Same location. Room 1612.

Giger responded:

What time do you want your purchases delivered?

Karl smiled.

Now.

CHAPTER TWENTY

Switch and delivery

"These girls will be leaving tomorrow?" I said as a sense of panic seized me when Stalder delivered the news.

Not now. I had hoped it wouldn't be this soon, even though Takamoto had informed me of the group of Chinese girls who had been ushered into the side door of the Elite earlier today. I thought I'd have at least two days. Or rather, I'd hoped I had that long.

"I do not need to repeat myself," Stalder said with his cool expression.

My brief feeling of panic turned into anger at his information. Not only because we could lose the girls here that we were trying to save, but also because we'd found no clues to Jenika's disappearance.

"Ms. Chandra and I haven't had a chance to fully train these girls." It sounded lame, but it was all I'd been able to come up with. "This is only our third day here."

"We have hired a group of young women from China who joined us this afternoon before you arrived," Stalder said. "They are currently upstairs. Resting."

Hired, my ass, I thought and tried not to scowl. And rather than resting, they were probably being "broken" so that they wouldn't try to escape in any way.

"Our customers like change." Stalder continued speaking in his precise English and looked as glacial as always as he added, "The Russian girls will work tonight then the Chinese group starts tomorrow."

"Where are the Russian girls being taken?" I asked, trying to keep my tone calm.

Stalder studied me with his icy eyes. "To another club."

I braved the cold. "Which one?"

From his expression I think I would have gotten frostbite if I touched him. Or maybe he was even cold enough that my tongue would have frozen to his jacket sleeve like a kid licking a metal pole during the coldest winter on record.

"It is none of your business," he said. "Your business will be strictly with the Chinese girls when they are brought to you." He tipped his head slightly. "If you are truly up to that task. I am not so sure of it."

I chose to ignore his comment because I had something more important to be thinking about. I hadn't expected Stalder to tell me where he was taking the Russian girls, but I had to try to figure it out. How could we help these poor girls, too, if we didn't know where they went next?

My agents would make sure they found out. *No worries, Steele.*

"I'm sorry." I tried to look innocent. "I did not know that where you are moving them to is a secret."

"The handlers will prepare the Russian girls for the move," Stalder said, his expression bland. "Your job is to concentrate on the new group."

My heart was beating like crazy as I thought about Jenika. Christ. If she hadn't already been moved, would they take her away, along with these girls? My entire *Little Red* team was on the job, trying to locating Jenika, but so far not a clue.

Yesterday Kerrison and I had slipped away, at different times, for "restroom breaks." We both did some fast searching when we were on our own, but no luck finding Jenika. We tried talking to the girls, but the handlers wouldn't let us anywhere near them, much less speak to them.

During last night's show, after her first turn to dance, the girl named Dasha passed by as we gave her handler her assignment. She looked at us with pleading eyes. There was nothing I could do but try to communicate back to her with my own gaze and hope she saw what I wanted her to see.

We'll help you. I promise.

She'd turned away and her expression went blank before she passed through the gap in the curtain that revealed the lap dance booths. I'd taken a deep breath and looked away, feeling impotent again. For that moment. Last night Kerrison and I had decent opportunities to plant a couple of bugs we'd kept hidden in our clothing. I put one bug by the door frame in the girls' common room on the fifth floor, and Kerrison placed one in the men's restroom.

With the bug I had planted the day before, three were all we had right now. We needed more, including one in the offices in the hall off the main floor. That's where Giger and his men seemed to spend their time when they weren't out on the floor.

Christ. Everything was going to hell. With Jenika gone, the Russian girls being taken away, plus the fact we had no definitive time and date when Anders Hagstedt would be arriving, we could be seriously screwed if we didn't make something happen. And make it happen fast.

Kerrison and I had heard whisperings about two of the handlers, Jorge and Mike. Neither had returned after his night off, and none of the handlers knew what was going on with the pair.

Jorge and Mike were Nick's hit, no doubt. Next step, he'd get in, and we'd close down these bastards a lot faster.

"Alexis." Giger's voice jerked my attention from Stalder to the back of the club, where Giger was standing. The dim light from a spotlight reflected on the lenses of his eyeglasses and I couldn't see his eyes.

"Yes, Mr. G?" I said. Stalder stepped back and got out of my way as I walked toward Giger. Maybe I could find out something about the girls from him.

Sure. As if he was going to start telling me every bit of the day-to-day activities of the trafficking operation without some of RED's special version of a truth serum.

When I reached him, I noticed again the flash of the thick gold band and the sparkle of what had to be at least a three-carat diamond ring. Guess diamonds weren't just a woman's best friend.

Giger motioned for me to follow him down the hall toward his office at the very end. Excellent. Maybe I could plant a bug in his office now. I started to reach into my bra where two of the bugs remained. But when Giger looked over his shoulder, I moved my hands to make it look like I was adjusting my neckline.

Now I could see his eyes behind his glasses and his gaze wandered over my breast. I held back what would have been an expression of total disgust. Alarm bells flashed in my head when his eyes met mine.

Was my cover blown—was he taking me to his office where he'd have his boys restrain me? At least he might think he could.

Getting a little paranoid, Steele.

Giger turned away again and opened the door to his office when he reached it. It swung open on well-oiled hinges. He walked through and didn't bother to hold the door open for me. It started to close in my face, and I had to catch it with one hand while I walked the rest of the way into his office.

He remained standing in front of the door when it closed and faced me. My heart thumped and my throat grew dry, but I let my body relax to aid me in defending myself if I needed to.

"You're going to make a special deliver." Giger's words were a clear demand, his expression as nasty as ever.

"What kind of delivery?" It had better be good, to take me away from the operation for any length of time.

Giger's flattop needed a serious trim. His gray hair

was starting to stick up like porcupine quills all over his head. "You'll take three of the Chinese bitches to a *special* client who just got into town."

I couldn't help the frown. "I didn't know you ran an escort service out of the Elite."

"I *don't* run a fucking escort service." He scowled and I went rigid and raised my chin rather than stepping back, as instinct would make any person want to. "I don't need to explain a fucking thing to you. Your job is to to what I tell you."

"Yes, Mr. G." I bit the inside of my cheek to keep from saying anything else.

It took one full second to realize what Giger was saying. What he was asking me to do. And who it might involve.

Hagstedt?

This could be our break.

"When?" I asked.

"Now." He opened his cell phone and turned his back to me as he pressed a button.

While he wasn't looking, I stuffed my hand into my bra and jerked out the card with the two remaining bugs.

With the ease in which any person speaks this native tongue, Giger said in Swedish, "Bring the virgins to my downstairs office."

I stiffened. Bastard. Not only was he taking innocent girls to the man, but he was taking girls who hadn't even lost their virginity yet.

I peeled one of the bugs off the card, gave a quick glance at his desk, and saw the pencil holder made to look like a pair of a woman's breasts. What irony.

"Spray some of that expensive perfume shit on them that you put away for the client," Giger continued in Swedish.

It took only ten seconds for me to draw the bugs out of my bra, stick one to the underside of the titty holder, activate it, and slip the one remaining bug back into my bra.

"Put the whores in those clothes the client sent over," Giger said. "Fucking hurry and get them to my office."

The client had to be Hagstedt.

Despite the fact that I was now primed to kill Giger and Hagstedt with my bare hands, I was standing quite innocently and demurely when Giger snapped his cell phone closed and swung his gaze to look at me.

"You are Swedish. You understood what I said on the phone," he stated.

I shrugged. "It was a personal call. I didn't pay attention. I heard something about clothes, I think."

Giger studied me for a moment as if gauging whether or not I was telling the truth. "The girls will be here in a minute or two. It shouldn't take that fucking long for them to dress." He pointed to one of the high-backed striped chairs on the opposite side of the desk from his large office chair. I sat.

He ignored me as he unfolded a copy of the *New York Times*. Having caught a glimpse of the headline earlier about an eleven-car accident in the Holland Tunnel, I knew it was today's edition.

The tangible smell of a newspaper practically hot off the presses reached me. His wire-rimmed glasses reflected the picture of the accident, and the Jägermeister wall lamp sent an orange glow across the page.

Today my white-blond wig was hair swept up into a French knot, which was nice because my neck didn't feel so hot from the weight of the wig's long, straight hair. Unfortunately it was still hot on my head. Kerrison had poked a sprig of holly with a couple of red berries inside the French knot, and I'd just rolled my eyes.

My dress was short and sexy, this time a sapphire-blue outfit with crisscross laces up the back. It was formfitting but stretchy material. It was a good thing I was in great athletic shape, because that dress showed every single curve. I had some cute high-heeled slides that Georgina had picked out to go with it. I liked them because if I had to, I could kick the heels off easily.

Earlier this afternoon, Kerrison had said I looked like a high-priced hooker. I told her that in the neon-green mini-nothing dress she was wearing today, she looked like a cheap leprechaun tramp. A tall leprechaun tramp.

Of course that wasn't true—Kerrison carried it off with style. Like Georgina, Kerrison looked great no matter what she wore.

The leprechaun description would fit *me* better if I was wearing bright green, thanks to my being height-challenged as well as the fact that I'm Irish.

Note to self. Never wear Irish green. Especially near St. Paddy's Day.

I crossed my legs at my knees and clasped my hands

around one knee as I looked at the opposite side of each newspaper page Giger turned as he read them.

While I waited, with him ignoring me, it gave me time to think about the entire op.

But more than the op, I thought mostly about my mother and getting home to her soon. Why did it have to be her? Why did it have to be Mama?

I made myself switch my thoughts back to the op. If the pervert waiting for the three virgins was Hagstedt, we could take down the bastard today. Tingles spread throughout me from my toes to my head as I repeated in my mind that it could all be over *today*. Once we had Hagstedt, the rest would fall into place.

We'd get the Russian girls before they were taken somewhere that we might not be able to find then. We'd save these new girls from China. We'd find Jenika. We'd take down Hagstedt's New York sex trafficking ring and bust every single club.

Giger folded another page of the newspaper when a small article's heading caught my attention:

DRUG-RELATED KILLINGS OR PROFESSIONAL HIT?

Cold prickles rushed over my skin. I took a slow, deep breath and hoped the article wasn't about Donovan's hit from last night. He was damned good at what he did. Still, mistakes could be made by anyone.

Donovan hadn't come to the apartment in Brooklyn in the wee hours after Kerrison and I got home from the Elite. I hadn't seen him since I'd tried to push him into talking about his past. I figured he wasn't in the mood to be pushed again, and I can't say that I wouldn't have tried to get the rest out of him.

The way Donovan had left the conversation, so cryptic, and on such a horrifying note, made me want to choke him. I could almost feel Donovan's big neck beneath my hands as I clenched my fingers . . .

Giger started to flip the page over and I held my breath, hoping he didn't see the article.

A loud knock at the door. Giger dropped the newspaper onto the desk, and I slowly released my breath.

"Come." Giger shook the paper again and closed it, hiding the potentially damning article.

The door opened. Stalder, one of the handlers, and a Chinese man herded three Chinese girls into the room. I don't know what to call it but *herded*, since they were pretty much shoved inside and in front of Giger's desk. The soft scent of lotus blossoms followed in the girls' wake, apparently the perfume of choice for the client.

The girls were gorgeous to a one. Their eyes were red, or at least those of the two girls who had their heads raised. The third looked down at the floor, her body visibly shaking.

"Do you speak any Chinese dialects?" Giger asked me.

I shook my head. I actually did speak standard Mandarin and some Cantonese, but I wasn't about to let him know. "Only Swedish, German, and English," I said.

Satisfaction was clear in Giger's eyes. He didn't want me to be able to speak to them. "The new girls are from Beijing." He gestured to the man in the business suit. "Jianjun will be their translator until you reach the hotel." The Chinese man adjusted the sleeves of his obviously expensive business suit, and I wondered how far up Hagstedt's trafficking ladder Jianjun worked.

Giger's shirt was so tight that his buttons looked close to popping off as he breathed out a tight breath and handed Jianjun what looked like a plastic hotel key card. The Chinese guy slipped the key into an inside pocket of his blazer.

"Alexis," Giger said, "on the way to the hotel you'll instruct the girls on how to make the client happy, and Jianjun will translate."

Oh, that should be fun. And awkward. Maybe I'd just off Jianjun in the limo—if there was a way to do it and not blow my cover.

"Of course," I said in Swedish.

Giger focused on the girls. They were dressed in surprisingly conservative clothing compared with what Giger's men forced the Russian girls to wear when they danced each night. I didn't doubt that this was for the client's benefit. Couldn't very well have three girls looking like prostitutes going to his hotel room.

Jianjun focused on the first girl, whose black hair hung at least ten inches below her small breasts and straight down her back. They'd dressed her in a bright multicolored handkerchief dress and reasonable two-inch sandals.

"What is your name?" Jianjun asked her in Mandarin. The man's voice was sharp and condescending.

The girl narrowed her slightly almond-shaped eyes. "I am Ai," she responded, also in Mandarin, her tone combative. The meaning of her name was "love." I thought about the parents who had given her such a special name and now probably wondered where their beloved child had gone.

Giger moved with surprising swiftness. "Fucking little bitch. Watch your fucking mouth." He slapped Ai's face hard enough that the sound of his hand against her perfect skin echoed in his office.

Fire burned along my own neck as Ai's head snapped back and the imprint of his fingers lingered on her fair complexion.

A touch of flame remained in Ai's dark eyes despite the reddening that I was sure was from crying. That flame and her small show of defiance told me that Giger's men hadn't broken her yet. I didn't plan to give Giger or Hagstedt the honor of taking that spirit from her.

"And you?" Jianjun said to the second girl who wore her short dark hair in a pixie haircut. She had more pronounced almond-shaped eyes, and her face was round compared with Ai's oval. She didn't look even close to being combative like Ai, but I could see her strength of spirit was also still there.

The second girl's voice wavered as she answered Jianjun. "I am Daiju." Black jade. Such a pretty name.

Her outfit was conservative like Ai's in that it covered her body fairly well. A halter-top dress fell to just above her knees. It was white with black polka dots, the style accenting her breasts and baring shoulders that looked tanned next to the other two girls.

With her head still bent, the third girl replied, "Ning." Tranquility.

"Look at me, bitch," Giger said in a snarl.

Ning raised her head, her eyes redder than the other

two. Tears rolled down her pale cheeks. She wiped them away with her fingers.

Of the three, Ning looked so very sweet and innocent, so young. I wouldn't have guessed her to be eighteen. Her features were soft, lovely, her hair long and lighter brown than the other two. Giger's men had dressed Ning in a snug wine-red, spaghetti-strapped dress with matching low-heeled sandals.

Giger paced in front of the three girls, starting with Ai and ending at Ning as he studied them. "You're all virgins?" he said in English.

My whole body tensed and heated at the way they were being treated and because of what Giger expected them to do. Soon.

Color rose in all three girls' cheeks. They each tried to avoid Giger's eyes, even Ai with all her bravado.

"Yes," Daiju, Ning, and Ai said, almost at the same time.

"You'd fucking well better be." Giger spoke so low and dangerous that I don't think the girls could help but look at him.

My insides contracted into a hard ball as he added, "If the client finds out you're not virgins, what he'll do to you will make you pray for a fast death."

CHAPTER
TWENTY-ONE

Giger

The softness of the Russian girl's cheek lent to the satisfaction Beeff experienced as he backhanded the naked slut and knocked her across the room.

He enjoyed the cry the blond made when he hit her and then the following sound of her head hitting the wall with a thud. She slid down to the floor and crumpled into a ball as her body shook from her sobs.

Beeff had decided he was in the mood for a blond instead of one of the new Chinese pieces. He'd pick out one of those later.

"Get the fuck up." Beeff finished zipping his slacks over his now flaccid penis. "I'm not finished with you."

The bruises already appearing on the girl's naked body would make her useless—except to the clients who preferred a dose of violence with sex.

Like he did.

Sometimes one of his clients got carried away and the girl ended up dead from drugs or strangulation. Of course that always cost the client a shit load of money afterward. He didn't give a fuck about what happened to this slut. As long as he made some decent cash off of this piece of merchandise, it didn't matter.

The girl avoided his gaze as she got to her knees, her entire body trembling. Blood trickled from a small cut above her eyebrow.

Beeff imagined what it would feel like to shoot the bitch and take her before she died. He'd thought about it with other used-up prostituted girls, but had never followed through.

The metal drawer of his desk scraped like finger-nails across a chalkboard as he opened the drawer. He needed to have one of the handlers do something fucking useful and fix it.

He reached into the back, and his hand found the grip of his favorite handgun. A German-made Walther that he'd had since the mid-1990s. A fucking great little gun.

He turned and took a step toward her, already imagining the satisfying feeling of shooting her in her belly. She'd die slower with that kind of wound. Slow enough.

A sharp knock on the metal door to his private second-floor office snapped Beeff out of his sexually brutal fixation on the girl. The knock could only mean business. *No one* would bother him in his second-floor office unless it was urgent.

Beeff shook from his head the pleasurable images of shooting the girl. The interruption had fucked up the moment. He scowled at her. "Get your clothes on."

He didn't know the name of the Russian girl he had just abused and almost killed.

From this point on, she might as well not exist as far as he was concerned. Cash. That was all she represented to him. That and she had been a good fuck when he'd needed it.

Not a chance he'd use her body again. He preferred a different piece of ass each time he indulged.

The room now smelled of sex and the cheap perfume the girls were forced to wear for the clients. He would have this office cleaned. He preferred the scent of Pine-Sol and Windex over that shit.

He swung his gaze to the door as he set his Walther on the corner of the desk. "Who is it and what the fuck do you want?" he yelled toward the door.

"Stalder" came the cool, even voice of the big Swede, telling Beeff nothing about how urgent this interruption was.

But Stalder never disturbed him unless it was important. Beeff grabbed his T-shirt off the floor. Americans called this style a wife-beater, and Beeff's frown almost turned into a smile at the irony.

He took his time putting on the rest of the clothing, his thoughts revisiting the arrangement with Hagstedt and the merchandise that was already paid for and had just arrived. Petite, dark-haired girls with slanted eyes. His penis started to grow hard at the mental images.

Hagstedt—or whatever the asshole's real name was—of course demanded the three best girls out of the lot. The bastard always timed his visits to coincide with a new shipment of merchandise and preferred the virgins. He liked to watch them cry and beg.

"Get the fuck out of here," Beeff said to the Russian girl, who had dressed in what was left of her torn clothing. She bumped into his desk and practically fell against the edge. "Clumsy bitch," he said as he held the door open and let her run to where her handler was waiting.

After the girl dodged past Stalder, Beeff motioned to his top man to enter. "You know you'd better have a fucking good reason to bother me."

"Jorge and Mike are not missing. They are dead." Stalder came to a stop as he spoke, and Beeff narrowed his eyes. "From what information I gathered from the police, the preliminary conclusion is that Jorge and Mike shot each other early this morning after leaving a bar on Fifth Street and Avenue B. The NYPD officers believe the men had an argument over drugs before drawing their weapons. Officers found two grams of meth on Mike."

"Fuck." Beeff clenched his fists and his temples started to throb. "First Cherie is strangled and now these two fuckheads shoot each other?"

"A single round from each gun was discharged." Stalder's face looked impassive. "However, several witnesses only heard one shot."

Beeff frowned, digesting what Stalder said. "These witnesses—did they actually see the fuckheads pull the triggers?"

Stalder indicated no with a slight movement of his head. "One of the local newspapers came to the same conclusion I did. I believe Mike and Jorge didn't kill each other. I am certain it was a professional job. The hitman intended it to look as if Jorge and Mike had murdered each other over drugs."

Stalder continued, "The killer staged an almost perfect scenario. If it had not been for other factors, including the single shot heard by several witnesses, it certainly would have been perfect."

Beeff folded his arms across his barrel chest as he studied Stalder. "Why don't you think they fucking did each other in?"

Stalder's cold blue eyes remain fixed on Beeff. "Without telling them of Jorge's and Mike's deaths, I asked the other handlers about the men. According to our handlers, and from my own observations, Jorge and Mike were considered friends. Neither man was known to be violent, even with the girls they handled. And neither man was known to use drugs."

Something wasn't right. Beeff mentally tried to put the pieces together. They didn't snap into place until Stalder added, "I believe someone is trying to get inside our operation and he created an opening. Two openings."

For a moment Beeff didn't move as he digested the information. Then potent rage came over him, thick and hot.

"Fuck." The metal side of the desk made a crumpling metallic sound as Beeff kicked it. The vibration traveled up his leg, but he felt no pain.

Hagstedt was here. Beeff couldn't take a chance of screwing up by bringing in some kind of fucking spy. Like that whore, Jenika. She'd be dead, soon, after she came out of the coma and after he knocked the fucking crap out of her until she told him what he needed to know.

Beeff almost shook with the desire to personally wrap a piece of wire around the neck of the man who had killed Jorge and Mike. He could practically smell the man's sweat and fear as Beeff took his life.

After a few moments, he managed to control the power of his anger. "No fucking way am I going to hire anyone until we get this fucking figured out."

"I have an idea." Stalder might as well have been a block of ice when it came to the way he spoke without inflection, a voice almost cold enough to freeze. Especially now. "We can put word out, very discreet, that we are looking for handlers. Then we see what bites."

Even if Stalder was an asshole, he was a damned good asshole.

They could handle this without the bastard getting to Hagstedt. Beeff nodded. "Do it."

"This also raises a question about Madame Cherie's death," Stalder said. "Is it possible the new madame and her assistant are plants?"

Beeff put his palm flat on the cold metal desk. "What about their backgrounds?"

"Impeccable," Stalder said. "Perhaps too much so."

"What in the fuck is going on?" Even more rage coursed through Beeff. He slammed his foot into the side of his desk again, the metallic sound ringing as he made another dent. Then another when he kicked it a third time.

Beeff tried to control his breathing. "Unless traffic is too fucked up, the fucking bitch will probably be with the boss by now with those three Chinese pieces."

"Lock Chandra in the basement," Beeff continued, his voice loud enough to hurt his own eardrums. "Take care of her."

Rage made Beeff's arms shake. "I'll make sure Alexis is eliminated."

CHAPTER
TWENTY-TWO

Dasha

Eddie studied the new bruises on Dasha's body and whistled as Stalder went into Mr. G's office and closed the door behind him. "He did a number on you."

Dasha did not wipe away the blood she felt trickling from above her eyebrow and down the side of her face. She gripped the metal in her hand tighter and kept it hidden in a fold of her torn clothing.

Over time, she'd gradually seen what happened to other girls once they were severely beaten. The abused girls never again showed up at the madame's practices. Those girls never danced again onstage. Instead they remained in their own rooms or the common room until they were called out for their next private appointment.

The girls might start out with more bruises from their following night of work. Then they might return with broken bones from their next appointments.

Sometimes they didn't come back at all.

Eddie was surprisingly quiet as he walked her up to the top floor. She would rather endure Eddie's abuse than what she had just gone through with that other horrible man.

Maybe Eddie knew she wouldn't be alive much longer.

Unless the slightest hope existed. A feeble strand she had been reaching for since her nightmare started.

Even as she gripped the gun in her hand, in Dasha's mind the strand of hope that she might live dissolved into black fog.

Then it was gone.

CHAPTER
TWENTY-THREE

Being a smartass is great for developing enemies

The warmth of my coat and the limo's heated interior amplified the heat of my anger as Jianjun interpreted my instructions to the three Chinese girls. Or rather, his version of what I was attempting to tell them. Jianjun and I faced the rear of the limo as we sat on a bench seat directly across from Ai, Daiju, and Ning.

The limo drove like liquid silk through holiday traffic on Broadway, as if the city weren't full of crazy, speeding, dodging, honking, aggressive New York drivers. Of course there was the occasional idiot who'd never driven in Manhattan before, the driver sitting in bewilderment in his car, holding up traffic, as New Yorkers zipped around him.

A dark window was raised between the chauffer and the group of us in the back. Jianjun had already checked to make sure the two-way speaker was off and secure.

They were short on handlers, so they'd hired a limo with a chauffeur rather than using their own driver. He made sure to keep the window up between us and the chauffeur so the man didn't hear what I was telling the girls via Jianjun's interpreting.

All the better. I only had one of Giger's men to deal with if this went down the way I hoped it would.

As I spoke to the girls in English, I gripped a cold glass of rum and Coke that Jianjun had poured for me after we were settled in the limo. What I really wanted to drink was a six-pack of Guinness. All at once.

Didn't matter, though, because I only pretended to sip the rum and Coke, just in case Jianjun had been instructed to drug me, for God knows what reason. But the heater in the limo was up high, and my throat was dry enough to make me want to take the chance.

Despite the heat and perspiration on my skin, my fingers grew colder as I held the glass and told the girls erotic things they would need to do to please the client we would be meeting soon.

My features were a mask, not showing my anger and my hurt for these girls. Tears trickled down their faces like the condensation rolling down the sides of my glass and dripping onto my bare thigh. I tried to keep my instructions tame, but there was no way of keeping my cover without telling the three poor girls things that would horrify them.

But I had no intention of letting "the client" actually get his hands on these girls.

What if he's not Hagstedt? pounded on the inside of my head. *You can't break cover.*

Breathe. It was him. It had to be him.

While the limo made its way through Manhattan and the thousands of holiday decorations and miniature white lights, I continued to keep an eye on where we were headed without looking like that's what I was doing. We were closing in on Central Park West.

As Jianjun translated what I said, he inserted his own additions, but in Mandarin. Of course he didn't know I was nearly fluent in Mandarin. I say *nearly* because speaking and reading Mandarin Chinese is one of the most difficult disciplines to learn. But I do a pretty damned good job of speaking the language.

I tried not to clench my hands around my glass or clench my jaws as Jianjun added something crude to what I said every time he interpreted one of my instructions. I think he was really getting off as he told the girls vulgar acts that they would be expected to perform.

The three cried harder and I wanted to kill Jianjun all the faster.

Breathe, Steele. Almost.

Two sharp beeps came from inside Jianjun's blazer pocket. He drew it out and opened the phone, then pressed a button and read a text message. He nodded, then snapped the phone shut and put it back into his blazer pocket.

Flashing emergency lights caught my attention as they approached from behind. An FDNY response unit was working its way up to and then past us through what was now a congested intersection. The huge truck's emergency lights flashed through the window and across the girls' faces. I glanced over my shoulder to look ahead of the limo and see what the holdup was.

Damn. An accident right on Columbus Circle. Looked like a carpet company truck had broadsided a white limo. I scanned the area and guessed where we were heading. I'd lay money the client was staying at Trump Tower.

Our black limo came to a stop. Jianjun looked in front of us and in back, then shouted several foul things in Chinese that I wouldn't say in any language.

The girls huddled together, as if somehow that would make them stronger. Invincible, even.

Yes, together you are stronger. But not invincible.

"We'll be late," Jianjun said, spittle flying from his mouth.

"Are you paid for punctuality?" I wanted to get this show on the road, too, but getting a dig in here in there wasn't going to hurt anything. Relieves the stress a little. "Or are you paid for getting the 'merchandise' to your client intact?"

Jianjun's face twisted into a snarl. "Shut up, bitch."

Being a smartass helps develop enemies.

I'm good at that.

And I planned to put it to good use with Jianjun.

I pressed a recessed button and one of the limo's beverage holders appeared. I set my rum-and-Coke glass into it and looked Jianjun in the eyes and smiled sweetly. "What were you saying?"

And then in Mandarin I proceeded to tell him a few unflattering things relating to his masculinity, or lack thereof, including the size of his genitalia—if he had any at all.

For a brief moment, the three girls' expressions showed that they didn't know whether to laugh at the blatant and embarrassing insults, or if they should continue crying from what they were about to face.

Jianjun, on the other hand, looked like he was ready to kill me. His face was a nice shade of reddish purple, like a Chinese plum blossom. His tendons stood out on his neck, drawing the muscles of his throat tight. His features seemed to bloat, his eyes difficult to see.

I gave him another sweet smile.

Jianjun started to make a movement toward me when his cell phone gave two shrill beeps again, no doubt another text message. He cursed at me in rapid Mandarin as he jerked his phone out of an inside pocket of his blazer. I had to admit it—he sure knew some creative insults.

He pressed a couple of buttons and started reading a text message. I could see the text, but couldn't read what it said from where I was sitting.

His breathing stilled for just a fraction and his body tensed. Something was wrong. Really wrong.

The tiny cell phone in my bra vibrated against my breast. Shit. That couldn't be a coincidence. My muscles tensed and my heart pounded faster.

Jianjun darted a glance at me then glanced at his phone before snapping it shut. He moved as if there were nothing to be concerned about and slipped the phone into his pocket as he looked at the girls instead of me.

Adrenaline kicked up in my system. He was going to come after me. I'd do him one better and go on the offense.

He twisted toward me and started to raise his left hand. I was sitting on his right.

Before he even turned his upper body, I had clenched

my fists together. With my power and strength, I rammed my elbow into his Adam's apple.

Jianjun gave a strangled gasp. I shifted my body and grabbed his hair in both of my hands. I jerked his head down and moved my knee upward.

I slammed his face against my knee and heard a satisfying crack.

He didn't have time to shout.

Holding on to a handful of his hair with one hand, I jerked his head all the way back then rammed the heel of my palm against his nose and jammed it up all the way into his brain.

Jianjun never made a sound. He slumped in the seat, his eyes staring upward in an expression of disbelief, his face bloody from his nose to his chin.

"Damn." I looked at my bare thigh as Jianjun's dead body slid sideways on the seat and his head thumped the window. "I got blood on my knee and my hand." I couldn't very well start digging around in his suit jacket or my bra with blood on my hands. I looked at the girls and continued to speak in Mandarin. "Do you see any linen napkins? I could use some club soda, too."

I closed Jianjun's eyes and adjusted his body in his seat so that from the back it might look like he was just sleeping—if it hadn't been for the blood all over his face.

Daiju found a small bottle of club soda and poured it onto a fine linen napkin that Ning handed her.

"Thank you," I said in her language and wiped up the blood that was on me. "I'm going to help all three of you get away from these bastards who've taken you." I talked and glanced at them while I cleaned up more blood on the leather. The fine white linen napkin was bright red. "Go along with whatever I say or do."

They stared at me before Ning and Daiju nodded. Ai had a wary expression, like she didn't know if she should trust me. But she said nothing as she watched.

The limo started moving again, past the accident. Traffic was still slightly congested, but if Trump Tower was our destination, then we'd be there within two minutes.

Now that I had blood off my hands I could get into my bra and Jianjun's pockets. The girls gave me a look like they thought I was weird as I dug in my bra for the mini cell phone. I ignored them and pulled it out of its pocket and immediately checked for text.

Cold washed over my body as I read the message from Takamoto. It was what I'd thought, but this confirmed it.

Blown. S-K-D abort. HQ.

"Shit." In other words, Takamoto just told me, Kerrison, and Donovan that we'd been made. He'd probably heard it over one of the bugs we'd planted. The three of us were supposed to head to our makeshift HQ in the hotel, and not the stakeout apartment or our Brooklyn apartment.

If there was any chance in the world that Hagstedt wasn't on to us—maybe he had his cell phone off—I wasn't about to abort my end yet. I was going to get in there, find out if he was our man, and take him down.

I hit reply to Takamoto's message and added Kerrison's and Donovan's coded cell phones as recipients.

Negative. Trump Tower. Wolf.

God, I hoped the Tower was right. My gut told me it was.

Takamoto, Kerrison, and Donovan would now know where I was and that I believed Hagstedt was here. RED's New York branch along with my own team would be all over the place within no time. Because I hadn't directly called for them, the agents would stay out of my way until either I signaled, or I was dead.

I shoved the mini cell back into my bra. "Like I said, I'm here to help you and the other girls," I told them in Mandarin as I slipped my hand into the dead man's suit jacket and found one bulge that had to be his cell phone. Farther down was his wallet. "I need you to go along with everything I say and do so that we can catch the men doing this to many girls."

Ning and Daiju nodded. Ai just stared at me.

I drew out Jianjun's cell phone and wallet. I opened his wallet, ignored his ID, and slipped out the key card Giger had given him. I tossed the wallet to Ning. "Hold on to that," I told her.

Then I looked directly at Ai. "Please, just cooperate. I can't help you if you don't help me."

A pause and then she gave a single nod. "I will help you," she said in clear English.

Thank God. "Another wet napkin, please." I held out my hand, and Daiju helped Ning by pouring club soda on the second linen napkin.

I grimaced as I hurriedly used it to wipe the blood off Jianjun's face. "Can you find a place to hide these?" I handed the cloths to the girls when I was finished.

Ning took them by the unbloodied corners, searched around her, then opened up a compartment on one side of the limo and dropped the napkins in there. Meanwhile I straightened Jianjun's suit, folded his hands in his lap, and tilted his head back against the window between us and the chauffeur. His nose was obviously odd in appearance. Hopefully the driver hadn't gotten a good look at Jianjun to begin with.

The limo pulled up to Trump Tower. My hands shook as I hurried to get a look at the message Jianjun had received.

Eliminate madame. Return merchandise.
Notifying client.

Shit, shit, shit.

I scrolled back a message. The message from Giger with the room information like he'd promised.

Deliver merchandise. Tower. Room 1612.

The limo had barely come to a stop when I shoved open the door to get out without waiting for the chauffeur to come around. Icy cold wind blasted away the almost unbearable heat of the limo.

Fortunately for me, Jianjun happened to be "sleeping" on the other side of the vehicle.

One of the hotel employees took my hand and helped me from the limo before I had a chance to do so myself. I clenched Jianjun's cell phone in one hand, the key card in my other, as I moved to let the three girls out.

The white-haired chauffeur, who sort of looked like Santa Claus, raised his eyebrows. Obviously because we hadn't waited for him to come around and assist us. He started for the rear passenger door on his side and reached for the handle.

"No." Heart thumping in my throat, I called out to

the Santa-chauffer. "The man does not feel well and is asleep." I nodded as I spoke with a heavy Swedish accent, and the chauffeur automatically nodded along with me. "He wants to stay in the car until I call for you."

"Yes, ma'am," Santa said and tipped his hat.

"Let's go," I said to the girls as I turned and headed into the hotel. "And smile along the way so no one suspects anything's wrong."

By now the girls' tears had dried and they made attempts at smiles that weren't very convincing, but better that than them walking through the hotel bawling. Like that wouldn't attract attention.

Trump Tower was impressive enough to just about take my breath away when I entered. Just about. I was on a mission and I'd appreciate the Tower a whole lot better with Hagstedt in RED's custody, or down and out.

I spotted the concierge. "We need to take the elevator to the sixteenth floor," I said to the man as soon as I reached him.

The concierge directed me to the elevator and I tried to look elegant and unhurried while the girls followed me. It was virtually impossible to do that and get to the elevator as soon as I wanted.

The four of us stepped into the first car that opened. Damn. Didn't have time to keep a couple from coming on. They looked American, so I thought I was going to be okay speaking Mandarin to the girls as the elevator went smoothly to the sixteenth floor.

"When we get there, I need you to act as demur as possible." I spoke quickly and noticed the couple watching me, as if a Scandinavian-looking silver-blond-haired woman speaking rapid, fluid Chinese was an oddity. "I'm hoping I can take him off guard, and I can only do that if you're with me."

The elevator stopped at the sixteenth floor. The four of us got off and the couple stayed on. I checked to see where room 1612 would be. Conveniently, it wasn't far from the bank of elevators.

My heart pounded, adrenaline revving up my whole system as I reached the door. My hand was steady as I slid the key card into its slot.

Three things happened at one.

Jianjun's cell phone vibrated in my other hand.

My cell phone vibrated against my breast.

The door was jerked open.

All thoughts of vibrating cell phones fled my mind at the sight of the man standing in the doorway.

He was pointing a handgun directly at my chest.

CHAPTER
TWENTY-FOUR

Chandra

"Like this, honey." Chandra Kerrison thrust out her breasts, her hands gripping the dancing pole behind her as she rubbed her ass against the pole and shimmied until she was squatting with her knees spread wide. She glanced at the handler not far from Klara before she looked back at the girl. "Put on a good show to keep the guys happy."

Chandra would have never guessed that her experience at stripteasing at a bar to pay for college was going to help her one day as a federal law enforcement agent.

Special Agent Chandra Kerrison. Specialties: weapons expertise, hand-to-hand combat, intelligence operations, master cryptanalyst . . . and striptease instructor.

What a nightmare for these girls. And she had to teach them to make a bunch of men want to screw them.

Not much longer, Kerrison.

Chandra sucked in a deep breath as she tipped her head back against the pole and shimmied her breasts. By the end, by bringing down Hagstedt, she would be helping to save thousands and thousands of women. That's what she had to keep in her mind, always.

Hundreds of thousands of women could be saved. Just by bringing down one man's multibillion-dollar organization.

Chandra eased up the pole with slow, sensual deliberation. Then she performed a few simple moves that would come off as enticing if done right.

She stopped and turned to the girl next to her on the stage. "Your turn, Klara."

Klara was so strung out on some kind of opioids, and had been prostituted to so many men, that she didn't seem to care what she had to do. She followed Chandra's directions and did a fair job. In some cases, the out-of-it, dazed expressions on the girls made them look like they desired whatever it was a man wanted to do.

"Good job, Klara." For the third day in a row, Chandra forced yet another smile as the girl stumbled back toward her handler.

Having to smile pissed her off. What she really wanted to do was start shooting every man in the place with her Sig Sauer P226. She didn't mess around.

Chandra cleared her throat as she cleared her mind of the satisfying images. "Vera, why don't you take your turn now?"

The girl's handler picked her up and swung her onto the stage, swatted her on the ass, and laughed when she fell on her hands and knees.

"That's the way," the dickhead shouted. "Just spread your knees more and let everyone get a better look at the goods."

Chandra's body shook as she made herself avoid the man's gaze so that he wouldn't see murder in her eyes. His murder.

She focused on Vera as she took the girl by the hand and helped her up. "Okay, sweetheart, why don't you try the first move I showed Klara?"

Despite the fact she hated most men—being raped by older stepbrothers could do that to a girl—Chandra had helped put herself through college working a few hours a week at a titty bar in Nashville. She'd always preferred women, but sexual abuse by males sealed their coffin.

Showing off her body and knowing that no man could touch her had made Chandra feel like she was getting a little revenge for what her two stepbrothers had done to her when she was in junior high school.

Vera was having problems staying on her feet. From the confusion in the Russian girl's eyes, the slowness of her breathing, along with the severity of the sedation caused by the narcotic, Chandra wondered just how much opioid Vera had in her system.

Chandra took a deep breath and instead of counting to ten, counted in her head the number of dicks she was going to blow off.

Then she tried to help Vera again.

Chandra could've done any number of other things to earn money while she was in college, but it had been strangely empowering to striptease at the Corral Cowboy Club in Nashville. As far as her income tax records were concerned, she'd been a waitress. She'd danced under a fake name.

No man had power over her body anymore. *She* held all the power.

That was a fact she'd gotten across to her two step-brothers one Christmas. She'd just graduated from her advanced training courses at FLETC, the Federal Law Enforcement Training Center.

Steve and Carl would never be able to father children.

Chandra looked at Vera's handler when the guy approached. "Vera's going to collapse from the amount of drugs she's used," she said in a low tone to the girl's handler. "She's overdosed, or she's close to it. You really need to get her to a doctor."

The girl's handler smirked. "Just do your job. I'll do mine."

"I'm serious." Chandra put more authority into her words. "She could die."

"Fuck off." The handler supported Vera and dragged her off the stage.

Chandra tried harder to slow her breathing and rein in her fury. But even counting shot-off dicks wasn't doing the job.

The mini cell phone in her bra vibrated against the side of her breast.

She went stone-cold sober.

The fact that it had just gone off had one meaning and one meaning alone.

She had to get the fuck out of there. Now.

"I need to take a restroom break." Chandra walked

down the steps from the stage, trying to look calm and casual. "I'll be right back."

"I do not think so." Stalder's voice came from the direction of the podium, directly behind her. "You have a meeting scheduled. And you are *late*."

CHAPTER
TWENTY-FIVE

Nick

"Word's out on the street according to Johnny." Takamoto snapped his cell phone shut. "Good job, Donovan. The Elite Gentleman's Club is looking for a couple of new bouncers."

Smithe snorted as he braced his hand on the back of the chair in the suite of their hotel room HQ. "Bouncers, better known as prostitute handlers on the inside of Giger's little Manhattan organization. So Hagstedt's man's bought it."

As he finished putting on his leather jacket Nick frowned. "But the damned *New York Times*—if Giger read that article, this could be a setup."

Takamoto slipped his cell phone into its clip on his belt. His starched shirt and unwrinkled appearance created an extreme contrast with the rest of the surveillance team, all tired as hell. "That does potentially complicate things."

Nick thought about this morning's *Times* and narrowed his eyes. How could he have made that mistake? Letting his silencer get damaged? It had been one fucking big mistake.

"Giger putting word out this soon could mean you're right, Donovan." Smithe fidgeted with a button alert sensor Nick would be putting on his jacket. That sensor would bring down the wrath of RED wherever Nick was if he simply pressed the device. "I expected at least a day before we'd hear anything," Smithe continued. "But then the dipshit Giger was in one hell of a big of hurry to hire a madame after we strangled the bitch."

Not actually strangled, of course—they'd just staged the act, and then shipped her out. Cherie was now tucked away in Nevada running a cathouse. Nick lightly touched the stiletto-heel-shaped cut and bruise on his cheekbone from the night they'd kidnapped her and he almost snorted. The madame wasn't happy about being in a place that was nothing like New York City. Nick had told her to deal with it or face being gunned down by Giger's men. Hell, Steele had told her she'd gun Cherie down if she got in their way.

Steele could be pretty damned convincing. And she usually followed through with her threats.

Cherie's situation wasn't like entering a witness into the Witness Security Program. With WITSEC, witnesses were given entirely new identities and lives, including being unable to take on any kind of job remotely related to their previous careers.

In Cherie's case, RED had just gotten her the hell out of Manhattan until they took down Hagstedt and Giger's local ring. She could come back when the op was finished. They wouldn't need her for testimony. RED didn't deal with red tape.

"We'll just have to see what happens when I meet up with Giger or his men." Nick checked to see if the slender blade he'd put into a hidden pocket right behind the thick leather lapel could be felt if he was patted down by Giger's men. One of the smallest handguns available, a Rohrbaugh R-9, was tucked into one of his shitkickers. With the thick leather of his boots, and the small size of the R-9 9mm, it wasn't likely to be detected.

He'd rather have his Beretta.

Smithe handed Nick the button sensor. He peeled off the backing so that he could stick the device behind the middle button of his leather jacket.

Nick couldn't shake the feeling that Steele was going to need his help. He had to be convincing and get on the inside of the club.

Takamoto gave Nick a slim cell phone. "If this thing vibrates, you know to get the fuck out of there."

Nick gave a short nod and put the cell phone into a belt clip, close to his hipbone where he'd be sure to feel it.

"Good luck, man," Smithe said as Nick headed out of the hotel room.

Nick was too focused to reply. He took the elevator to the lobby and walked toward the entrance and its floor to ceiling wall of crystal clear, unsmudged glass. The brass around the revolving glass doors shone as if it had just been polished. It reflected the holiday decorations in the lobby as the doors turned.

He stopped twenty feet short of the hotel entrance

and focused on the situation with Giger, calculating the risk of trying to get on as a handler to back up Steele's ass. And Kerrison's, too.

Around Nick the expansive lobby was decorated with holiday lights, massive wreaths, huge bouquets, and an enormous evergreen tree with shiny gold bulbs and white satin bows. It even smelled like the holidays. Pumpkin pie spices and pine.

Outside the floor-to ceiling windows, the day had turned blustery. A stiff wind bent trees and caused holiday decorations to swing. A crumpled newspaper and scraps of garbage tumbled along the sidewalks.

If he concentrated hard enough, he could almost feel the late-November sunshine and mild climate in Arizona. He'd practically made his home into a fortress in a small community in Bisbee. The fortress was there in case his past caught up with him. In Boston with RED on this op he didn't feel as vulnerable as he had when he settled down in one location and worked as a PI. With RED he was always on the move and mostly underground.

Or maybe it was his determination to get that fucking bastard, Hagstedt.

After Hagstedt was brought down, Nick would return to Arizona. This time his sister would live with him, safe from harm and far from the place of her nightmares. If he hadn't had such pure hatred toward Hagstedt for what the sonofabitch's organization had done to his sister, Nick would have returned to Bisbee after he recovered Kristin.

Nick closed his eyes for a moment. But Lexi was in Boston. He pictured the petite woman taking down men two or three times her size and beating the shit out of the dickheads who deserved it. He smiled to himself. Lexi was one tough little chick, something no one would argue about. He pictured her wicked grin, her don't-get-in-my-face expression and attitude.

But then in his mind he saw her features soften into a smile in the flickering candlelight from their recent night together. His gut clenched as the feelings returned that always stirred inside his chest when she was around. She'd kill him if she knew how much he wanted to protect her.

Him and Lexi?

He opened his eyes again and started for the front doors as he shoved the images out of his mind. From the start, Lexi had made it clear she didn't do long-term relationships, especially after her last one ended with the bastard cheating on her.

Hell, he didn't do long-term either.

Before Nick reached the revolving glass doors, the small RED cell phone vibrated against his hip.

Fuck. Something was going down. And it had to be bad.

He jerked the cell phone out of its clip and flipped it open. His heart started pounding as he pressed speed dial for Takamoto then raised the phone to his ear.

"You're all blown." Takamoto started talking without giving Donovan a chance to speak. "One of the bugs Steele planted caught a conversation between Giger and Stalder. They're on to the handlers' killings, and they suspect Kerrison and Steele as plants."

Nick started jogging toward the revolving doors and ducked into them. "Shit. Where are they?"

"According to the GPS devices, Steele has reached Trump Tower. We got a text from her confirming that—and she says she's still going after the man she thinks might be Hagstedt." Takamoto sucked in his breath. "Kerrison is at the club, or she was. We lost signal. She didn't trip her alarm."

"Goddamnit." Icy wind blasted into Nick as he ran toward the street where a Christmas-red Ferrari was running, its exhaust jetting out puffs of fog from the cold. Its owner, who looked like he was probably a millionaire computer geek, was standing by the curb talking with a bellhop from the hotel.

"You go after Steele," Takamoto said, "We'll cover Kerrison."

"Got it." Nick flipped the phone shut as he reached the owner of the Ferrari. He rammed his shoulder into the slender geek, knocking the guy hard into the bellhop and sending them both onto their asses and sprawling onto the sidewalk.

"Police," Nick said as he slid into the vehicle and tossed the phone on the passenger seat. "I need your vehicle," he added before shutting the door, gunning the powerful engine, and shooting straight into a narrow gap in traffic.

CHAPTER
TWENTY-SIX

Chandra

Prickles ran down Chandra's spine as she sped through options in her mind.

First option—run for the door and make it past the two muscle-bound bouncers.

She eyed the door. Those two muscle-bound bouncers were blocking that means of escape. She could take them one-on-one, probably. Two-on-one with those guys, possibly.

Second option—go with Stalder, get him alone, and rip his throat out.

The third option wasn't an option at all. Fight her way out. There were too many men to have much of a chance of defending herself. She could take on a few. Not a dozen.

Option two seemed her most likely bet. And could be much more satisfying if she did manage to rip out Stalder's throat.

Even as her heart started pounding, she kept that

image in her mind and didn't have to fake a smile as she turned and faced Stalder. "Somehow I missed the memo. Maybe you can fill me in on this meeting I'm late for?"

"Now." Stalder kept his face expressionless but his eyes told her she was in deep shit.

"Sure." Best she could do was go along, try to get with as few men as possible, then use every means she could to escape. She walked toward Stalder in a slow and deliberately sensual pace and smiled at him. "No problem. The restroom can wait."

Chandra followed Stalder around the drapes behind the podium and out of sight of the girls and their handlers. Two men in suits were waiting in the lap-dance hall on the other side of the curtain. Men she'd never seen before.

One of the guys was typical hired muscle. Built like a linebacker, blond, blue-eyed, and he wore a diamond stud in one of his ears. She'd put him at around thirty-five. His arms were folded across his chest, and veins stood out on his hefty biceps. Yes, hired muscle, not brains. The kind of guy who used his size and appearance to intimidate, his strength to cause pain.

The other was a very young Japanese guy. Maybe twenty. She couldn't tell if he was American Japanese or a Japan native. He was of slighter build than both Blondy and Stalder, dark-eyed, with stylish shaggy black hair. The way he stood, a casual but ready stance, told her he was extremely confident in his abilities. He was probably a black belt in some form of martial arts. Out of the three—the Japanese, Stalder, and

Blondy—the Japanese was likely the one to watch out for. But she didn't intend to underestimate any of them.

Stalder would pull a gun on her rather than wasting his breath on physical contact.

Blondy would be the one to *try* beat the shit out of her.

The Japanese—he could probably break her neck in one move.

To the men, Stalder gestured toward Chandra with a *handle the girl* motion.

Chandra took a step back as the blond headed for her. The guy had plastic zip cuffs. For one second she considered tripping the alarm on her jewelry and having RED come down on the place. All she'd have to do was unfasten the catch on her bracelet. She could use the narcotic in her rings to knock the men out and then she'd make her escape.

No, not yet. Their team was too close to getting Hagstedt and she couldn't jeopardize the *Little Red* and *Big Bad Wolf* ops. She'd play along with this and see where it led. Their RED team wasn't after shutting down one single club. They were after the bigger picture.

She ignored the increasingly rapid beat of her heart as she looked at Stalder in feigned surprise. "What's going on?"

"We will find out soon," Stalder said in a tone that made her want to shiver. "Won't we, Chandra?"

Blondy reached her and took one of her wrists. He smelled of Stetson cologne but it didn't do a good job of masking his body odor, a heavy smell of testosterone and sweat.

"What the hell?" she said, putting as much confusion as possible in her words.

Stalder said nothing as Blondy forced her to turn her back to him and handcuffed her with the plastic zip restraints. He wasn't rough like she'd expected, but he did a damned good job of making the cuffs tight.

Stay calm, Kerrison.

"Tell me what's going on," she repeated as she looked over her shoulder and narrowed her eyes at Stalder, this time putting anger in her words.

Stalder ignored Chandra, and Blondy took her by her upper arms so that she was facing Stalder. The asshole ignored her and walked in the direction of the restrooms and the stairwell.

The Japanese man followed. She considered flipping him off since her wrists were bound behind her, then thought better of making a possible martial arts expert Enemy Number One.

She couldn't hear a sound coming from him, but Blondy made enough noise for them both as his boots clumped on the black-and-white-checkered linoleum. The four-inch stilettos she wore today had rubber heels so they didn't make any clicking sounds.

Chandra expected the men to take her up the stairs, probably to the room on the second floor where Steele had found the room Jenika had probably been interrogated and beaten in. But Stalder slid his hand down one of the metal rails of the staircase.

A click and then a grinding sound as the four-foot-wide wall to the right of the staircase rose and revealed a staircase leading down to a basement. A wave of

cool, musty air pushed its way toward her. A damp
scent that included the smell of rust.

What? This part of the basement wasn't on the schematics.

Chandra closed her eyes. She and Steele had missed
this altogether. Jenika was probably down there and
that was why they hadn't been able to find her. If she
was still alive.

And this was where she and Jenika could both die.
Since this part of a basement hadn't been on the building's schematics, RED would never find them.

She'd figure out her escape for herself.

Chandra opened her eyes as the blond guy drew her
toward the basement entry. Stalder stared at her with
what she thought was the hint of a cold smile. The first
sign of a real expression from him she'd seen.

She let herself be guided toward the entrance to the
basement, then Blondy helped her walk down the
rickety staircase. The stairs swayed and made it difficult to walk in her high heels. She might have fallen
a couple of times if Blondy hadn't kept a good hold on
her arm. His grip was firm, but he didn't press his fingers too hard into her flesh. He was acting more like
an escort than someone who might be about to torture
her.

She and Blondy finally stepped onto a filthy dirt-
and oil-spotted concrete floor. They paused at the
bottom of the stairs. To their left, a series of single
lightbulbs ran the length of the basement.

The damp, rusty smell obviously came from the
multitude of pipes running along the walls, many of
which had water-moistened rusted joints, showing

small leaks. Some of the pipes themselves were covered with rust, too. A dusty, dirty, and oily scent made it difficult to breathe until she got acclimated to it.

Stalder was on the step behind Chandra, and his cold voice made her spine stiffen. "Take Chandra to the girl so that she can see what happens to spies who don't cooperate."

"Spy?" Cold prickled her skin. Chandra put as much *what the hell are you talking about* into her voice as she could. "You think I'm a fucking *spy*?"

No one answered.

Blondy guided her farther into the basement, past crude oil heaters and containers of fuel. Odds and ends were tossed or arranged everywhere, but there was no method to their madness as far as she could tell. Deteriorating cardboard boxes were stacked randomly, the box labels long since faded and unreadable. Blondy took her past piles of wooden planks, and near a new white chest freezer that had to be at least twenty cubic feet.

Rusted tools were tossed in a pile on some baling wire next to the freezer, and she cataloged those she could define. A pair of pruning shears, flathead screwdriver, ball-peen hammer, and heavy-duty pipe wrench.

After Chandra notated the tools, she fixated on the freezer. Oh, God. They hadn't put Jenika in there, had they?

Blondy guided her on. Then they came to a full stop.

Horror swept through her at the sight of Jenika on a bare mattress, flat on her back, naked, and unmoving.

Most of her face was bruised and swollen, and there was an indent where something small but brutal had been rammed into the side of her head.

An image of Giger's three-carat diamond ring rushed to her mind. Anger at the sight of Jenika's unmoving body swept through Chandra.

She wasn't supposed to know anything about Jenika so she tried to keep the fury out of her voice, even though it was burning her up inside. "What did you do to this girl?"

"She is in a coma. I'm sure you already know her name. Jenika, I believe." Stalder walked close to Chandra as Blondy made her face him. "Who is she to you?"

"I've never seen her before." Chandra didn't break eye contact. "Goddamnit, what's this all about?"

Stalder studied her with what seemed like an impartial expression. "This is your one and only warning. Tell me who you work with."

Chandra shook her head. "This is crazy. I don't know what you're talking about."

Stalder gave a slight nod to the blond guy who'd been so gentle with her. Blondy stood in front of her and her heart plummeted as he pulled back his arm, his hand balled into a fist. Instinctively she wanted to use her skills to protect herself and dodge at the same time.

The Japanese guy gripped her upper arms from behind.

Blondy's fist headed straight at her face.

Chandra couldn't hold back the cry of pain as his fist slammed into her eye and cheekbone.

Black spots and white sparks burst behind her eyes.

With her hands cuffed behind her back, she would have fallen if the Japanese guy didn't have a good grip on her.

"Are you ready to talk?" Stalder looked her over as if he were assessing a work of art.

"What the fuck is going on?" She had to give it to Blondy. That had been a good one. Chandra felt tipsy as the faint tickle of blood rolled down her throbbing cheek from where the skin had split under her eye. "I don't know this girl. This is all crazy. I—"

Stalder gave another nod and Blondy slammed his fist into the side of Chandra's head.

Her knees buckled. Her mind swam. Images of blowing off these three bastards' dicks circled her head like chirping birds.

They were so dead.

If they didn't kill her first.

Fuck them. She'd had enough.

Before Blondy could punch her again, she jerked out of the Japanese man's loose grip and slammed her head against Blondy's forehead.

At the same time, she hooked one of her ankles around his and jerked.

Blondy fell hard and started to get up but she rammed her stiletto heel into his scrotum. She jammed her heel so hard it ripped through his suit pants and probably pierced one of his balls.

He screamed and held his hands to his now bleeding crotch. His throat worked like he was about to throw up.

As Chandra immediately went back into a defensive position, Stalder nodded to the other man.

The Japanese darted around so that he was facing her, definitely in a martial arts offensive pose. At least he wasn't attacking her from behind.

Honorable, then. Good. She wasn't.

His first move was a strong kick toward her thigh. Chandra anticipated it and dodged to the side while going on the offense and darting close to him, something she could see he hadn't expected. She twisted just enough to ram her elbow into his sternum.

He didn't make a sound, just reacted with a fast blow to her collarbone. The blow would have broken the bone if she hadn't adjusted her position in time. But the pain from where he'd struck her made her stagger and she cried out.

Then another burst of adrenaline made it easy to focus on him, not the pain.

In time with his strike, Chandra dropped and rolled away on the filthy cement floor, toward the rusted tools.

Blondy was still screaming. The Japanese followed her at a confident, sedate pace.

She twisted during her roll and with her limber body was able to bring her arms from behind her back, under her feet, and then her bound wrists were in front of her. Years of yoga came in handy. Having practiced this move a hundred times made it fast and easy.

Chandra was on her knees in a second. The Japanese guy looked surprised, but she didn't have time to use the jewel on her ring with the narcotic. He came at her too fast with a side kick. He struck her temple, and the power of his kick sent her reeling, tumbling backward. The back of her skull struck the freezer. More Tweety dicks circled her head.

She rolled onto her belly, close to the tool pile. She twisted and with her bound hands reached above her head to grab the closest tool. The ball-peen hammer. She gripped it tight.

This time the man kicked her ribs. If he'd been intent on killing her, she'd have several broken bones by now, and it was very possible she'd be dead.

But the Japanese guy was toying with her. She met his gaze as he shook his arms and legs, limbering up for another round. A slight but almost crazed smile was on his face.

She'd been wrong about the young guy possibly being a black belt. He was too slow. He was an overconfident wannabe. Perhaps a brown belt, working his way up, but he was no expert.

He moved toward her as she got to her knees, her side facing him and her body holding the hammer.

Hold. Not too fast. Not prematurely.

When he started to put weight on his back foot to lash out at her with another kick, she twisted her upper body and put her own weight behind her swing as she went after his ankle with everything she had.

Satisfying cracks from the sound of bone shattering in his ankle.

The young man screamed and screamed. Ankle injuries were among the most painful injuries anyone could suffer. There were fourteen ankle bones and thirty-two foot bones. She slammed the hammer down on his ankle again and shattered a few more of them.

The man screamed long and loud as he held his knee tight to his chest.

Chandra gasped as the ball-peen hammer was jerked out of her hands in a motion that caused her to fall onto her back. Pain shot up her spine. She looked up to see Stalder's icy expression as he swung the hammer toward her head.

Her movements were automatic. She ducked as she rolled toward his legs, but only in time to avoid getting her head smashed in. Instead, the hammer struck her collarbone, which snapped.

Chandra cried out as nearly blinding pain ripped through her. Only her adrenalized body kept her from losing consciousness. Barely.

She ground her teeth against the pain as she twisted again so that she was half under Stalder. She brought her knee up hard enough to hit the back of one of his knees. At the same time she levered herself so that the top half of her body pushed against the front of his at an opposite angle.

Stalder gave a furious shout as he dropped. Breath rushed out of her lungs when his legs landed half on her waist and half on her hip. The movement rocked her whole body so that more pain shot through her collarbone, bone grinding against bone.

Chandra reached out with her bound hands and tried to grab the screwdriver. Stalder was still lying on her, but from her peripheral vision she saw him reach beneath his suit jacket.

He was going for his gun.

Fear gave her the strength to reach higher for the rusted screwdriver.

Slow motion.

Stalder had his hand on his gun and was drawing it.

Chandra gripped the screwdriver in both hands.

A click as he undid the safety catch of his handgun.

Chandra screamed the pain of her broken collarbone as she turned her upper body.

Stalder started to push himself off her.

She didn't give him a chance. She jabbed the screwdriver with enough power to ram the tool into Stalder's eye. And buried it in his brain.

He collapsed on her body, his deadweight pinning her legs. The other men were whimpering, but not screaming anymore. They probably had guns, too.

With her still-bound hands, Chandra grabbed Stalder's .380-caliber handgun and pointed up just in time to see Blondy, his face oxblood red, as he lurched forward and started to raise his own handgun.

She nailed him in the heart with three rapid shots.

He dropped. Soundless until his body thumped against the concrete.

The young Japanese man was sobbing and cursing in Japanese. He sounded closer now. Chandra tried to keep consciousness; her mind wanted to fade to black due to the pain in her shoulder.

She cried out as she worked her body to get Stalder off her legs. Finally she was free. But she didn't take time to congratulate herself. She rose just enough to see the young Japanese crawling toward her, involuntary tears flowing from his eyes but deadly determination in his gaze. He probably intended to break her neck with his bare hands because he didn't have a gun.

Chandra forced herself to her knees even though she wanted to collapse.

The man kept coming toward her. She had the strange flashback of an old movie she'd seen called *The Terminator,* where the humanlike machine kept going and going, even with his body in pieces.

This was no Terminator.

And she was finished screwing with these bastards.

She aimed the handgun at the Japanese and shot him between the eyes.

CHAPTER
TWENTY-SEVEN

China dolls and the bull in the shop

Oh, shit. The handgun the man pointed at my chest was a wicked-looking Sig Sauer P210-3, the kind issued to the Swiss police.

Hagstedt. I would bet this man's life on it. Hell, I'd kill him just for intending to abuse these girls, even if he didn't turn out to be Hagstedt.

But there wasn't a doubt in my mind who he was. In my gut I *knew* it.

"What is going on?" I laid on the Swedish accent really thick, as well as giving the the best look of in-nocence and confusion I could muster. Well, innocent for a woman who oversaw prostitutes.

He narrowed his snow-pale blue eyes, and I saw a flicker of indecision in them. Kill me now or kill me later?

Not a chance in hell I'd let him do it one way or another. Since I wasn't already dead, he likely wanted to drill me with questions about the organization

I worked for—yeah, whatever—before drilling me
with a bullet. Plenty of time for me to come up with a
plan to get out of this mess as I faked innocence and
stalled. Takamoto would have RED agents here in no
time, too, thanks to my response text.

I'd forgotten to text Takamoto the room number
after I checked Jianjun's messages. At least RED
could pinpoint me with the GPS tracking device in
my mini cell phone.

The three Chinese girls probably couldn't see the
gun, only the man's head. Ai, Daiju, and Ning stood
obediently behind me and I felt the thickness of their
fear in the air and heard their sniffles and low sobs. My
own fear had my heart pumping, but my anger kept my
hands steady at my sides and kept my gaze fixed on the
man's strange eyes, which reminded me of snowstorms
followed by pale blue skies.

Go, go, go! I wanted to yell to the girls. I didn't say
the words because I'd be taking the chance of getting
a hole blown in my chest, or the chance that the man
might shoot the girls.

"Get inside the room," he finally said in Swiss-
French-accented English as he gestured with the gun.
So, the man was likely from a French-speaking part
of Switzerland.

"My girls do not role-play with men who want to
use weapons," I said as I passed him. Not likely he was
taking my innocent act for anything but what it was.
An act. "These girls are too young. Too inexperi-
enced."

"Quiet for now." He looked calm, arrogant, and

sure of himself as he gestured with his gun again for me to get into the room. "I have questions that you will answer. Soon."

I cataloged his appearance as I stepped past him into the large sitting room of a luxurious suite.

About six-one, the man was anywhere from mid- to late forties, possibly fifty. His hair was dark brown, sleek, and he managed to appear handsome while holding a gun on me. He actually looked debonair in a black tux and starched white shirt, complete with a bow tie. What, he dressed up to abuse young girls? That or he had a special occasion planned.

Oh, I had something special in mind for him, too. Lots of special things.

Even though this man was older, he reminded me a lot of a very young, fit, athletic Roger Moore when the actor had played James Bond 007 in the 1970s and early '80s. I'd always enjoyed a good spy movie.

I didn't like this guy ruining my mental image of Moore's 007. Another mark against Hagstedt. Not that he needed any more marks. He was as good as dead already.

When I'd walked away from the girls, his gaze moved over them. They gasped and cried harder as they saw the gun that he still had fixed on me. Greed and lust flickered in his eyes along with anger.

His gaze was only partly diverted to the girls, because a good portion of his attention remained on me.

My body was tense, alert. Adrenaline flushed through my body and made me intensely focused on the man. If he'd been near enough, I could have broken the wrist of his gun arm by closing in with a quick combat move, which would also disarm him. Hard to hold a gun with a broken wrist.

Unfortunately he was out of range. And he was the one with the gun.

He slammed the door shut when we were all in the room. Gun still trained on me, the man pointed his free hand in the direction of a couch and two chairs. They were arranged behind a coffee table that had a huge clear glass vase holding a brilliant bouquet of flowers.

As he pointed to the furniture he told the girls, "Take off your coats and throw them into that corner." He nodded to the corner farthest from me and the girls. "Then sit."

The girls tossed their coats into the corner and walked with stiff but hurried, frightened movements as they obeyed him. He was amazingly patient.

"Take off your coat." The man met my gaze again as he spoke to me. "Slowly. Do not put your hands anywhere near your pockets or I will put a hole in your pretty head."

I managed a huff of indignation. "Sir, what is—"

The weapon made a clicking sound as he cocked it and gave an evil smile.

I shrugged off the coat while he kept his gun pointed at me. I threw it where the other girls' coats were.

Still holding the gun on me, he reached into his tux pocket and withdrew his cell phone.

He flipped it open one-handed, pressed a speed-dial number, then put the phone to his ear. A pause, and then he said, "I require your services immediately at the prearranged location." Another short pause. "Do not be late." He finished the call by snapping the phone shut before he put it back into his inside tux pocket.

"Sir—" I tried to get in another innocent plea.

"I will ask the questions." His voice was smooth and almost casual. Definitely self-assured. "Who do you work for?"

More faking confusion. "Mr. G at the Elite, of course."

"Remove the wig." The man raised his gun so that he'd be putting a bullet between my eyes if I didn't figure a way out of this soon. "You are the fucking bitch responsible for ruining my Boston enterprise."

Hagstedt.

It didn't really surprise me that he knew. Bet he'd seen some kind of surveillance vids when we took down his Boston sex slave auction ring.

"So you're Hagstedt." I jerked off the white-blond wig. I dropped the wig, the Swedish accent, and all pretenses. "Not so great to make your acquaintance," I added as the wig landed on the carpet in front of my right foot.

Since the hair of the wig was in a French knot, and the hair itself was pretty heavy, the wig made a thumping sound when it hit. I didn't take my eyes off Hagstedt when it landed.

"Of course when I kill you," I added, "things will be terrific."

Hagstedt didn't seem surprised, either, by my response or that I knew who he was. "Before the hotel maids find your body," he said, "you will tell me who you work for."

I smirked. "Of course. Easy as that I'm going to spill everything then let you shoot me."

"Yes, easy as that." As if he was enjoying a casual conversation with a business associate, he stepped back, farther out of my reach, and pointed the gun at Daiju. She stiffened, her face even more pale, her eyes wide with fear. "I will shoot one of the girls each time you do not answer a question to my satisfaction.

"When I run out of these precious little china dolls—" He smiled as he glanced at them, then at me again. "—I will start shooting at different parts of your body and cripple you slowly. First I'll put a bullet in one of your thighs, and if I'm not satisfied I'll shoot the other. A bullet in your shoulder should be painful, as well as a wrist . . . and so on."

I sucked in my breath as old terrors ripped through my gut. Images filled my mind of what the Nigerians had planned to do to me after my screwup in Army Special Forces and I had the nearly uncontrollable urge to throw up.

If I hadn't taken the ultimatum given to me by the Fucking Asshole Sonsofbitches—to be an assassin for their ghost of an operation—FAS would have turned me over to the Nigerians.

The Nigerians had planned to tie me to a public post, cut me up a day at a time, then patch me up enough that I'd live, tied to that post for the next mutilation. Something that was beyond a long, slow, painful death.

Through torture and threats, FAS had broken me in just about every way possible. The waterboarding finally did it after several beatings and three days of sleep deprivation. After the water torture, I could agree to nothing but turning into one of FAS's assets, an assassin.

Before Karen Oxford saved my life and brought me into RED.

The remembered fear and terror from my past balled up with the anger I felt now. Here, facing Hagstedt, I had no choice but to speak, because he was going to kill the girls, and he'd do it without remorse. I could see that in his unnerving snow-blue eyes.

I had to tell him *something*.

"Okay," I started then almost screamed as a shot rang out.

Daiju slumped on the couch, a hole in her forehead and a single trickle of blood nearly reaching her wide-open dark eyes, the whites red from the constant tears she'd been shedding.

The other two girls did scream.

My heart thundered and I had to force myself to look away from Daiju's body. To pretend she had only been a pretty china doll and not once an innocent, beautiful young woman.

"Why did you kill her?" My fury raised my voice so that I was almost shouting. "I was just about to tell you."

"Too slow." He aimed the gun at Ning before looking at me again. "Faster this time."

Fuck, fuck, fuck. No matter what I told him, even if it was the truth, he was going to kill the rest of us, too.

"I work for a covert organization." I practically spat out the words. I was going to kill him anyway, so I decided it wasn't going to hurt to tell him a little truth.

"We specialize in recovery of persons who are trafficked into prostitution or slavery."

"That has been more than obvious." He cocked the handgun. Ning sobbed harder and trembled as she stared at the weapon. "Tell me something that I haven't guessed already."

I could tell him the truth or I could make shit up. He wouldn't believe any of it, or at least he'd pretend not to and just keep shooting.

I had a better idea.

"The truth is," I said slowly, "you're going to die."

I kicked the wig I'd dropped in front of my foot. The French knot and the heaviness of the wig gave it enough weight and balance that it sailed straight for his face.

He tried to duck out of the way. The French knot hit him on the side of his head and he shouted as the sprig of holly nailed him in the eye.

A little holiday cheer, courtesy of Kerrison.

His first shot went wild.

I'd already dived to the floor the moment after I kicked the wig. I propelled myself toward him as I moved. His wild shot rang out over my head.

The carpet burned my arm as I tucked my body into a fast, evasive roll. Thank God the dress I'd worn was made of a stretchy material, similar to Lycra, and didn't restrict my movements.

I rolled toward his left side to avoid his second shot. That one wasn't even close, either, and I knew I'd taken him by surprise again by my movements.

When I was tucked in, I was able to slip off one of my high-heeled slides. Before he had a chance to get off a third shot, I made it to my haunches and swung the heel of the shoe at his Achilles tendon.

I missed and only grazed his anklebone.

Hagstedt bent and jammed the barrel of his gun to my head, the metal pressing into the skin right behind my left ear.

The pain from the pressure made me wince even as I went still. Sweat beaded my forehead and dripped alongside my face as my heart rate continued to ramp up.

I had to control my breathing. Take deep breaths. Analyze the current situation.

"Ready to die, little girl?" Hagstedt's voice was even, smooth, elegant.

With the gun pressed so hard behind my ear, I couldn't look up to see his face. "No thanks," I said in an almost casual tone, then winced again when Hagstedt pressed the weapon harder against my head. It felt like the metal was now tearing the delicate skin behind my ear and starting to drill a hole into my skull.

Enough of this crap.

I snapped my hands up and shoved the handgun away from my head so that the muzzle was pointed toward the wall. The loud retort of the gun echoed in my ear as the shot buried the bullet in the plaster.

In the instant that followed, I twisted my body so that I rose to my knees, facing Hagstedt. In the same smooth movement, I aimed the side of my hand at his in a long-perfected jujitsu move.

Several bones shattered in his hand.

Hagstedt screamed and dropped the gun. It was impossible to maintain his hold with a broken hand.

I dove for his Sig Sauer. He snapped his good hand

out too fast and grabbed the tail of my French braid. Pain splintered through my head. He jerked me away from the weapon and dragged me several feet as I clawed at his hand.

Braids and ponytails were a no-no for this exact reason—it gave him something solid to hold on to. He could swing me around and seriously hurt me. I'd had my hair in the braid to keep it tucked more easily under my wig. I should have taken my chances and just shoved it in.

He landed a blow to my gut as he kicked me with one of his polished black evening shoes.

My eyes watered from the pain but it wasn't going to stop me. I grabbed at air for a moment, trying to reach his injured hand. It was too far from my groping movements.

With his pull on my braid I lunged upward. I hit his broken hand with the same move I'd used before and probably shattered the rest of the bones.

Hagstedt screamed. He stumbled as he released his hold on my hair.

I pushed myself to my feet, fast, and kicked off my remaining high heel. I started to go after him—then I saw the strangest sight.

A bouquet of flowers rose in the air behind Hagstedt.

Then I saw Ai.

Ai was gripping the clear glass vase from the coffee table in her small pale hands.

She swung the vase and flowers at the side of Hagstedt's head.

The vase shattered against his face.

He screamed as glass sliced into the right side of his model-fine features, flaying open that side of his face. Skin flapped from his temple, down his cheek, all the way to his chin.

Blood flowed onto his once spotless starched white shirt and down his black tux. The right side of his upper lip was also torn, his eyelid shut tight and bloody. The top of his right ear was gone.

Hagstedt's handsome face was ruined.

Water and blood covered him and his tux. Flowers tumbled onto his shoulders and the carpet around his feet.

He gave something between a howl and a scream. I started toward him again.

Hagstedt moved faster than I expected for a man who had just been mutilated by a glass vase.

He whirled and grabbed Ai, wrapping his arm around her neck and jerking her against his chest.

Ai gasped and coughed as she fought him with her fists and landed kicks to his ankles. Water and his blood dripped onto her hair, face, and clothing.

"I'll snap her neck." His face was hideous, his voice menacing as he stepped back from me. He was moving toward the door.

Ai let out a strangled sound as he gripped her tighter by her neck. Her fair skin started to turn purple. She grabbed at his arm, but he held on to her.

I heard a single chime as he slid one hand inside of his tux. My heart jerked. He was drawing another gun.

Instead he pulled a cell phone from his pocket and flipped it open. He continued to hold Ai by her neck and keep his gaze on me.

He brought the phone to his left ear, which was on the side of his face without wounded flesh, the side not covered in blood.

"Are you here?" he said in a guttural, furious voice. A single pause before he added, "Stay on the pad. I'll be there shortly.

"Grab a towel and give it to me," Hagstedt shouted at Ning.

She hesitated only a moment before she rushed into the bathroom. He took position so that he could see both me and the bathroom and was out of reach of any more surprises.

Hagstedt still had a tight grip on Ai, but her chest rose and fell in short pants, which told me she could still breathe.

I wanted to go for his Sig, which was maybe five feet from me, but I didn't dare. He'd follow through in a heartbeat with his threat to break Ai's neck, and then he'd go after Ning.

Ning rushed back with a thick white bath towel but didn't get close to Hagstedt. She tossed the towel to him and it landed on the arm with the broken hand. His ruined right hand, ruined like the right side of his face.

Hagstedt cursed then shoved Ai so that he now held her with his right arm. His hand might hurt like a sonofabitch, but he still had her in a tight stranglehold in the crook of his elbow. He held her firmly and she couldn't struggle. She looked so close to passing out that I didn't think she could move.

Hagstedt made guttural sounds like a wounded animal as he used his good hand to wrap the towel around his bloody face, leaving only his nose and his left eye open. What I could see of his face was almost the same snow blue as his eyes. Blood stained the towel in bright red blotches as it seeped through the cloth.

When he finished, Hagstedt started dragging Ai past me to the door. Her face was so purple, I was positive she was close to asphyxiation.

"Open the door, bitch," he said to Ning. His voice was muffled by the reddening towel, but I still heard the fury in his voice.

To me he said, "Don't follow. You know I do not care if this girl lives or dies."

My breath caught in my chest and I remained motionless as Hagstedt jerked Ai past Ning and through the doorway.

The door slammed shut behind Hagstedt.

I heard the ding of one of the nearby elevators that must have just opened along the bank of elevators.

Shit. I hoped it was one filled with RED agents.

I heard another elevator ding as I scooped Hagstedt's gun from the carpet. I dodged glass as I ran barefoot toward the closed door.

Wood and debris flew in every direction as the door frame splintered and the door exploded inward.

CHAPTER
TWENTY-EIGHT

Exit stage left

The crash echoed in the suite like an iron ball shot from a cannon.

My heart leaped into my throat as I stopped in my tracks. I trained Hagstedt's Sig Sauer on the doorway.

Ning whimpered.

Relief rushed through me as Donovan tore into the room. He charged through the shattered doorway after the battering ram that had been used was jerked out of the way.

I lowered the Sig. Donovan's expression was furious, his face contorted into primal rage.

He came to a halt as he saw me and Ning. He swept his gaze over the room and took in the broken vase, the blood, the flowers, and the dead girl, then me and Ning again.

He gave me a swift look-over and seemed satisfied that I wasn't hurt. "Was the man Hagstedt?" Donovan said in a low, menacing voice. "Where's the bastard?"

RED agents in raid gear were with him, but I couldn't tell how many. I didn't recognize the agents and knew they had to be from the local RED branch. We never brought in any other law enforcement agencies. Never.

Our raid gear always had POLICE on everything—it's the universal word for law enforcement. What would the bad guys think if you were on a raid and started yelling, "RED! This is RED! Put your hands up!" They'd probably laugh their asses off.

Not to mention, RED didn't officially exist.

"Hagstedt called someone and said something about a pad." I reached Donovan at the shattered doorway. "I'm betting he has a helicopter landing on the pad at the top of the condominium part of the tower. And Hagstedt has a hostage."

"Fuck." Donovan whirled to face the agents. "Hancock, contact victims' response unit, scene control, and cleanup."

There must have been quite a few agents because Donovan then shouted in a booming voice, "Everyone else get to the lobby then to the condominium elevators. Head to the roof. Suspect has a copter and a hostage."

Several agents responded that they were on their way.

"Hold the elevator for me, Donovan," I called out as I started following.

A young agent, apparently Hancock, hurried through the doorway after the other agents rushed out. The young man stopped just inside the door, holding his FN A2 RED standard-issue rifle with the barrel pointed toward the carpet.

"Stay here," I said to Ning as I headed out of the doorway, still gripping Hagstedt's Sig. "This police officer will help you."

No time to see if Ning acknowledged my order as I bolted out of the suite. One door in the bank of elevators was being held open by Donovan as he growled, "Hurry, Steele."

Several apparently very wealthy civilians, outfitted in what was no doubt thousands of dollars' worth of clothing, were backed up against one wall. They stared at the elevators with jaws dropped, eyes wide. They'd probably been jerked off elevators that had been headed down so that RED agents could pile in.

I ignored the people and dodged spots of blood on the rich carpeting as I ran in my bare feet to the elevator. Donovan grabbed my wrist and yanked me inside. He, along with New York branch RED agents wearing black raid gear, crowded the small space.

No doubt more RED agents were already headed to the lobby, then to the bank of private elevators that take residents to the condominiums. Guest rooms only went as high as the seventeenth floor, the condos taking up the eighteenth through the fifty-second stories.

"How about Kerrison, the girls, and Jenika?" I looked up at Donovan. "Are they okay?"

"I hope to hell they are." Donovan's expression was grim. "Our team should be there now."

My stomach tightened into a knot at the thought of what could be happening over at the Elite.

Focus on this part of the op, Steele. Trust your agents.

Deep breath. *We should be reaching the lobby soon.*

Considering that we were a bunch of agents, most dressed in full raid gear and all handling guns—it wasn't going to be pleasant running through a lobby full of guests.

I could already hear the imagined screams in my ears.

The eight agents in the elevator, including me and Donovan, were so pumped to go after Hagstedt that we could barely contain ourselves. I was practically bouncing on my bare feet with impatience.

The air felt heavy and thick, charged with adrenaline and testosterone as the elevator seemed to take freaking forever to get to the lobby. I realized my glove of a dress was hiked up to my ass and tugged it down with the hand not holding the Sig.

I almost screamed—with frustration—the three times the elevator stopped at floors for guests who had wanted to head down to the lobby. Each time the people were smart enough to take one look at us and back off.

On the ride down, Donovan stuffed the little Rohrbaugh R-9 into his boot. One of the agents holding a rifle handed him a Glock G22 .40-caliber handgun.

That was more like it. Big man. Big gun.

Me, I'd be happy to shoot Hagstedt with his own Sig. Yes, that would feel really good. Of course I wouldn't kill him with it—that would be too easy. Injure him then go after him with my bare hands. Yeah, that was the ticket.

"We need Hagstedt for questioning to bring down

his organization." Donovan looked at me as if reading my mind. "You can't kill him, Steele. Yet."

"Damn." I scowled. "You took long enough. Did you have a hard time finding me?"

"Yeah. Too fucking long." Donovan's jaw was tight. "We had a difficult time homing in on what floor you were on. Once we did, it was no problem locating the exact room he had you in," Donovan said.

I gave him a quick run-down on what had happened in the suite with Hagstedt. "I didn't learn crap about him." My voice rose with my anger. "All I know is what his face looks like. Well, that was before Ai tore him up with that glass vase."

Donovan frowned. "Did she get his entire face?"

"No." I shook my head. "But with the extent of the damage on the one side, I wouldn't doubt that he'll be getting some serious plastic surgery. At his level, after a face-to-face with a law enforcement agent out to get him, he'll probably change his features altogether while he's at it." I gritted my teeth. "But he won't get the chance because we're not going to let him get away."

"He's probably got one hell of a lead on us." Donovan banged his fist on the closed metal elevator door. The sound was loud and vibrated in the cramped space. "Fuck," he said in a growl.

"Word of the operation," I said.

Finally the elevator came to a stop at the lobby. Yup. It was already a madhouse thanks to the first elevator full of RED agents who had charged out. The guests had probably been unnerved to begin with after seeing a man with a bloody towel wrapped around his head and face as he dragged a nearly unconscious girl toward the condominium elevators.

Add a second bunch of agents with guns and we have an episode of *Cops* come to life.

The screams were louder than I'd imagined as we bolted through the crowded lobby. Donovan was shouting, "Police! Move!" as we ran.

People moved. I imagine that getting a good look at the wicked FN A2 special police rifles was a big incentive. Somewhere ahead, the other group of agents was shouting at people to get out of the way. Damn. Their elevator ride down had apparently been slow, too.

Hopefully Hagstedt's had been equally so and we'd catch him before he hopped on a resident elevator.

My heart pounded like a battering ram as I bolted through the maze of people. Being petite, barefoot, and not weighted down by a heavy rifle or raid gear made it easier for me to dodge and weave around people.

I might be small, but I have a hell of a voice when I need it, and you bet I could be heard just about as well as Donovan as I shouted, "Get down! Police!"

Despite all of the screaming and freaked-out people, we didn't have to worry about the NYPD or any other law enforcement organization crashing our party. All calls to LE—law enforcement—regarding this situation would instantly be rerouted to RED. All cell phone calls from anyone from anywhere within the building, even people who were calling family or friends, would hear constant "call failed" messages.

I was getting closer to the other elevators. Shouts of the RED agents ahead of us sounded louder now.

Despite being clandestine—as in, RED didn't exist

beyond the knowledge of a certain handful of people—RED had grown pretty damned powerful.

It was well backed by Very Important People, which included the President of the United States, one influential U.S. Senator, and the Director of the NSA. With that kind of leverage behind us, RED easily arranged for any and all other LE agencies to back off.

The Vice President and members of the President's cabinet, as well as all LE agencies, were in the dark when it came to RED. No other way to be as clandestine as RED had been designed.

Shoving our way through crowds of shrieking and screaming people made the run to the condo bank of elevators seem to take forever and a day.

Condo residents had their own private elevator code. I reached a desk close to the condo elevators. The desk had RESIDENT CONCIERGE imprinted in gold in the rich wood. "Police! Give me the code for the elevator that goes to the top-floor penthouse." I pointed my Sig at the flustered-looking man behind the concierge desk. "And the code for the stairs to the rooftop."

The concierge's face looked waxy and his whole body trembled as he fumbled behind the desk with a pen that probably cost three digits. He wrote down two sets of numbers on a sheet of paper with gold-foil lettering.

The shocked and even terrified expression on the concierge's face probably came from having a man with a bloody towel and a hostage demanding the codes from him, then the first group of RED agents—no doubt at gunpoint like I had him.

Maybe Hagstedt hadn't thought to ask for a code to the rooftop.

"Hurry!" My voice was nearly a scream. "Christ. Come on."

The concierge almost dropped the sheet of paper before he thrust it into my outstretched hand.

"Thank you," I said as I bolted away from him without looking back.

It didn't hurt to be nice to the poor guy. He was obviously paid to cater exclusively to the Tower's condo tenants. If I were him, I'd be thinking about asking for a raise.

When we reached the small bank of luxurious elevators, stunned residents had already backed away. A set of doors was just about to close behind agents in black raid gear.

Only one elevator went up to the fifty-second floor. Blood was smeared on the wall beside it and partially on the code pad.

"Hold that fucking door," Donovan's voice boomed out. One of the agents stopped the pair of doors from closing by stepping between them.

Shit. They'd probably had to wait for the elevator to come back down after Hagstedt took it up. He could be in the helicopter by now.

There had to be ten agents crowded into that one little elevator. Donovan and I stuffed ourselves inside, too. They'd had to have used a code just to get into this elevator, too, so I didn't need the paper I was carrying anymore.

"Got the rooftop codes?" I asked the agents in the elevator.

One of the agents beside me said, "Right here."

I handed my own sheet of paper with the codes to an agent right behind me who couldn't fit on the elevator. He and the others in no way could cram in with the twelve of us already packed inside.

As the doors closed, I said to the agent who had it, "Give me the roof top codes."

He handed me a paper that matched the one the concierge had given me. Shaky handwriting and all. The paper crumpled some in my fingers as I gripped it.

I thought about the blood on the wall beside the elevator. If we didn't get Hagstedt this time, we'd at least have his DNA. Maybe we'd get a hit if he had any priors.

It wasn't likely at his level, but the DNA record would go into all law enforcement data banks. If a match popped up in the future, RED would be alerted immediately.

But we're going to get him, now. *We have to get him.*

I was practically trampled by the other agents in the elevator who were all, of course, six feet or more taller than me.

"Back off," I shouted with a serious pissed-off note in my voice. "You're crowding me." The agents moved.

If I thought the last elevator had been overcharged with adrenalized agents, it was nothing compared with how we felt on a fifty-two-floor elevator ride. Personally I was ready to yank out the speakers that were playing highbrow elevator music.

"Christ." I wanted to kick one of the twin metal

doors, but I also didn't want to break any of my bare toes. "Can this elevator go any slower?"

"Don't jinx us," one of the NY RED agents said.

I squeezed the grip of the Sig. Maybe I'd shoot him just to relieve some of the stress.

As soon as the elevator door opened, I bolted out into an incredibly luxurious penthouse foyer that would leave most people gaping. Whoa. I cataloged the foyer in one sweep of my gaze.

A glittering crystal chandelier hung from a twenty-foot-high ceiling, and blue light glowed upward on the walls from hidden lighting in the floor. Real trees were strategically placed in front of the blue lighting. The paintings on the wall were probably authentic and famous. A large crystal vase with an incredible floral bouquet rested on a circular table with gold-leaf designs. Even the door that would open into the penthouse was amazing.

I would have stopped to stare but I had a man to kill.

Priorities.

"Try to take him alive, Steele," Donovan said. The man was a damned mind reader.

"You're ruining all the fun," I muttered.

The emergency stairwell was next to the elevator. Thank God. Donovan was beside me and jerked the door open before I could. The stairwell wasn't blocked going down to our left. To our right there was a door with NO ADMITTANCE on it, obviously the door to the rooftop and the helicopter pad. I imagined that the top-floor residents did have the code to it for emergency situations or to catch a helicopter.

The life of the wealthy.

Very fancy door and stairwell, too, including the NO ADMITTANCE sign. Worthy of the Tower's residents.

After glancing at the paper that had been given to me, I pressed the sequence of numbers on the keypad beside door. A red light flashed instead of green. Christ. I looked at the paper and saw I'd mistaken a one for a seven thanks to the man's shaky handwriting. The lock clicked when I reentered the code. I yanked the door open and charged up the stairs in a heartbeat.

I reached another door that had ROOFTOP printed across it. A hollow metal fire door with a red EXIT sign above the door. It didn't need a code.

At the same time, Donovan and I pushed down on the exit bar and opened the door.

Freezing wind blasted us and goose bumps immediately pebbled my skin—I didn't have my coat and felt like my skin was coated in ice.

At that moment I didn't give a damn. Hagstedt, bloody towel still wrapped around his head, was climbing into a gold-trimmed black helicopter even before it had finished landing. I recognized the manufacturer—Eurocopter. Fast little sonsofbitches. We couldn't let it off the pad.

Ai was lying motionless near the helicopter. My rage ramped up impossibly more.

The helicopter made the air even colder and windier as the rotors turned. I rushed toward it.

The heat of my anger and adrenaline pushed me faster. When I was close enough to get off a good shot, I stopped and in a second had spread my feet shoulder width and steadied the Sig with both hands.

I aimed and pulled the trigger. Once, twice, three times.

My aim was off, because the power of the wind was making it almost impossible to keep my arms steady.

The first shot chipped the paint near the cockpit. The second hit the rudder.

The third shot nailed Hagstedt in the thigh.

If Hagstedt shouted, it vanished in the noise of the helicopter. But he slipped and lost his footing so that he was half in and half out.

He still managed to cling to a handgrip with his good hand. The bloody towel tore from his face and sailed with the power of the push of air straight toward me. I had to bat it away with one hand, which unsteadied me even more. It caught on my arm.

I didn't realize Donovan was at my side until Hagstedt looked over his shoulder, and his eyes narrowed as he looked past me.

When I shook off the damned towel I realized it hit Donovan square in the face, blinding him before he flung it away.

In the seconds it took to me get rid of the towel, Hagstedt had made it almost all of the way into the helicopter. I ran closer, firing my weapon. Bullets pinged off the metal and shattered passenger windows.

Damn. I couldn't get off a decent shot. Something had to be off with the Sig.

I realized the agents behind us couldn't take the chance of hitting Donovan or me in these conditions before they reached us.

Everything happened in seconds, before the agents could get to our position.

Donovan drilled a bullet into Hagstedt's foot. Blood dribbled from his shoe onto the rudder and onto the pad.

I emptied the Sig's magazine. I flung the weapon aside and my heart started to hurt my chest as hard as it was beating.

The helicopter began lifting from the rooftop.

"No!" I shouted and shoved my hand into the top of Donovan's boot where I'd seen him stuff the little Rohrbaugh.

I yanked the handgun out and ran toward the copter, shooting into the side even though I couldn't see Hagstedt anymore. All I could do was hope that with luck one of the bullets made fatal contact.

When the helicopter was off the pad, there was no way we could safely stop it. I sank to my knees. A feeling of hopelessness dropped away my mental shield that had kept me from thinking about the freezing air.

I felt every bit of the cold as I watched the helicopter fly away from us like a black-and-gold honeybee.

Donovan had indicated to the other agents to stand down. We couldn't take the chance of the helicopter tumbling into Manhattan and taking more lives.

Innocent lives.

Like Hagstedt was taking every single day.

CHAPTER
TWENTY-NINE

Dasha

She was going to die anyway. Dasha knew it with everything she had.

Before she passed on, though, she was going to kill the man who was responsible for forcing all of these girls into prostitution and in some cases letting them die.

If the man they called Mr. G was gone, then the other men would have no one to tell them to murder her parents. At least she would save them and maybe the girls around her.

Some kind of chaos was going on somewhere below the fifth floor. She could hear it all the way to the common room. All but one handler, Eddie, had left. He was standing outside the door instead of inside.

It was the perfect time.

Most of the girls in the common room were talking, but in whispers, since their handlers weren't there to punish them. Dasha ignored the other girls and walked to the big closet.

She looked for the loosest and most modest clothing she could find. *Modest* was almost impossible because they were always forced to wear something revealing. *Loose* would be easier, because she hadn't been eating. She'd lost so much weight that her ribs and hipbones now showed.

Dasha was naked in the closet where all of the scraplike clothing was kept. She found two black pantyhose legs and tied both around her waist, making sure the makeshift belt was secure.

Then she searched and located what Jenika had called a short black babydoll top. It hung just below Dasha's waist and over the pantyhose belt, so it was good enough. The babydoll top had circles where her breasts were, but she didn't care. She just needed its length.

There wasn't much of a choice for a pair of bottoms. Thongs and G-strings were all they had. She picked up a black thong to match the babydoll and climbed into it. She wasn't going to wear shoes.

Dasha went to a corner in the closet where she had pulled away the old carpeting and stored the gun beneath. She had piled her torn clothing on top of the bump in the corner.

She retrieved the gun and arranged it so that it fit in her pantyhose belt. Since she'd tied two of them around her waist, she was able to slip the muzzle of the weapon between the legs of the pantyhose while the grip remained up at the top. She tested it and found it to be secure enough.

She had checked and there were six bullets in the gun, including one in the chamber.

That was all she needed.

Dasha flicked off the safety. A long time ago, when she was young, her father had taught her how to use a gun. She hadn't had many lessons, but maybe they'd been enough.

It was odd how calm she was. She felt numb more than anything else. Smells were dull, her hearing muted.

This must be what it was like to know that soon she wouldn't be seeing, hearing, or feeling.

Dasha walked past all the girls in the common room, her legs steady. Her sight had dimmed, and she saw only through a tunnel. Just the door in front of her.

When she reached the door she raised the hem of the babydoll and drew the gun out of her pantyhouse. The weight of it was like a feather in her nerveless hand.

She leveled the gun with one hand and opened the door with her other. She pulled the door open.

Eddie turned to face her. She saw his scowl. Then his look of surprise just before she pulled the trigger.

Vaguely she heard the sound of the gun firing and was barely aware that her arm had jerked from the recoil. He dropped to his knees, but she felt no curiosity, no concern. She just wanted him dead.

Blood flowed, making the dirty white T-shirt turn red near Eddie's heart. Like a blossom.

He stared down at his chest. Now he had a shocked expression as he watched blood spreading and soaking the cloth so fast that it almost looked like he was wearing a red-and-white shirt. In a slow movement, he brought his hand over the wound then fixed his gaze on his blood-coated palm.

Eddie raised his head. His eyes were wide when he met Dasha's. He fell backward, his body twisted at a curious angle.

His eyes were still wide as she walked past him, but she knew he saw nothing anymore, would never hurt anyone ever again.

Dasha felt nothing beneath her bare feet. Not the cool tile or the rough cracks.

She tucked the gun back into her pantyhose belt and left the safety off. She held on to the railing to make sure she didn't fall. Through her tunnel vision, all she could see were the stairs as she walked down.

The noise grew louder. She was aware of that even though it was muffled in her ears.

Dasha reached the second floor and unfastened the rope that blocked it off. The sign clanged to the tile as she passed. The room where Mr. G had hurt her was not far down. It was an office he used. Somehow she knew he was there.

Dasha drew the gun out again. Her hand was steady as she reached the door and raised the weapon. The door was slightly open and she heard his voice, that hated voice. He was yelling. Screaming at someone.

Dasha pushed open the door. It squeaked as she opened it. He was talking on his phone as he stood at his desk and searched the drawer he had taken the gun from earlier. If she cared, she would have smiled. He'd forgotten that he'd taken the gun out to kill her.

Mr. G looked up, his face red with rage. He dropped the cell phone as his mouth widened.

"You fucking b—" he started right before Dasha shot him.

The bullet buried itself in his belly. The second shot in his arm. The third shot in his chest. The fourth shot in his chest again.

He dropped to the floor. His screams would have hurt her ears if her hearing wasn't muffled.

Now he would die. No one could save him.

She had one bullet left. She'd had plans for that last bullet from the beginning.

Dasha put the gun to the side of her head and pulled the trigger.

CHAPTER THIRTY

Bachmann/Hagstedt

Karl screamed as he writhed on the floor of the helicopter. His wounds wouldn't kill him, but the pain was excruciating.

The shattered bones in his hand caused it to throb as if someone was continuing to hit it with a hammer. His ruined face felt like it was on fire. The bullet that had passed through his thigh had gone through muscle and exited the back of his leg. The shot hadn't come close to bone or arteries.

But his foot—the bullet that pierced his shoe had lodged in bone, and he almost felt like he would die from the pain of it combined with everything else.

When Karl had glanced over his shoulder, he'd had a good look at the man next to the bitch. He was the same man from the auction surveillance tapes.

As the helicopter headed to a prearranged hidden location, Karl imagined putting a bullet between the man's and the woman's eyes.

NSA? CIA? FBI? No. The agents were of some unknown clandestine organization.

But Karl now had a clearer image in his mind of the pair who had taken down his Boston auction ring. He knew exactly what both looked like. He would find them.

Plastic surgery would be required to fix his face, which the stupid Chinese bitch had ruined. While he was at it, he would have his surgeon remake his features. No one at the unknown agency would be able to recognize him.

His skin chilled as he realized that his image had likely been captured on security tapes at the airport and the Trump Tower. They would be able to locate him by his real name.

Karl gritted his teeth from the pain and applied more pressure with his good hand to the wound in his thigh.

Because he couldn't put on a headset, the deafening sound of the helicopter made it difficult to think clearly. The pain didn't help.

A new identity. He would have to find someone whose life he could assume. The plastic surgery could give him a face nearly identical to someone of his social stature. Karl's smile was no doubt cold looking as he thought of the exact person whose life he would assume. The man was unmarried, no children, and fairly reclusive. A billionaire whose looks were close enough to Karl's that it would be easy to become his identical twin.

Then Karl would have the man eliminated and take over his life.

His thoughts churned over what would have to be

done. He would have his financial adviser liquidate the balance of his wealth immediately and store it with the rest of his money in his bank accounts in the Cayman Islands.

Then Karl Bachmann would disappear.

When he did, he wouldn't stop until he found and destroyed the man, the woman, and their organization. Whatever agency they worked for couldn't possibly have the manpower or financial resources to easily locate him.

No, there was not an agency in the world that had billions in cash that they would be willing to spend looking for one man.

Karl did.

CHAPTER
THIRTY-ONE

Going home

The plane couldn't get me back to Logan Airport in Boston fast enough to see my mother. And then the sluggish pace of the people getting off the plane just about made me scream. Dear God.

I wished my legs were longer so that I could walk faster as I pulled my red carry-on suitcase through the much-too-crowded airport. I'd left the rest of my luggage to be brought back with my team so that I could get home sooner.

My RED cell phone vibrated against my hip and I drew it out without slowing down. When I flipped it open the screen said *Unknown,* of course. Covert is covert.

This better be good. "Steele."

"You okay?" Donovan's voice, low with concern. "Where are you?"

"Just landed at Logan and trying to get the hell out of the airport." I dodged a reunited family hogging up my path. "I'm heading out to get to long-term parking where I left my Cherokee."

"I hope your mother is doing better," he said.

She's got to be. She's is going to be okay. It was like I was mentally ordering all the gods anyone believed in to make it right. "Mama is tough. She's a survivor." My chest hurt the more I spoke. "She'll be okay."

"I know she will," Donovan said. "With you around, I don't think anything would dare hurt her."

If we didn't change the subject I felt like I was going to fall apart. It was hard to believe *Operation Little Red Riding Hood* had just gone down yesterday. This was the first time I hadn't been around to wrap things up and make sure everything was finalized.

I rubbed my forehead with my free hand. "How are Kerrison and Jenika?"

"Both are in the New York branch of RED's infirmary. They're doing fine." Donovan sounded ready to punch a wall. "Considering the trauma they both went through."

RED agents never went to the hospital, always to an infirmary that was unknown to any agency.

"The other clubs?" I paused inside the terminal instead of walking through the automatic sliding doors and I closed my eyes. "The girls?"

"Everything was on Giger's hard drive. He had it all well documented, including where all of his clubs are in the city," Donovan said. "Not to mention his accountant, a guy named Andreas, was more than willing to cooperate.

"The New York branch of RED and our team are in the process of shutting all of the clubs down and arresting every trafficker involved. We've worked it out so that the NYPD is handling that end of it."

Because of what his sister had been through, I could imagine the pain in Donovan's eyes when he continued speaking. "We're getting the girls out of the clubs and to hospitals to be thoroughly checked out, along with psych evaluations and treatment before we send them home."

"I just can't imagine," I said as I opened my eyes and stared out the floor-to-ceiling glass windows of the terminal. "Is everything okay with bringing in the NYPD and other outside agencies to take care of the girls without letting them know about RED?"

"Yeah," Donovan said. "The agencies are doing their best to help the girls and notify their families that they're okay."

I swallowed. "The girl, Dasha. I promised to save her."

"Dasha was the one who killed Giger, and she killed her handler as well. A guy named Eddie. Apparently with Giger's own gun." Donovan sounded like there was something he was holding back.

"And how is she?" My voice was hoarse as I thought of the girl the last time I'd seen her.

Donovan's sigh was heavy. "After she killed them, Dasha turned the gun on herself."

My legs nearly gave out. "Christ," I whispered as I thought of the pretty blond Russian. Takamoto had briefed me on Giger, Stalder, and the other employees who were dead. But I'd left New York without knowing every detail. And the fact that Dasha had killed herself was a big detail. One that tore at my heart and made my chest hurt like someone was taking a hammer to my ribs. I'd promised. Even with only my eyes, *I'd promised to help her.* I'd failed.

That wasn't like me, not to be in on everything to do with an op. But getting home to Mama was more important, and I didn't regret not being back finishing up the op in any way. I wasn't about to feel guilty for leaving everything to the team and Donovan to clean up.

I needed to be with Mama.

The automatic doors parted, and I went through them into the cold but clear November day. I hugged my coat tighter to me with my free arm.

Mental exhaustion wanted to weigh me down, but I wouldn't let it. Not until after I'd seen my mother and after I climbed into my own bed in Southie.

I thought of Hagstedt, the sonofabitch I wished I could have killed. I didn't care about needing him for information. I wanted him dead. Now.

"Any breaking news on Hagstedt?" I pictured his face before and after the mutilation.

"We're going to need you as well as the two girls who were in the suite to ID him on hotel and airport security tapes," Donovan said. "You three are the only ones who have seen his face—before it was mutilated. Once you ID him, we'll know where to start looking. Even if he changes his appearance and identity." The air in Boston usually smelled good to me, but right now everything seemed foul while thinking of Hagstedt.

"We'll get him," Donovan added.

"Soon," I said. "I can't believe Ai survived." I remembered her motionless body by the helicopter. "If it wasn't for her, I'm not sure what would have happened to all of us."

"You would have found a way, Steele," Donovan said.

"Yeah, I would." I caught sight of the transport for the long-term parking. "I'd better go. I'll catch up on the rest after I see Mama."

"She's going to be okay," he said quietly.

"I know." I nodded as I said it, even though I was scared to death that neither of us was right.

During the drive to my parents' home in Cedar Grove, I probably broke a dozen traffic laws.

When I parked and climbed out, I didn't bother to lock the door of my Jeep. I bolted from the Cherokee and ran up the walkway to the blue-trimmed white house. I cut across the fall-yellowed grass and hurried past the basketball hoop where I often played three-on-three with my brothers and new sister-in-law. I ran up the stairs without bothering to knock and I let myself in through the front door.

Neither Mama nor Daddy was in the family room and I ran straight through the swinging door to the kitchen. I came to a stop. My mother was using a pair of hot pads to take a baking pot out of the oven. I caught the wonderful smell of her rice pudding.

"Lexi." Mama beamed as she set the baking pot down and left the white-and-blue-checkered hot pads on the counter. "I made your favorite. Rice pudding."

"Mama." The word came out choked as I ran to my mother and fell into her warm embrace. "I've missed you so much."

"I've missed you, too, pet." After a huge hug, Mama drew away and stroked the side of my face, her look tender and concerned. "Is everything all right?"

It was hard to meet her gaze. It was so hard to see the dark green cloth wrapped around her head, hiding the fact that her hair must have fallen out from the chemo. I didn't want to picture her beautiful gray hair falling out in chunks, leaving her bald.

And she was thin. Way too thin.

"Of course I'm fine." I tried to smile, for her.

That's what she wanted. She didn't want everyone to walk around worried and afraid. That had never been her way, and I knew that in my heart. But I didn't think I did a very convincing job of not looking worried or afraid.

And angry. My anger at the cancer that was inside her was eating away at me, too.

She frowned as I met her blue eyes, and her Boston Irish accent was strong. "Don't you go moping around on me, you understand? I want to see you out there playing basketball with your brothers and Willow, kicking their arses."

I hugged her again, feeling the softness of her clothing, breathing in her familiar scent. Apples along with the spices she used for cooking.

"I could use your help, pet." Mama put her hands on her hips as she looked at me. "Start peeling those potatoes on the cutting board by the sink. I'm putting together a couple of Irish lamb and potato hot pots."

"I'm on it." I can't cook, but peeling potatoes I can do. I went to the sink and picked up the potato peeler, then glanced back at her. "Do you like your doctors at the cancer center?"

Mama gave a nod and smiled. "The doctors and nurses at Massachusetts General are fine indeed."

My stomach turned at the thought of her having to go there. I turned and started peeling a potato. "What do the doctors say?"

"The cancer is shrinking." The sound of cabinets opening and closing followed her words as I still faced away from her, making myself focus on the potato. "It may be soon enough that the doctors will go ahead and perform the surgery," she said.

I stared at the potato and stopped peeling it. The ache behind my eyes made the pressure in my head almost unbearable. "How much longer before they can get the cancer out?"

"Pet, stop." Mama rested her hand on my shoulder, and I looked up at her. She smiled. "Your brothers are coming over for dinner, so I need your attention on getting those potatoes peeled."

I tried to smile back, but failed miserably. "Okay."

"Now tell me about your trip to Stockholm." Mama moved to the fridge, and cool air brushed my bare arms. She grabbed two bunches of green onions before closing the door. "Did you enjoy yourself?"

I studied the potato in my hand. "Not this time."

CHAPTER
THIRTY-TWO

Black ops. Blacker mistakes

"I missed your cooking." I leaned back on the couch and patted my stomach. We were in Donovan's living room in Back Bay. The brownstone he had bought was incredible. It looked like he'd hired an interior designer for his floor and for Kristin's. "That Ben and Jerry's Chunky Monkey ice cream was a nice touch."

He spooned the last of the banana ice cream with walnuts and chunks of chocolate into his mouth before answering. "You only missed my cooking?"

"The sex." I grinned at him. "I definitely missed the sex over the last week while you've been wrapping things up in Manhattan."

"That's what you always say." Donovan set the empty container and spoon on the serving tray by our plates. "You miss the sex when we're not together." He brought his hands to my face and cupped my cheeks with his fingers, which were cool from holding the ice cream container. "I wonder if you missed me."

He kissed me before I could say anything in return. His kiss was soft, sweet, delicious. He tasted like banana ice cream and chocolate.

When he drew away, he rubbed his thumb over my cheek. "Are you sure you want to know about my past?"

Surprise made me blink. He was offering to tell me?

"You were right." Donovan brushed strands of hair from my cheek. "You shared your past with me, and I should be willing to do the same."

"About damned time," I said with a pretend grumble. But in some ways I was worried for him because of that cryptic thing he had said the last time we talked.

He gave me a half smile. More a sad smile. Probably because of what he was going to tell me.

"As you know, I was a SEAL before I left the Navy to take care of my sister when our parents were killed," he said.

I nodded, studying his brilliant blue eyes.

"No one knew, but I was still active duty while I raised Kristin." He lowered his hand from my face and leaned back against the couch. "I did local jobs that wouldn't take me away from my sister." He paused. "As a mercenary. Mostly I did private security work guarding senior U.S. diplomats, but there were other more secretive operations that I took care of."

"Mercenary," I said, the word seeming strange when it came to Donovan and the United States, not some foreign country. "But that changed when your sister graduated and went to college? Or did you continue your work as a mercenary?"

"When Kristin headed off to Harvard," he said, "I went into black ops." Donovan shook his head. "It was like being a mercenary ten times over."

I put my hand on his knee and squeezed, but he didn't seem to notice.

"Our missions were quietly approved and funded by a branch of the military," he said. "My job was recovery. To rescue specialist kidnapped soldiers and kidnapped operatives that no one knew existed. I didn't just recover people, though. I recovered objects, military secrets—anything that needed recovery."

"That's probably one of the reasons why Oxford wanted to hire you so badly." After all, we were RED, the Recovery Enforcement Division.

Donovan nodded. "I was good at what I did. Damned good." His brilliant blue eyes seemed to dim as they clouded with what had to be memories I wasn't sure anymore were something I wanted to know about. "Too good," he added softly.

"What happened?" I asked.

He looked down at my hand, which I'd rested on his knee. "One of our ops had to do with going after a major terrorist responsible for . . . tragedies that we as a country still have not come to grips with."

Chills prickled my spine. I didn't know what was coming, but it wasn't going to be good.

"Except we weren't supposed to just recover him." Donovan met my gaze again. "We were ordered to eliminate him."

"Something went wrong," I stated.

"We were fed bad intel." His eyes seemed even

more clouded with pain. "I was captain of our squad and I trusted our source."

I held my breath.

Donovan looked at me with so much remorse on his face that I wanted to bring him into my arms and hold him tight. "I should have had my men do some of our own recon."

He blew out his breath. "We were given a building and a specific time that the terrorist would be meeting with followers in an Afghan village."

Christ. Here it came.

"My squad prepared hours ahead of time," he said. "We had that building wired with so many explosives, they wouldn't find any pieces left to identify.

"One of my men was ready to blow the whole fucking place with the single remote." Donovan's throat worked as he swallowed, and my chest was hurting like an elephant was standing square on it. "I picked up my long-range binoculars and adjusted them so that I could see better.

"It wasn't until then that I saw the children being herded into the building."

Horror built up inside me, welled like boiling water in a pot.

"I yelled at my man to abort, as loud as I could." He gritted his teeth before he continued. "I didn't give a shit who heard me even though there were Afghan soldiers all around us who hadn't been aware we were there."

I closed my eyes, knowing what was coming.

"My operative didn't hear me." Donovan's throat

worked again. "And we blew those children all to hell."

Donovan braced his elbows on his thighs and put his face in his hands. I didn't know what to do. What to say. The horror of what his team had done, what he'd had to live with, was too great.

"The Afghan soldiers captured every man on my team," Donovan said when he raised his head. "We were beaten, tortured. A couple of men were killed. For a while I was too numb to care. I felt like I deserved it.

"After a while I realized I had to get my men out of there. I couldn't let them continue to be brutalized." He shrugged, a very noncasual shrug. "I escaped, helped to get every one of my men out of there. My men who were still living.

"I never saw the children's faces. The children we killed." Donovan looked at me again. "But I see face-less children in my dreams and my waking thoughts. Every single day of my life."

I buried my face against his shirt and slid my arms around his waist and held him. Soon he gripped me tight in his arms and we clung to each other for a long time.

We slept together that night, but all we did was hold each other.

In the morning I woke to see Donovan propped up on his elbow looking down at me. His face was so serious as he met my eyes. "I don't know how you've done it, Lexi," he said, and I knew he was really serious because he'd used my first name. "But I care for you in ways I've never cared about another woman."

"Donovan," I started, but he put his hand over my mouth.

He moved between my thighs and spread them apart before he thrust his erection into me, hard.

He took me so deep and fast and so unexpected that I came within moments. My cry surprised me, and with every stroke my body vibrated.

When he climaxed, he shouted out my name. He throbbed inside me and I kissed his jaw as his breathing came in ragged puffs. A drop of his sweat splattered on my chest.

Donovan rolled over onto his side, bringing me with him. "I love you, Lexi," he said, his voice soft, quiet.

Shock rolled through me. I couldn't move.

I didn't say anything. I couldn't say anything. All I could do was close my eyes and pretend he hadn't said those words.

AUTHOR'S NOTE ON
HUMAN TRAFFICKING

My accounts are fictionalized, but the truth is human trafficking is a very tragic fact of life around the world.

As of this date, the U.S. Department of Justice's Web site states:

"Trafficking in persons—also known as 'human trafficking'—is a form of modern-day slavery. Traffickers often prey on individuals who are poor, frequently unemployed or underemployed, and who may lack access to social safety nets, predominantly women and children in certain countries. Victims are often lured with false promises of good jobs and better lives, and then forced to work under brutal and inhuman conditions.

"It is a high priority of the Department of Justice to pursue and prosecute human traffickers. Human trafficking frequently involves the trafficking of women and children for sexual exploitation, a brutal crime the Department is committed to aggressively investigating and prosecuting. Trafficking also often involves exploitation of agricultural and sweatshop workers, as well as individuals working as domestic servants."

The most recent information on the Federal Bureau of Investigation Web site states:

"According to the State Department, up to *two million people* are trafficked worldwide every year, with an estimated 15,000 to 18,000 in the U.S."

You can report suspected instances of trafficking or worker exploitation by calling the Department of Justice or contacting the FBI field office nearest you.

As an author, my hope is that by making more people aware of human trafficking, we will have the strength to save more human lives.

FOR CHEYENNE'S
READERS

Visit Cheyenne's Web site at www.CheyenneMcCray .com. Please feel free to e-mail her at chey@cheyen nemccray.com. She would love to hear from you.

Keep reading for a sneak peek
at Cheyenne McCray's

LUKE
An Armed and Dangerous Novel

*Coming soon in trade paperback
from St. Martin's Griffin*

Hair prickled at Trinity's nape, as though she was being watched from a totally different location, and a slight shiver skittered down her spine. She knew she was acting slightly rude to Guerrero, but she couldn't help pivoting, searching for the source of the sensation—and she came to an abrupt stop.

Caught her breath.

Heard Navaeh's voice bouncing through her mind, whispering, *One gorgeous hunk of cowboy.*

Okay, yeah, this must be the guy.

Because he was the most rugged, most handsome cowboy she'd ever had the pleasure of viewing.

He was standing a few yards away from her, sometimes hidden from view by the flow of the crowd. The look on his face was nothing short of feral.

Instinctively she took a step back, bumping into Guerrero, who caught her and her wine both this time.

He didn't keep hold of her, and Trinity noticed that he seemed angered by the cowboy's scrutiny.

"My apologies," Guerrero murmured. "I had no idea you were attached. Please forgive my boldness."

He was gone before Trinity could correct the mistake, not that she could have managed a single word with the cowboy staring at her so intently.

She raised a trembling hand and drained her wine.

The cowboy moved toward her.

Was it her imagination, or was the crowd parting for him?

You're losing your mind, Trin.

He came closer, closer, a few feet away from her. Now a few inches. She tried to back away again, but in a quick movement he caught her wrist, drawing her closer to him. Her flesh burned where he held her, and her mind went entirely blank. She would have dropped her wine glass if the cowboy hadn't slipped it from her limp hand and placed it on a server's tray.

His expression was so intense that Trinity's knees almost gave out. And those blue eyes—God, the way he was looking at her made her feel like he was making love to her right on the spot.

She tried to pull her wrist out of his iron grasp. "I—let go."

The man shook his head, the look in his eyes possessive and untamed. "No, Sugar," he murmured, his liquid-hot Texan drawl flowing over her. "You're not going anywhere."

Sensual heat scorched Trinity in a rush. It shot up her thighs and waist, straight to her breasts, and on up to the roots of her hair. He had to be the one she'd seen getting out of the truck earlier. Even without the cowboy hat and duster, he seemed just as dark and dangerous. Maybe even more.

Dang, the man was tall. And sexy. He had a strong, angular jaw line shadowed by dark stubble, and the most intense gaze that refused to let her go. And God, but he smelled good. Like spicy aftershave, the clean scent of soap, and a hint of malt beer. The way the man was looking at her, she could just imagine his touch, his mouth—

Hold on. Who the heck did he think he was, telling her she wasn't going anywhere?

Yet she couldn't speak. Couldn't move.

Like a deer trapped by headlights . . . only what had captured her was a pair of wicked blue eyes and a steel-vice grip on her wrist.

The man pried the wine glass from her hand and set it on a table beside them. "You keep some hazardous company, Sugar."

"Excuse me?"

"Guerrero." The man nodded in the direction Guerrero had taken. "All hat and no cattle—but lots of guns and drugs."

The man's expression faltered, like he hadn't meant to say exactly that. Then he seemed to come to some decision, and added, "Francisco Guerrero is a dangerous man. If I were you, I'd stay far away from him."

The man's expression was so earnest and fierce that Trinity actually felt a thrill of fear. "I–I never met him before tonight."

The man's eyebrows lifted. "Is that so?"

"Are you a detective or something?" Trinity studied the man, searching for any clue that might help her get a grip.

"I'm a ranch foreman," he said, and Trinity almost laughed, despite the fact his fingers seemed to be burning straight into her skin.

"Yeah. At *this* party?"

His expression looked tense again. Very near to rattled. Trinity felt proud of herself.

He cleared his throat. "I'm standing in for my boss. Now, back to Guerrero. You think about what I said, Sugar. And tell me your name."

Trinity swallowed and mustered a defiant look. "Well, it's not Sugar." Her voice came out sounding small and hesitant, and she forced herself to put some muscle into her tone. "Let me go."

"Name's Luke Rider." His firm mouth curved into a sensual smile that met his eyes, and she thought for sure her knees were going to just up and give out on her. "It's most definitely my pleasure to meet you . . . *Sugar*," he drawled, sounding every bit as lawless as he looked.

Oh. My. God. Trinity MacKenna had *never* come across a man that she wanted to jump, then slap— then jump all over again the moment she'd met him.

Uh . . . uh . . . uh . . . Take me now, I'm yours.

Okay, she'd set a new record. She'd become a complete and total idiot in less than two minutes.

The man—*Luke*—placed a possessive palm on her waist and took her other hand in his. Before she had gathered her thoughts—what few she had left—Luke drew her into the crowd of people dancing at the

center of the room. "Do you two-step?" he asked,
even as he led her.

"Uh, yeah." *Brilliant, Trinity.* "It's, ah, been a
while." She glanced down at their feet as they moved,
and promptly embedded her three-inch spiked heel
into the leather toe of his boot, bringing them to a
halt. Her gaze shot to his and to his credit he didn't
even flinch. "A really *long* while."

He grinned, a dimple appearing in one cheek, and
she instantly became a dithering idiot. Again.

A-duh-duh-duh.

"Well, then," he murmured, moving his mouth
close to her ear, "we'll just have to keep at it till it all
comes back to you. All right?"

"O–" Trinity shivered and almost moaned at the
feel of his warm breath along her cheek. "Okay."

And can I have your babies, too?

What the heck was the matter with her, she wondered as Luke drew her smoothly into the throng of
dancers. Sure, she'd gone ga-ga over guys before—
when she was a *teenager*, for goodness' sake. And
those had been the ones in *Teen People* and *Rolling
Stone.* The adorable and unobtainable.

But this was a *man.* And God, what a man. Certainly just as unobtainable as her childhood crushes,
only now because she was spoken for. More or less.

Er, good ol' whatshisname . . .

Her pulse rate zoomed past the legal speed limit as
they two-stepped to a country-western tune that had
been popular back when she'd lived on the Flying M.
Funny how she could still remember all the words.
Yet right now she had a hard time remembering what

her almost-fiancé looked like. All she could picture in her mind was this sexy hunk of cowboy whose mere presence had fried all the circuits to her brain.

Cowboy. Jeez! She didn't do cowboys. Well, not to mention she shouldn't be doing *anyone* but the man she'd been with for the last couple of years.

"Are you going to tell me more about you?" Luke's baritone rumbled as the tune came to an end and a much slower song started. "Or am I gonna just have to keep making things up in my imagination?"

Uh . . .

Trinity's whole body went on high alert as he brought her into his embrace for the slow dance. She placed her hands lightly on his shoulders—like she was afraid to touch him. His jean-clad hips moved so close to hers that she felt the brush of denim through her silky skirt. She gulped, and her gaze shot up to his. That couldn't be his . . . he couldn't be . . . it had to be her imagination. He wasn't aroused, was he?

Amusement glittered in Luke's blue eyes as he guided her in a slow and easy turn to the music. "Did you drop your voice into that incredible cleavage?" he murmured.

Trinity blinked and then smiled. "Now that's one I haven't heard before."

"Well, what do you know?" He gave her that sexy grin again. "The beautiful woman does remember how to speak."

Beautiful. Sheeee-yeah.

"I–I'm Trinity." Trinity gave her "new" name, her Europe name, wishing like hell she could find that newer, confident version of herself.

"Nice." Luke rested one hand on her hip, but she didn't know if he was referring to her name or her body. His palm felt so hot that it was like he had it pressed to her bare skin, rather than against her dress. "Where have I seen you before, Trinity? You're not from 'round here, are you?"

She caught her breath as he twirled her to the song, and he somehow managed to bring her body even closer to his. "I used to live in this area, ages ago. I'm visiting."

"Very sexy." Luke brought one hand to her left ear and lightly ran his thumb down the row of earrings. His expression turned thoughtful. "Your eyes . . . I never forget a woman's eyes. Hell, I've never forgotten a face. So why are you so familiar, yet I can't place you?"

"We've definitely never met." Trinity managed a smile. "I'd remember you."

"Yeah?" He moved away from her and took her hand, his palm hard and callused against her softer skin. "And why's that?"

With a start, Trinity realized Luke was drawing her through the open doors of the sun room. "I really should get back to Navaeh," she said, her words rushed and her heart beating furiously as he led her toward the Christmas tree in the corner. "She'll wonder where I am."